PRAISE FOR

The
Cypress
Maze

OTHER TITLES BY FIONA VALPY:

The Storyteller of Casablanca

The Skylark's Secret

The Dressmaker's Gift

The Beekeeper's Promise

Sea of Memories

Light Through the Vines (previously published as *The French for Love*)

The Recipe for Hope (previously published as *The French for Christmas*)

The Season of Dreams (previously published as *The French for Always*)

The Cypress Maze

Fiona Valpy

LAKE UNION
PUBLISHING

Text copyright © 2023 by Fiona Valpy
All rights reserved.

Published by Lake Union Publishing, Seattle

www.apub.com

Amazon, the Amazon logo, and Lake Union Publishing are trademarks of Amazon.com, Inc., or its affiliates.

ISBN-13: 9781542035200
eISBN: 9781542035217

Cover design by Emma Rogers

Cover image: © yvonne oswald / Alamy Stock Photo;
© bubutu © Roman Voloshyn © Click Bestsellers © photomaster
© Ilya Sirota / Shutterstock

Printed in the United States of America

Per Jerry e Linda, con amore e amicizia

Nel mezzo del cammin di nostra vita
mi ritrovai per una selva oscura
ché la diritta via era smarrita.

-x-

In the middle of life's journey
I found myself in a dark forest
Where the straight path was lost.

The Divine Comedy
Dante
Inferno, Canto I, 1–3

Tess – 2016

It may have looked as if I was still alive, still breathing and walking and going through the motions of some semblance of a daily routine, but my life stopped the day yours did in that bleak room at the clinic's apartment in Switzerland.

Now I know, though, that there can still be hope. A life after a death. I know it is possible to find a way through the torturous maze of grief.

It was Beatrice Crane who showed me the way.

Chapter 1

Tess – 2015

You'd love this place. That's my first thought as I stand looking at the view across the valley. Behind me, the dust hangs on the still air as the taxi disappears along the rutted track, making its way back down the avenue of cypresses to the wrought-iron gates marking the entrance to the estate, before heading for the *autostrada* to Florence.

The evening light bathes the Tuscan landscape in gold, the sun's lingering rays burnishing fields of ripening wheat. On the far hillside, another neat, zigzagging line of cypress trees stitches its way upwards to a more unruly copse of oaks.

You would have stood here beside me in silence and taken my hand, listening to the sound of the cicadas sawing away at their high-pitched symphony, taking in the lie of the land. Your map-maker's eye would have noted the broad valley – far wider than the parched river running along its floor – and the weathered slopes of the hills beyond it. You'd have told me – instead of my having to read it for myself in the guidebook I'd bought at the airport – that this region is known as the Crete Senesi.

I can hear your voice. And, to my surprise, it really is your voice. Not the robotic, artificially synthesised one you had to rely on as the illness paralysed your vocal cords, but your calm, deep tones, so serious when you were talking about your work and so quick to reveal the warmth of your sense of humour when you relaxed. *See those bare clay cliffs running along the rim of the valley? They've been designated a special conservation area*, you tell me. *It's an incredibly fragile environment, despite the greenery around us.*

It sounds so real that I want to turn to see if you're standing by my side, but I resist the urge, knowing it will break the spell. There's nothing there, I know, only the wall of the villa and a neatly cut box hedge.

I survey the view, stretching before me for miles. If you were here, you'd have turned your gaze to the hazy blue bulk of Monte Amiata in the far distance off to the west and pointed out that the brooding mountain is actually an ancient volcano. Your eyes would have lit up as you spoke of tectonic plates and abduction zones, of rivers of red-hot magma and the unimaginable forces that had created the rocks all around us, and you'd have planned a trip to the geothermal springs a few miles away, reminders that the earth beneath our feet is never as solid as it looks.

A faint breath of breeze stirs the strands of my hair that have escaped from their messy chignon, tickling the side of my neck. For a moment, I close my eyes and let myself imagine it's your breath. I lift my chin, wanting more, longing for your lips on my skin. But the movement breaks the fragile spell, and you are gone again.

Rousing myself, I pick up my bags and turn towards the villa. Its ochre walls mirror the fields of wheat, and the shutters on the windows are the same dark green as the cypresses, complementing the natural landscape of hills and trees. But there's an elegance to it too, the hand of mankind evident in the sweep of stone steps leading to the door and the finely carved finials along the balustrade running the length of the front of the house. I want to pull out my camera and photograph it all straight away, automatically thinking how I'll frame the pictures. But there'll be time for that later. It wouldn't feel right to begin to capture the place before I've even announced my arrival.

I knock at the door and the noise echoes in the silence. No reply. But Miss Crane had told me in our email exchanges that she would probably be in the garden and I should come and look for her there. I follow the stone-paved path to the back of the villa, completely unprepared for what awaits.

In the mellow evening light, the formal gardens take my breath away. The precise lines of clipped box hedges, casting their long black shadows across sun-bleached grass, are softened by lemon ·trees in huge terracotta pots and cascades of red geraniums that tumble from intricately carved stone urns. Beyond the far hedge, the land slopes gently upwards and a path leads the eye through into a less formal area.

Here, a wooden pergola drips with wisteria, providing respite from the glare of the Tuscan sun. On either side, curving beds overflow with billows of purple lavender, and dancing white flowers, like butterfly wings, float above them. Spikes of phlox punctuate the softness, giving structure to the planting, and scented tobacco plants release their perfume to tempt night-flying moths into their heady embrace. To the left, just visible in front of a cluster of tall oak trees, the path forks, ending at a dense wall of pollarded cypresses. It looks impenetrable, forbidding, and I wonder why it's there, an abrupt dead end in the otherwise sweeping view. Instinctively, I turn my eyes away from it, back to the more open stretch of garden. The lavender-lined pathway ends at an arbour, draped with more swathes of wisteria, and a wooden bench sits beneath it facing the view of rolling hills beyond, layer upon layer of them, fading from blue to mauve to grey.

A tall, slightly stooped figure appears, meandering slowly down the path in the less formal part of the garden, and I blink to make sure I'm not hallucinating. In her long smock and broad sunhat, she looks like a relic from the beginning of the previous century. She carries a trug over one arm and a pair of secateurs in the other hand, which she brandishes at the rose bushes here and there, snipping off dead flower heads. When she sees me, she raises the clippers in a salute.

'Ah, there you are, Tess. What perfect timing. I was just finishing up here and I've cut a few stems for your table in the cottage.' She speaks in the style of a BBC announcer from the early days of radio, her very proper tones – with just the faintest hint of a Scottish accent softening their edges – adding to the impression that I've fallen through a gap in time and landed slap bang in the nineteen forties. The wording of her emails had been similar – each message set out as if it were a handwritten letter, the language precise and polite. But, for all her formality, her manner is friendly and relaxed as she slips her secateurs into a pocket in her smock and reaches out to grasp my hand, her grip surprisingly strong for such an elderly woman, despite her fingers being gnarled and lumpy with arthritis.

Beatrice Crane is an old schoolfriend of my grandmother's, both of them having long ago been packed off to a rather austere Scottish boarding school beside the North Sea, and it was Granny who'd organised my escape to Italy. I suppose she'd seen how I was struggling to find my feet again in the suffocating embrace of my family after you'd gone. I tried to keep my pain from them, but I could see it every day, reflected in their faces as they tried – so hard and with so much love – to support me. They worried about me. But their care became a sort of additional burden as I forced myself to smile for their sakes, to join in the walks and the outings and the Sunday lunches, those kindly meant diversions to pull me from my solitude and distract me from my grief. The trouble was, every single one was another reminder that you weren't there. You should have been sitting across from me at the dinner table as Mum insisted on slipping an extra Yorkshire pudding on to your plate. You'd have taken my hand on the walks, your fingers gently squeezing mine to tell me how much you loved me, even as you discussed the rugby with Dad. You'd have pointed out the lie of the land as we climbed the hill behind the house. I loved the way you could make sense of the landscape, showing us how it had been formed and shaped over the millennia by fire and ice and rivers and humans. To me, a map was always simply a two-dimensional sheet of paper; to you, it was more than just your work – it was the living, breathing world, right there in your hands.

Granny, who is still as sharp-eyed at ninety-four as she'd ever been, noticed how difficult I was finding it. Or maybe she's just lived long enough and experienced enough grief of her own to understand mine. She seemed to know that what I needed was not what my family was offering. What I yearned for was space and peace, the luxury of not having to protect the people I love from the unbearable agony of losing you to that cruel illness. I don't know whether Granny contacted her old schoolfriend first. Or perhaps Beatrice Crane mentioned in one of her letters that she could no longer drive and was frustratingly isolated at the Villa delle Colombe. Either way, the plot was hatched and arrangements made, once I'd agreed to them, for me to come and spend a few months in Italy as a companion of Miss Crane and to drive her to the shops when needed.

What really clinched it for me – as if the offer of a few months in Tuscany wasn't enough – was when Miss Crane explained the accommodation. A little apologetically, she'd written that she lived in an apartment in one wing of the main villa, but that there was a small cottage on the estate that would be available for my use. When I read that, I'd looked up from the email on my laptop and gazed around the cramped sitting room of our Southampton flat, the home we'd bought all those years ago so as to be close to your work at the Ordnance

Survey offices. A whole cottage to myself! But it wasn't the prospect of Italian sunshine and Tuscan views I was thinking of. It was the thought of a space where you weren't missing. A place where each room wasn't filled with your absence, where there weren't the constant, jolting reminders of you – or rather of the loss of you – every time I made the bed or took a mug down from the shelf. I could simply lock that front door and walk away, leaving behind the rooms where we'd battled for so long against the terrible disease that was consuming you a little bit more each day. Where your world and mine had closed in, inch by inch, until all that was left were these four walls and the clutter of medical paraphernalia. The equipment had allowed us to keep you at home for a few more months, then a few more weeks, then just a day at a time until the nurse told us gently it was too much for us both and suggested that it was time . . .

So, before I could start to think of all the reasons why I should really stay in England, I clicked 'Reply' and wrote that I'd book my flight for one week's time as suggested.

The flat in Southampton feels a world away as I stand in the garden on that first evening. Trug and secateurs in hand, Miss Crane leads me back through the formal parterre, pointing out the *limonaia* beside the pool, a sort of glasshouse where the lemon trees in their terracotta pots are kept safe from winter frosts. In a section of wall above its glass panels are a series of small holes, forming a dovecot where the *colombe* that give the villa its name make their homes. She shows me a discreet side door set into the end of the east wing of the villa, which is the entrance to her own apartment, before ushering me through an archway in the high stone wall.

We step into a wide yard, enclosed on two sides by an L-shaped block of stables. Through the open top halves of their doors, I can see they stand empty. 'Once upon a time, this is where Francesca kept her horses,' Miss Crane says, with a wave of her hand. 'Of course, they all went in the war . . .'

She leads me beneath another stone arch at the end of the yard and into a roughly paved lane. I gape at the views and she says, 'Impressive, isn't it? Everything you can see – the fields, hills and woods as far as the horizon over there – it all belongs to the estate.'

A mouth-watering smell of frying garlic wafts from the open doorway of a red-tiled farmhouse, its stucco walls peeling here and there with age. 'Giovanni and Vittoria live there,' Miss Crane tells me with another wave of her hand. 'He's the gardener and she helps me look after the villa. You'll meet them tomorrow.'

A dusty track runs down the side of the hill and she leads me along it, past the farmhouse, to a little stone cottage. With its rough walls and lichen-spotted roof tiles, it appears to be as much a part of the natural landscape as the rocky earth from which it rises. A stone *loggia* runs along the front of the house, shading the stone flags of the terrace below, and an ancient vine twists its way up one of the pillars to spread its leaves to the sunlight.

Pushing open the weathered wooden door, Miss Crane gestures for me to enter. I step across the threshold into the cool of a shadowy kitchen. It's simply furnished with a cooker and sink, a painted dresser and a scrubbed pine table with spindle-backed chairs. In one corner, a comfortable armchair sits beside a smoke-blackened stove, redundant in the summer heat but probably a welcoming place to sit, I imagine, when the autumn winds make the terrace a less inviting prospect.

'Your bedroom is up the stairs there. And the bathroom's next to it. I'll just put these in some water and then leave you to settle in.' Miss Crane takes a pottery jug down from the dresser and fills it from the tap, then begins arranging the flowers from her trug. I watch her for a moment, struck by the beauty of her face as she settles each stem in place. There's a serenity about her, her features softly highlighted in the last light of the day that filters through the kitchen window. A little gold brooch, in the shape of a cupped flower, glints where it's pinned to her smock above her heart and her hair is as pure as the white roses in her hands. But beneath her quiet calmness there is something else – a sense of sadness as deep and dark as the shadows behind her. I feel as if I've stepped into a *chiaroscuro* painting by Titian or Tintoretto and my fingers itch to capture the portrait with my camera.

When she's satisfied with the arrangement of roses, forget-me-nots and lemon verbena, she sets it in the middle of the table where it will breathe its sweet perfume into the room.

'Will it do?' she asks, with a sweep of her hand to take in my accommodation once I've taken my bags upstairs to the bedroom under the eaves.

'It's perfect.' I hadn't realised how tense I'd been feeling but, as I let my luggage fall to the floor and set down the heavy case containing my camera and lenses on the bed, it feels as if I'm setting down some other burden, one I've been carrying on my shoulders for a long, long time. 'I'm so grateful to you, Miss Crane, for having me here.'

She places a bony hand on my arm and smiles, the lines of her face contracting into deep creases. 'Better call me Beatrice, my dear, since we are to be companions. And it's a pleasure to have you here.' Her eyes are a piercing blue against the tan of her skin, which is mottled with sun spots. 'I was so sorry to hear about your husband . . .' I nod, perhaps a little too curtly, and she seems to understand my reluctance to talk about you. She gives my arm a gentle squeeze, then says, 'You remind me a lot of your grandmother, you know. Dear Philly, what a faithful friend she's been to me down the years.'

She turns away abruptly, and I wonder whether it's to hide the sudden upwelling of emotion that I think I glimpsed. Despite the villa and its grounds being a corner of paradise on earth, it must still have been very lonely for her, here on her own for so long. Granny had told me that she had help, of course, from the elderly gardener and his wife, who maintain the house and grounds, but otherwise I imagine she's pretty isolated by a combination of geography and old age. I wonder why she's been living here alone, seeing out her years in this beautiful but solitary place, rather than returning to Britain or moving to simpler accommodation in a town where there'd be more support. But she seems capable and determined and perhaps she prefers it that way. Maybe my company will be enough to fill whatever gaps there are in her life, for the next few months at least.

She fishes a lawn handkerchief from the pocket of her smock and blows her nose loudly, then busies herself showing me the fridge stocked with cold meats and cheese and a bottle of wine. 'There's bread in the crock and some grapes in the bowl there. Enough to get you started. Perhaps tomorrow we can drive to the shops so you can get anything else you need and I can show you the lie of the land. We have a kitchen garden, too, so you can pick tomatoes and salad leaves whenever you need them. And *zucchini* and peppers by the bucketload.'

We arrange that I'll come up to the villa at ten the next morning and then she leaves me alone to settle in. I unpack, stowing my clothes in the ancient wardrobe that sits in one corner of the bedroom, and putting your compass on the little table beside the bed. I carry it with me wherever I go, perhaps in the hope it will help me find a sense of direction as I drift on the sea of my grief.

As I sit at the little wrought-iron table on the terrace beneath the *loggia*, condensation dewing the glass of wine before me, I watch the sun set beyond Monte Amiata. For the first time in many months, I feel a sense of calm seep through my limbs. Looking down at my hands, I see that my fingers are clenched into their habitual fists. Slowly, one by one, I allow them to relax as the dusk softens the outlines of the hills and the last swallows slip into their nests beneath the eaves.

Chapter 2

TESS – 2015

Next morning, I make myself a cup of coffee and wander outside, drawn by the promise of the morning sunlight and the newness of the day. I retrace the route Beatrice Crane showed me the evening before, through the arch in the wall and back into the garden. It's still early and I have the place to myself, giving me the chance to explore it more thoroughly. I imagine you walking beside me as I approach the *limonaia*. Its glazed door is unlocked, the wrought-iron handle moving soundlessly as I open it and step into the glasshouse. The windows are hinged open, but already the heat is building inside. I'm sure by midday it will be like an oven. The floor is tiled in a pattern of blue and white stars, but otherwise the space is empty apart from a pile of cushions in one corner. They look as if they belong on the pair of loungers beside the pool, which will be a tempting place to come and sit later in the day.

The soles of my sandals slap quietly against the terracotta slabs surrounding the pool as I make my way past several lemon trees in their pots and through to the formal parterre at the back of the villa. This is the classically Italian part of the garden. Apart from the rectangular planters of scarlet geraniums lining its outer edge, the palette is restricted to cool shades of green and white, the clean lines of clipped box hedges adding a demure formality in perfect keeping with the architecture of the villa. Tall holm oaks on either side help shade the house from the summer heat and white plumbago spills from a carved stone urn, forming a soft cloud at the geometric centre. In one corner, water trickles quietly into a deep stone trough, encrusted with lichen, where a single white waterlily is just beginning to unfurl its petals to the morning sun.

Look, I say to you, knowing you'll wonder at its perfection too.

But I'm drawn onwards, to the less formal part of the garden. It had all been a bit of a blur on the previous evening as I tried to absorb my new surroundings, but I have a distinct memory of the path leading to that sudden, forbidding wall of green-black cypress branches and it intrigues me. It had seemed out of place against the relaxed abundance of the planting up there, blocking the view that was such a feature in the rest of the garden.

It doesn't make sense, I hear you say. *What do you think it is?*

Still nursing my coffee cup, I retrace yesterday's steps through the gap in the hedge, taking the left-hand fork that leads up the path beneath the oaks.

On closer inspection, I realise the cypresses have been kept carefully trimmed to form the dense walls of a maze. It's impossible to see its layout from any other point as it sits on top of the highest knoll in the gardens. I find a narrow opening at one corner and step through, leaving the sunlight behind as I enter the dark alleyway. I follow it a little way, but soon come to a place where the pathway splits. I glance back the way I've come, half expecting to see you there. But you've gone and the loneliness washes through me again.

A prickle of fear creeps up the nape of my neck as I realise I'm unable to see the gap through which I'd entered. The shadows cast by the cypresses are as black as ink, creating a sort of twilight, even though I know that just the other side of the branches there's light and warmth and a garden filled with flowers. But the walls seem to close in around me and I think if I take one step forward, in either direction, the maze will swallow me up and I might never get out. I realise the hand holding my coffee cup is trembling and I give myself a little mental shake, telling myself not to be so silly. But I can't put one foot in front of the other to move forward, deeper into the convoluted tangle of pathways. Taking a breath to steady myself, I turn and walk back the way I'd come, thinking I'll ask Beatrice Crane about the maze later and get her to show me the way to navigate it.

I emerge, blinking, into the brightness beyond the walls of cypress and glance at my watch. It's nearly nine o'clock and the sun's heat has already ratcheted up a notch. I need to get back to the cottage and tidy away my breakfast things, making myself presentable in time for meeting Beatrice at the villa at ten.

As I hurry back through to the formal part of the garden, I hear voices. My Italian is very basic – just good enough to get by on a trip to the shops or a restaurant – and to my ears it's a language that usually sounds filled with rapid-fire urgency even when simply ordering an ice cream. I can hear a woman's excited tones, although I can't understand everything she's saying, followed by a deeper and equally vehement-sounding response.

Rounding the side of the villa, I find Miss Crane in a state of some dishevelment, her white hair floating about her face like a puff of thistledown, clutching the sides of her thin cotton dressing gown together in one hand and brandishing a letter in the other. An elderly man in dusty blue overalls – Giovanni the gardener, I guess – is gesticulating with a large pair of shears in response to something she's just said.

'Miss . . . er . . . Beatrice?' I say. 'Are you all right?'

She turns to face me, all traces of the sad serenity I'd noticed the previous evening now banished, replaced by a look of unadulterated joy.

14

'I'm better than all right, Tess,' she beams, waving the letter at me. 'I've just received some very good news indeed. The owner of the villa is coming at last. After all these years, we've finally found him.'

Her words make no sense to me. All I know is that she lives here in her small apartment in the role of a custodian for the place. I struggle to recall what Granny had told me about the original owner . . . She'd been a good friend of Miss Crane's, I think, and had died some years ago, leaving Beatrice to take care of the villa and its grounds with the help of the few remaining staff. But whoever the owner is now, Beatrice is clearly delighted at the prospect of his arrival.

She smooths out the letter, which has become crumpled in her excited grasp, rereading it. 'He's coming in a week's time! Och, we have so much to do to get everything ready.' She turns to the gardener. 'Gio, *di' a Vittoria di venire subito!*' And then back to me, saying, 'Tess, I shall need your help as well. We need to open up the villa, think about meals, tidy the garden, prepare his room . . . we must write a list!'

Very gently, I lay a hand on the sleeve of her dressing gown. 'Shall I come up to the villa in half an hour, once you've had a chance to get dressed?'

She looks down in astonishment, having clearly forgotten that she's dashed out in such an unseemly state. She lifts a hand to her hair, its unkemptness taking her by surprise. 'Dear me, what am I thinking. Of course, that will be perfect.' And with that she hurries back into her apartment, pushing the door closed behind her.

Before I turn to go back to the cottage and get myself ready, I glance across at the gardener, Gio, unsure how to introduce myself. He's stooped to pick up a rake that had been lying on the parched grass and, as he straightens up, he raises his eyes and nods at me briefly in acknowledgement.

15

'*Buongiorno,*' I begin haltingly, but then I stop short, catching a glimpse of the expression on his face.

His eyes are kind, but his knitted brows and the grim set of his mouth speak volumes. Gio is most definitely not thrilled at the news Beatrice has just delivered. I don't get the impression he's angry, though, as he walks off towards the vegetable garden; more just a man who is very, very worried.

◆ ◆ ◆

The next few days pass in a flurry of activity inside the villa. I write lists for Beatrice, whose hands are too swollen with arthritis to hold a pen comfortably and whose laborious two-fingered typing on her ancient computer makes me realise how long it must have taken her to write those emails to me and compose the letters she sent to Granny.

Before we start work, she tells me about the long-lost owner of the villa, whose impending return has prompted our efforts.

'His name is Alfredo Verlucci. He lived with us here in the war years, one of a number of children we took in as refugees from the bombing in the cities further north. But as the war escalated it became too dangerous for him to stay. He had to leave. There was an accident . . .' Her words tail off as she remembers, as if some of the memories of that time are too painful to tell. And it seems the pain isn't only emotional but physical too. Unconsciously, her hand goes to the small of her back before she gives a little shake of her head, recalling herself to the present, and resumes.

'We lost all contact with him. Francesca Robbia, the previous owner, died childless and bequeathed the estate to Alfredo, who'd been a great favourite of hers. It broke her heart not to have been able to find him. When she knew she was dying, she asked me to stay on as custodian here. She gave me a home for life. In return,

I promised her I'd keep up the search for Alfredo and never give up until I'd tracked him down. Now, at long last, the lawyers have found him.' She shows me the letter she's received, translating the official Italian phrases that give notice that the legal owner of the Villa delle Colombe has now been located and will be coming to take formal possession of his inheritance on Monday 11 May 2015 at 14.00 hours.

As she traces the words of the letter with her gnarled forefinger, I notice how it shakes slightly and how her eyes shine with excitement – and maybe just a little relief – that Alfredo has been found. She's done her duty, fulfilling the promise she'd made to Francesca all those years ago. But I can't help wondering what it will mean for her once he takes over the estate. Will he be happy for her to stay on in her apartment in the east wing, or will he want to take full possession of his new home? Was that what had been worrying Giovanni on the day Beatrice received the lawyer's letter? Was he worried, too, that he and Vittoria might be evicted from their farmhouse, replaced by a younger set of staff? And will I find myself back in my flat in Southampton, staring at the walls instead of the Tuscan views that I've scarcely had time to explore and photograph?

As I shake a long feather duster at a chandelier in the formal drawing room, dislodging a fine shower of dust, I mentally give myself a dressing-down as well. My own concerns seem selfish compared with the upheaval that might be about to be inflicted upon Beatrice, Vittoria and Gio. And Beatrice is so radiant with happiness at the prospect of seeing Alfredo again after all these years that it gives me hope. Perhaps he'll be pleased for it all to carry on as it is, joyfully reunited with Miss Crane, back in the villa that had offered him a sanctuary from the storms of war in his childhood.

We work from dawn to dusk, and she ticks off each item as it's completed. We fling open the shutters in each room in the villa, letting the light flood in to rooms that look as if they've been in a state of half-darkness for decades. We take the dust sheets off one beautiful piece of furniture after another, revealing silk-covered settees, mahogany tables and an intricate rosewood sideboard inlaid with mother-of-pearl. Vittoria sweeps the floors and then polishes the oak floorboards with a righteous vigour until they gleam, leaving in her wake the scent of beeswax and the few rebelliously dancing dust motes that manage to escape her ministrations. I climb a rickety stepladder and fish for cobwebs in the furthest corners of the cornicing with the ancient feather duster, while Beatrice sits on the bottom rung to steady the ladder and points out the bits I've missed. Her hands may be crippled and her back bent and stiff from years of gardening, but there's certainly nothing wrong with her eyesight.

She talks non-stop, as if Alfredo's return has unlocked a long-sealed vault of memories, not just from the war years but from her childhood too. Perhaps it's my presence and the fact that I remind her of my grandmother that makes her recall her school days, growing up in pre-war Edinburgh with her two best friends. 'We were so inseparable they nicknamed us The Triplets, though we didn't look anything like each other. And we were very different in temperament too. Your grandmother, Philly, was the ringleader, of course – always organising the rest of us. It was no wonder she was made head girl. Ella was far gentler, the prettiest girl in the school, popular with everyone. French was her passion, and anything to do with France. She went on to spend quite a bit of time over there. She surprised us in the war by joining the Women's Auxiliary Air Force, working on Hurricanes. You couldn't have imagined anything less likely. But that's another story . . .'

She leans forward from her perch on the ladder and says, 'Just give that corner another going over, would you, dear? I think there's still a bit of a cobweb stuck there.' Then she continues, 'Philly excelled at all her lessons, loved languages but was good at mathematics as well. You probably know about her exploits in the war. I believe they've been declassified now?'

I nod, handing the feather duster to her and stepping down to move the ladder to the next section of the room. Only recently have I learned about my grandmother's role, but, as Beatrice says, that's another story too.

'My family was less well-off than Ella's and your grandmother's. Not that they ever rubbed it in. Philly and I loved going to stay at Ella's family house in Morningside for exeat weekends. The three of us would be allowed to get the tram into town, as long as we stuck together and only went into Jenners for a cup of tea and a scone. That was the height of our daring back in those days. Funny to think that now.'

As we work together, I get more of a sense of who Miss Beatrice Crane really is. She may be old and somewhat crippled with her arthritis these days, but I realise the spirit of the schoolgirl whose photograph she's shown me, laughing alongside her two best friends on a windswept Scottish beach as they prepare to run into the sea, is still there just below the surface. It must have been very lonely for her, living here alone for so long, sustained only by her determination to keep her promise to Francesca in tracking down Alfredo.

◆ ◆ ◆

At last Monday morning comes and everything is ready. The villa has been restored to life. Beatrice and I go from room to room, making the final checks and pulling the shutters to so that the furnishings will be protected from the midday sun. She's placed an arrangement of fresh flowers in the entrance hall, roses and honeysuckle from the garden, and the front door stands open ready to welcome Alfredo.

At one o'clock, we retreat to Beatrice's apartment and I try to encourage her to tuck into a makeshift lunch of cheese and salami, but she's too excited to eat much. She keeps glancing at her watch, as if willing the hands to move faster and two o'clock to arrive. I've just made her a tiny cup of espresso and set it on the table in front of her when we hear the sound of a car pulling up. She leaps to her feet, coffee forgotten, and hurries through to the main villa so that she can be at the front door to welcome Alfredo. I follow close on her heels, in time to see the dust settle over a sleek black Ferrari that has been parked beneath an umbrella pine. The driver's door opens and a man gets out. But he is young – surely far too young to be Alfredo?

And then I hear Beatrice Crane's stifled gasp and turn to see her face crumple, as her heart breaks into a thousand pieces.

Chapter 3

TESS – 2015

His name is Marco. Marco Verlucci, the son of Alfredo. He has a file of papers from the lawyer to prove it. His father died five months ago, he tells us over the glasses of water I bring out to the table we'd set up beneath one of the holm oaks the day before, in anticipation of a far more celebratory meeting.

I can see Beatrice is struggling to conceal her emotions and listen politely to what this elegantly dressed man is saying. Her gaze wanders repeatedly to the gap in the hedge leading to the informal part of the garden and I wonder what memories are drawing her back there. The piercing blue of her eyes is clouded with rheumy tears, and she seems suddenly very old and vulnerable. As I pass her the glass of water, I briefly put my hand on hers, trying to communicate my concern. She smiles at me and seems to make an effort to pull herself together, my touch bringing her back to the here and now.

Marco is good-looking in that smooth, classically Italian way, his dark hair falling in expertly cut layers to the collar of his crisp white shirt. His forearms are deeply tanned where he's rolled up the sleeves, after removing his jacket and hanging it carefully over the back of his chair. Once we settle in the shade beneath the tree's spreading branches, he removes his sunglasses, revealing eyes of a deep brown that might have been warm had the expression on his face not been one of such guarded coolness. He hands each of us a business card with his name and contact details. The address is in Rome.

With exaggerated politeness, he insists on speaking English, even though Beatrice had welcomed him in her fluent Italian. Was it really a courtesy, though, I wonder as I watch him talk, or is there a faintly aggressive edge to it? It's almost as if he's trying to emphasise our foreign-ness, asserting his ownership of the estate and reinforcing the feeling that we are the guests, our presence here purely temporary.

He gives away very little about himself. He tells us he's driven up from Rome that morning, and yes, thank you, his journey was an easy one. No, he's never been to this particular part of Tuscany before although, of course, he's visited Florence and Siena in the past. His eyes only leave Beatrice's face once or twice, but in those brief glances I see how they sweep the whole area, taking in the villa and the parterre. Of course, it's only natural that he'd be champing at the bit to see round the estate, this surprising inheritance that he'd never known about during his father's lifetime. But the stoniness of his expression unsettles me again. There is no apparent wonder at the beauty of this place, nor any real enthusiasm for the gardens, and he shows no curiosity in asking Beatrice anything about herself or the other employees on the estate. I am clearly of no interest to him whatsoever, as he's ignored me completely after a single appraising glance that made me feel very aware of my baggy T-shirt hanging slack on my frame after all the weight I've lost, and my long skirt, which I'm sure he sees as dowdy and unsophisticated.

I reach for the water and my wedding ring clinks quietly against the side of the glass, loose on my finger. His eyes flicker towards my hands at the sound and I become conscious of the roughness of my fingernails, scruffy and broken after our week of cleaning the villa. His own are neatly manicured. Somehow, I can't imagine those hands pulling weeds from the flowerbeds or digging in the vegetable garden.

He drinks the last of his water and shifts his chair back from the table slightly, the scrape of the metal legs over the stone slabs a clear hint. Beatrice rises to her feet. 'Come,' she says. 'You must be longing to see the villa. We'll show you round and then leave you to explore at your own leisure if you'd like?'

He nods, gathering up his file of papers and tucking it under one arm. I stand back to let him go first but he gestures to me to go before him, saying, '*Prego, signora.* Please lead the way.'

During the tour, Beatrice points out the master bedroom. The previous day, Vittoria and I had made up the bed with crisp cotton sheets and Beatrice had hung little bunches of fresh lavender in the wardrobe in preparation for our visitor's arrival. But Marco just raises his eyebrows and shakes his head when she tells him we're expecting him to stay. 'Thank you, Signorina Crane, but I have a hotel room booked in Pienza and will be basing myself there for the duration of my visit. I don't wish to intrude on your space.' Once again, his words are perfectly polite but the coldness with which they're delivered belies their courtesy. I see the hurt in Beatrice's eyes as she turns away, pushing open the shutters to show him the view of the gardens.

Once we've shown him around, we leave him alone to wander through the villa taking notes in a small leather-bound notebook.

Beatrice and I retreat to the garden. She's distraught. I lead her away from the house, along the path to the bench beneath the arbour, hoping that the view and the sweet scent of wisteria will help calm her.

Her face is a picture of misery as she sits there and she seems lost in her grief, unreachable despite the hand I lay on her arm to try to offer her a little comfort.

'I'm so sorry,' I say. 'About Alfredo. It must be a huge shock to you, learning about his death like that.' Inwardly, I curse the lawyers for their obtuseness and the way they'd written in such formal terms, following procedure I suppose, but with no thought for the distress their letter might cause.

A single tear rolls down her lined cheek and she fumbles in her pocket for a handkerchief. Her hands are trembling uncontrollably, and the lines of her face seem to have deepened in the past hour, since Marco's arrival.

'I've failed him,' she says. 'I've failed Alfredo. And I've failed Francesca too.'

'But Beatrice, you've done everything humanly possible. For all these years you've kept searching for him. Perhaps he didn't want to be found. And now that Marco's here, you've fulfilled your promise to Francesca, haven't you?' I hope my words will cut through her grief and ease her distress a little, but she shakes her head.

'You don't understand,' she says. 'And he doesn't understand, either. What do you think he's doing right now, going through the villa, writing things in that notebook? He has no love for this place. I don't think he has the slightest intention of keeping it, do you?'

I have to admit she's probably right. Marco's appraising glances and his refusal to stay at the villa have given the distinct impression he's viewing his inheritance simply as a piece of real estate to be disposed of at the earliest convenience. Evidently, his life is in Rome, driving his fancy sports car through the city streets. What would he want with the villa and its gardens? But that's his prerogative, after all. I know it will be a wrench for Beatrice to have to leave, but perhaps it'll be for the best, at her time of life. And maybe whoever buys the estate could be persuaded to keep Giovanni and Vittoria on, so they won't have to move out of the farmhouse.

'I know it's a lot to have to come to terms with so suddenly,' I say. 'Perhaps there's a chance Marco will change his mind and come to love this place as you do. But if he does decide to sell it, it sets you free in a way, doesn't it?'

She turns to look at me then and I'm surprised to see how her expression has altered. Her mask of grief has been replaced by something else and it unsettles me to my core. She looks utterly terrified. And then she says, 'No, Tess. It doesn't set me free. In fact, it does the complete opposite. You can't begin to understand what this might mean for me now.'

With an effort, she pulls herself together and rises to her feet. 'Forgive me,' she says, 'but I think I need to go and lie down. The heat of the afternoon, all this emotion . . . it's been a bit much, hasn't it. I'm sorry, my dear. None of this concerns you. Do you think you could see that everything is locked up, once Marco leaves?'

'Of course. I'll handle it.'

I help her back to her apartment and make sure she's safely settled, putting another glass of water for her on the bedside table. And then I go back to sit on the terrace beneath the holm oaks, leaving Beatrice in peace.

As I wait for Marco to finish taking his inventory of the villa, I mull over the events of the day while the white doves flutter in and out of their dovecot above the *limonaia*. Their quiet cooing seems to be a mourning song for both the past and the future of the estate. I wonder about the ones who have left already – Francesca, Alfredo and the other children Beatrice mentioned who had found a sanctuary here as refugees from the war. If I listen carefully, I imagine I can hear faint echoes of past laughter and childish voices, playing hide-and-seek among the lemon trees. And I think of Beatrice, Vittoria and Gio, the ones who might now have to leave too.

My conversation with Beatrice echoes in my head. What did she mean when she said I couldn't begin to understand what this meant for her now? Why is she so frightened? What other memories have been stirred up by the news of Alfredo's death? And, most of all, why is the potential sale of the estate such a threat to her freedom?

My troubled thoughts are interrupted by the reappearance of Marco. He takes his jacket from the back of the chair and slips the notebook into one of the pockets before hooking his forefinger through the loop at the collar and slinging it over his shoulder. His gestures are a little less careful now he's apparently got what he wanted from his visit.

'*Grazie, signora*. And please give my regards to Signorina Crane as well.'

I shake the hand he's extended, but there's no warmth on either side. 'Will you be coming back again, Signor Verlucci?' I ask, making an effort to keep my tone neutral.

'No doubt,' he says. 'Clearly, I have some decisions to make. I'll be staying in Pienza for a few days before I return to Rome. But please don't make any special arrangements on my behalf. I have my own set of keys now, so I shall come and go as necessary.'

I swallow my irritation at the edge of arrogance in his tone. He is the rightful owner of the Villa delle Colombe, after all, and he's entitled to come and go as he pleases. But I'm angry on Beatrice's behalf: it would have been more respectful to let her know when he intended coming back. He's emphasising once again the fact that this is no longer her home and she'll only be here as long as it suits his plans for the estate.

I watch as the black sports car spins off down the drive, the roar of its engine leaving a shimmer of turbulence in its wake, long after it has disappeared into the distance.

Chapter 4

Tess – 2015

I take my camera into the garden to shoot some pictures in the evening light. The sun hangs low over Monte Amiata as I frame a view of the receding silhouettes of purple hills, and I feel you there beside me again. You often seem to stand alongside me when I'm taking photographs. The camera helps me feel I'm taking a step back from the real world and perhaps that helps me step into the place where you are. No-man's land. A place where we can be apart together.

He was awful, I tell you, still smarting in the wake of Marco's visit.

Yes, you say. *But why? If his father – Beatrice's beloved Alfredo – was so adored, so wanted here, why did he never return after the war? And if Alfredo's memories of the Villa delle Colombe were fond ones, why would Marco be so disinterested in the estate?*

I walk slowly along the path to the bench, trailing my hand across the tips of the lavender flowers to release their scent. You stand by my side when we reach the arbour and wait while I swap lenses to take some close-ups of the bees collecting their final drops of nectar for the day from the clusters of purple wisteria.

It'll be sad if she has to leave. She doesn't have another home to go to, does she? I know you're thinking about Beatrice Crane. *And you've hardly arrived. You're not ready to leave here either, are you?*

I shake my head. I don't want to go back to England. I've only just got here, but I'm already discovering what a relief it is to have left our flat behind, shutting the door on those rooms filled with the anguish of your illness. Here, it seems to me your presence is stronger than it has been for a while. I'm frightened that going home will mean I'll have to face the fact that you are gone. I'll have to lose you for good. You're right, I'm not ready for that.

Ask her, you say. *Ask Beatrice what happened. Perhaps then you'll be able to help her.*

Your voice sounds so real that I turn to look for you, expecting to see you there. But you are gone, and I'm left alone again as the cicadas play the final notes of their daily symphony.

◆ ◆ ◆

Beatrice makes it very plain that she doesn't want to talk about Marco – or anything else much – when I go to the villa the next morning. She's up and dressed, although the lines of her face are drawn and tired so she clearly hasn't slept well. She's regained a bit of her composure, even if one wayward wisp of hair hangs loose from the severe bun in which she normally wears it.

Her demeanour is determinedly brisk, and she focuses on the jobs that need doing in the garden. 'The first cherries are ripe, and we'll need to pick them and pit them so Vittoria can make preserves. Then there's asparagus to cut and sweet new peas and fava beans to pick in the vegetable garden behind the farmhouse. We'll ask Vittoria to cook us a risotto with them this evening. The early summer vegetables are always a treat,' she says.

I suppose it will be a good distraction. I'm rapidly discovering the garden is an endless source of work, demanding and rewarding in equal measure. Wearing broad-brimmed straw hats, we set to and soon fill the baskets we carry. Beatrice and Vittoria work quickly, their arthritic fingers defter than mine, their movements spare and efficient. At first, I squash some of the fruit as I pull it from the branches and break the vine of a pea plant as I snap off the pods, but Beatrice gently shows me the right way to harvest each crop and I soon get the hang of it.

The sun is blazing through the thin cotton of my blouse by the time we retreat to the villa. Ordinarily, the women would cook in Vittoria's farmhouse kitchen or the compact galley in Beatrice's apartment, but today we need the extra space and the use of the vast cooker in the main house. It's evidently stood dark and quiet for months, but now the cavernous kitchen comes alive as we pit the cherries and pop the peas from their pods, the windows flung open to let the steam escape as the room begins to fill with the sweetness of simmering fruit. Watching Beatrice and Vittoria work is a little like watching a dance. Their movements are so well rehearsed and choreographed that they never get in each other's way, each sure of her own role. I perch on a stool at the big pine table, staying out of their way and trying to keep up with the efficiency of their pace as I work an ancient-looking gadget that takes the stones out of the heaps of cherries we've gathered. The tips of my fingers quickly become stained with juice, turning them the same deep ruby red as the fruit itself.

The two women don't talk much. They each seem preoccupied, not just with their work but with their thoughts too. I wonder whether this is the final time the pair of them will be doing this. Will this be the last time they'll carry out this first harvest of summer? Who are we preserving the fruit and vegetables for, if the

29

estate is to be sold and they have to move out by the time the seasons turn and the autumn leaves begin to fall?

The kitchen is filled with the noises of cooking, the clattering of pans and the bubbling of boiling sugar, and so we don't hear the cars pull up on the opposite side of the house. We only realise Marco has returned when we hear the sound of voices through the open window.

I look up from my work just in time to see Beatrice and Vittoria exchange a glance and a frown. 'Shall I go and see what they want?' I ask, wiping my fingers on a cloth.

'No,' Beatrice replies. 'It's his house, after all. He can come and find us if he needs anything. We have work to finish.'

And so we do our best to ignore Marco and the other two men who are with him, although we see how they consult sheets of paper that look like plans and snap photos on their phones of the villa and the grounds from every angle as they walk past the windows of the kitchen. Catching sight of us, Marco gives a peremptory wave of acknowledgement, but doesn't stop to talk or to introduce the other men.

We work on in silence, each engrossed in our own thoughts, until the last jar is filled with the preserved cherries, and the peas and beans have been blanched and packed into bags for the freezer. Green and red, the fruits of our labours are lined up on the table like the colours of the Italian flag. It's midday now, and we hear a car engine start up in the distance and then drive off.

'I think I'll go and have a little lunch in my apartment, then a lie-down,' Beatrice says. 'We've done a good morning's work. Thank you for all your help, Tess. The afternoon is your own. Perhaps you'd enjoy a dip in the pool to cool down.'

Dismissed from my duties, I head off to change into my swimming things, the thought of spending some time beside the pool a very tempting one after the steamy heat of the kitchen. I retrieve some of the cushions from the *limonaia*, shaking off the dust, and lay them out on one of the wooden loungers, spreading my towel over them. Then, with a sigh of relief, I lower myself into the water, relaxing into its embrace. I dive to the bottom of the pool and swim a length, wanting to submerge myself completely and wash off the sticky heaviness of the day. Marco's presence has once again created an atmosphere as oppressive as gathering thunderclouds and the cool water is a release.

But when I resurface at the other end, I find I'm not alone. A pair of feet, clad in soft leather loafers, stand at the edge of the paving. Above them rise neatly pressed white jeans and, as I blink the water from my eyes, I find myself looking up at Marco.

'I'm sorry – *mi dispiace*,' I say, flustered. 'I didn't realise you were still here.'

His eyes are amused. He seems to be in a better mood than he had been the day before. '*Prego, signora*, don't apologise. I'm pleased to see you are making the most of your time here.'

He seems in no great hurry to leave, and I'm not enjoying the sensation of him looking down on me from where he stands, so I swim to the far end of the pool and climb out, wrapping myself in my towel. Then I slip my feet into my sandals and walk back to talk to him.

'I hope your visit today has been productive, Signor Verlucci. Did you find everything you needed?'

'Please, call me Marco. And yes, I did, thank you. Although I think yours has been even more productive – was that jam I saw you making in the kitchen earlier?'

I nod. 'You should take a jar with you. I'm sure it's better than anything you can buy in the shops in Rome. And they are your cherries, after all.' Little rivulets of water run from my hair down my shoulders, where they evaporate quickly, burned off by the hot sun.

31

He inclines his head in a gesture that is at once gracious and non-committal.

'Are you interested in gardening, Marco?' I persist, making the most of this opportunity to try to get a bit more information out of him.

He shrugs. 'I can appreciate beauty when I see it, *signora*.' He smiles and, for once, his eyes show a glint of warmth. He waves a hand at the parterre. 'This section, for instance, I find very elegant. In keeping with the villa.'

'And the rest of the estate?'

'It's very attractive too, in its way. That less formal bit – the English garden, as I suppose one could call it – and the woods beyond it. But they don't really fit with my plans.'

'I know it's not really any of my business, but may I ask what exactly are your plans? You and your – er – associates seemed to be taking a lot of photographs this morning.'

He looks at me appraisingly, holding my gaze for a few seconds. 'You may indeed ask. I'm putting together a consortium and we will develop the estate into one of the most exclusive golf courses in Tuscany. Or perhaps even in the whole of Italy. The villa and farmhouses will be perfect for accommodating guests and staff, and the setting is second to none. This area is ripe for it.'

I stare at him, stunned. He must have given the project a great deal of thought already if he has people lined up to invest in it. He certainly hasn't wasted any time, in the wake of his father's death.

'A golf course? But how will you fit that in around the gardens? And won't it demand a lot of water? It isn't exactly in plentiful supply around here, in case you hadn't noticed. And the Crete Senesi is such a fragile environment. Surely there are laws prohibiting developing it like that?' I can't help the slightly acid note that creeps into my voice and it seems he's heard it too as he raises his eyebrows slightly, his expression cooling rapidly again as the spark of warmth dies out from his eyes.

'The gardens will be removed,' he retorts briskly. 'That will free up both space and water. As for the laws, I hardly think you are in a position to lecture me about what is or isn't possible here in my own country. And you were correct, *signora*, when you began by saying it's none of your business.'

I bite my lip, not wanting to annoy him further, fully aware that he could tell me to pack my bags and get off his property any time he pleased. But I can't bear to picture the flowers and paths being bulldozed. Even worse is the thought of the distress that will cause Beatrice. All these years, she's stayed on here, working in all seasons to preserve the gardens. Doing it in the belief that Alfredo would one day return. Doing it for Marco, too, in a way.

He turns away from me, as if to go, and I reach out a hand to stop him, trying to placate him.

'I'm sorry to hear that,' I say. 'I don't mean to cause any offence. I'm just a bit surprised – I know Miss Crane had hoped the estate might be preserved in its current form, the way the original owner would have wanted it. I've heard how much this place meant to your father when he was young. I think she hoped it would bring you the same joy.'

He wheels back to face me and his mask of cool civility has completely gone now, replaced by a dark fury. 'You know nothing of my father,' he spits. 'He hated this place. It blighted his life, brought him nothing but misery. Why do you think he never returned? He wanted to forget it ever existed, that's why! The very best thing I can do is to bulldoze the lot. I would never live here – it would be a betrayal of his memory.'

I take a step back, stunned, recoiling from the force of the hatred written on his face.

'Enjoy your swimming while you can,' he says, his words still hot with anger. 'You should all count yourselves lucky I'm letting you stay on here for the time being. Out of courtesy, I was going to tell the old lady myself, but I'm not wasting any more of my time here now. So perhaps you would be so kind as to inform her? She has the summer. But I will be expecting everyone to be out by the start of September. A letter from my lawyers will follow soon.'

He stalks off and a minute later I hear the roar of his sports car as it speeds away down the drive. I sink down on to the lounger and stare, unseeing, at the sunlight crazing the surface of the pool. How could I have got it so wrong? How can Marco's interpretation be so far removed from Beatrice's? One of them must be misreading the situation – but which?

I raise my eyes to the view, feeling completely wretched. I'd been trying to make things better, but all I've succeeded in doing is making them far worse. And now I have to be the one to deliver the news to Beatrice, Vittoria and Giovanni that they need to start looking for new homes for themselves.

◆ ◆ ◆

I tell Beatrice that evening. I find her sitting on the terrace. She'd been turning the pages of what looked like a sketchbook on the table before her, which she sets aside when I join her in the shade of the oak trees. I expect her to be distraught when I deliver Marco's message, but she seems almost deathly calm. There's a helplessness in her eyes, but the fear she'd shown before has been replaced by something else. It's a sort of exhausted resignation, a surrendering of something she'd fought for or struggled against for a long, long time. She slumps into her chair momentarily, but then – with an effort – she pulls herself together, lifting her chin and squaring her shoulders like someone condemned, accepting their fate with all the dignity they can muster.

'Perhaps you could try phoning him, ask him to reconsider?' I suggest. I know I'm clutching at straws. He'd been adamant that he wasn't prepared to discuss his plans any further. Earlier in the afternoon I'd tried calling the mobile number on the business card he'd given me, just to see if I could ask him to come back and talk to us, give us a chance to persuade him out of his plans perhaps. But it had repeatedly been switched to voicemail and then gone dead as if he'd blocked me – presumably realising it was me with my UK number.

Beatrice looks away, as if watching some memories from long ago play out between the box edging of the parterre. She sighs. 'I've failed, Tess. I've let them all down. It's too late. And now I have to accept whatever comes next. I wish I could tell Marco my story – his father's story. Perhaps if I had a chance to tell him, he might listen and understand. Not that he seems like the listening type . . .'

She picks up the sketchbook and turns back through several of the pages. 'Look,' she says, pushing it towards me. 'This was one of Francesca's paintings.'

It's a watercolour sketch of children at play. I recognise the stone urn at the centre of the parterre and the outline of the *limonaia* in the background. Two white doves peck at the paving by the pool and a little girl jumps with a skipping rope, her pigtails flying, while several boys crouch over a game of marbles in the foreground, utterly absorbed. The execution of the painting is simple but skilled, capturing a sense of life and movement in the scene almost as well as a photograph can. Beatrice points to one of the little boys. 'That was Alfredo.' Her finger trembles slightly and she lets it rest on the page to steady it, as if she were stroking the child's dark curls, which seem to shine in the sunlight.

I puzzle over the page. 'They look so happy. It's such a peaceful picture. But Beatrice, Marco told me his father hated the villa. He said it had blighted his life. I don't understand. Looking at this painting, knowing how much the children were loved and looked after here . . . how could it have turned so sour?'

Beatrice draws the sketchbook back to her side of the table and turns a few more pages. She shakes her head. 'It's a long story, Tess. Terrible things happen in a war. And sometimes it's impossible to protect the people you love, no matter how hard you try.'

'I wish you'd tell me, Beatrice. I know there's probably nothing I can do to help. But at least if you tell me what happened I can try to understand. Perhaps we can even try to make Marco understand, if there are two sides to Alfredo's story.'

She raises her eyes to mine and blinks away the tears that are pooling there. Then she nods, slowly. 'Would you do that?' she says. 'Would you listen and write it down for me? Then at least I'll be leaving behind the truth that I've kept safe for so many years. It will be here, even if I am not.'

'Of course,' I say. She looks so frail, so vulnerable as the evening shadows lengthen towards her across the grass. This will be her last summer at the Villa delle Colombe. And suddenly it feels very important indeed that I should try to help her tell her story. Before it is gone for good.

Chapter 5

Beatrice's Story – 1940

In 1940, I found myself trapped in Italy. There were worse places to be stranded, of course, although the war made things less than ideal.

My life had been rather sheltered until that point. I was born in 1921, in a large house just outside Edinburgh, and had a comfortable upbringing that included my education at a girls' boarding school, where I studied subjects deemed suitable for a young lady. Needlework and domestic science were never my strong points, but I adored Italian and history of art. I also met my two life-long friends there – Ella Lennox and Philly Buchanan. We were inseparable, as close as sisters, and were known as The Triplets. But they were from better-off families than mine and by the time I left school at the age of seventeen, the economic situation had taken its toll on my parents' finances – as well as paying my school fees, no doubt – and there was no money to stay on for higher studies. Nor could my parents afford to send me to one of the finishing schools to which so many of my peers were headed, where I'd have learned how to become perfect wife material and been matched with a suitable young man. Instead, I said a tearful goodbye to Ella and Philly, packed a suitcase and boarded the boat train, in order to take up a position as an English tutor to the children of a wealthy banking family in Florence.

The job was hardly an onerous one. My young charges were well-mannered pupils, dutifully engaging in their English conversation classes when they returned from school, leaving me with much of the day free to explore the city. I spent hours wandering through streets lined with stuccoed buildings, where around every corner there was another fresco or statue to gaze at in awed reverence. Such casual, ubiquitous beauty was something I'd never come across back at home. I climbed the four hundred and fourteen steps of the Campanile and drank in the views across the Florentine rooftops, watching the pigeons flutter and settle, and listening to the chiming of the bells marking the passage of time as they had done for centuries. I remember tiptoeing round the narrow walkway high in the embrace of the Duomo as a flock of choirboys rehearsed evensong hymns far below, their voices soaring to fill every inch of the golden dome rising above me. I spent hours there, examining the extravagant frescoes depicting the Last Judgement, with its choirs of angels on high and its scenes of hell below. The works of art I'd studied in the pages of books and on blurry slides projected on to classroom walls were all around me, everywhere I went. After a childhood spent in the sepia light of Scotland, this gilded city was a revelation. I revelled in it, immersing myself in its sights and sounds.

In the cool of the evening, once my teaching duties were over, I often walked along the Arno, crossing the Ponte Vecchio to stroll in the Boboli Gardens and look back at the hustle of the city as the lights came on, before returning to my host family in time for the evening meal.

Within a few weeks, I'd met other British girls who'd come to Florence to study the art in the Uffizi or teach English, like me, or generally improve their minds while hoping to meet some similarly occupied young man. We would meet up for coffee or a *gelato* in the Piazza della Signoria and spend ages giggling over our experiences of the forwardness of Italian men or the funny things our young charges had come out with while grappling with English colloquialisms.

At first, when the news came in 1939 of Germany's invasion of Poland, and Britain and France declared war, there were announcements on the wireless that Italy had no intention of taking any military action. I suppose that gave us ex-pats a false sense of security, because, for all his promises and posturing, Mussolini had ambitions to reclaim much of the long-lost Roman Empire and he soon decided an alliance with Adolf Hitler could well be the easiest way to achieve this.

In the spring of 1940, many foreigners packed up and left, as the country's slide into the war became more and more likely. The tone of the daily reports on the wireless had begun to change, becoming more approving of the rapid advance of the Nazis. But two things made me ignore the warning signs. One was the simple optimism of youth. Perhaps some would call it naivety. I found it hard to believe a country so filled with art and beauty and thousands of years of civilisation could be drawn into the senseless destruction of war. And in any case, at that point not much seemed to be happening, other than a good deal of political posturing. Ignorance is bliss, I suppose.

The second thing was Luca. He was a student of philosophy at the University of Florence, and we'd met standing in front of Botticelli's *Birth of Venus* in the Uffizi. The gallery was empty, the museum about to close, but I couldn't tear myself away from the astonishing beauty of the painting. I heard footsteps behind me and turned, supposing it to be one of the attendants coming to tell me it was time to leave so they could lock up for the night. Instead, I found myself looking into the eyes of a beautiful young man, who wore a blue cotton jacket and carried a bag of books slung over one shoulder. Blushing, I turned back to face the painting again to hide my confusion. He stood next to me, not saying a word at first. Finally, he spoke. '*È un miracolo.* I thought for a moment you had stepped out of one of the paintings. *Una vera Botticelli.*' Corny, I know, but not bad as pick-up lines go. And I was certainly very flattered to be picked up at all. I towered over most Italian men, but this tall, curly-haired bohemian was different. The most startling thing about him was his eyes, which were as blue as the sky in the painting in front of us. I'd never seen anyone so exotic. And perhaps he thought the same about me, a tall *ragazza scozzese* with Titian hair.

As a museum guard finally shepherded the two of us towards the exit, Luca asked whether I'd care to join him for a drink. Two glasses of wine later, I thought I was in love.

It was a very innocent relationship, involving little more than holding hands and stealing surreptitious kisses on our evening strolls in the Boboli Gardens. I was never invited home to meet his family, who'd probably have disapproved intensely of this gangly British girl with few prospects. But Luca was enough of a distraction to blind me to the growing risks of my becoming an enemy alien in a country at war. He himself told me that Mussolini's alliance with Hitler was purely tactical, and that when it came to it the Italians would never side with Germany, not after they'd been such bitter enemies in the Great War. I chose to believe him and to ignore the letters from my parents suggesting maybe it was time I came home. The thought of returning to cold, grey Scotland, with the prospect of a dull typing job in some back-room office somewhere, was hardly very tempting when set alongside the blue sky promise of another Florentine summer.

If I'd known then that my parents were right – and that my irresponsible reluctance to return meant I'd never see them again – my life would have been very different. But I stayed, and then it was too late. Because on the tenth of June came the announcement: Italy had entered the war on the side of the Germans. The news was greeted with a sort of fatalistic calm in Florence, although there were reports of furious protests in some other regions. It all felt slightly unreal at first. Then my host family announced that my services as an English tutor were no longer required, and it suddenly became very real indeed. In fact, not only was my Britishness an embarrassment to the family, it was also their duty as paid-up members of *Il Duce*'s Fascist party to report me to the authorities. I had a few hours to pack my bags, the *signora* informed me, and then the police would be coming to collect me.

The children cried when I was taken away. I spent the first three nights in a cell in the monastery of Santa Verdiana, which was being used as a women's prison, while the Italian authorities satisfied themselves that I wasn't a British spy. I was one of the lucky ones. Those three days and nights were filled with the weeping of a woman in the cell next to mine. I tried to talk to her through the grille in the door, but the guard struck the grating viciously with his baton and screamed, '*Silenzio!* Leave the filthy Jew alone!' I shook with fear then, realising the full horror of the Fascist regime that had festered and grown in the past years, while I'd been sipping lemonade in cafés and wandering around looking at art. How could I have been so ignorant? I felt wretched. And it was even worse when the sound of weeping from the next-door cell stopped, the day they took her away. I don't know where she went. Her place was taken by another woman, who didn't make a sound after the door slammed shut behind her.

Once my time in the cells was up, I was moved to a large dormitory in the jail, with about fifty other women – mostly English and a few French – where we were put in the care of the nuns. Some of the other girls complained about the harshness of our treatment at their hands and the lack of food, but for those of us who were used to boarding school it all felt rather familiar, apart from the bed bugs that infested our lumpy mattresses.

After three weeks, we were told to gather our belongings together again and summarily turned out on to the streets. Some of the girls were handed transit papers and told to make their way to the railway station. However, my passport had gone missing when my belongings were confiscated on arrival at Santa Verdiana and the likelihood of being able to apply for a replacement in a country that had severed all diplomatic ties with Great Britain had evaporated. I had nowhere to go. For a fleeting moment, I toyed with the idea of trying to get in touch with Luca. But I realised his family would be even less likely to approve of me now, and he had made no attempt whatsoever to find me when I'd disappeared from his life. That in itself was enough of a message. War had transformed me from a fantasy into a liability: his walking-talking Botticelli vision was now a poor, shabbily dressed enemy alien.

One of the English girls told me about a Red Cross office in the city and so I made my way there, dragging my suitcase, trying not to scratch the bites the bed bugs had left on my arms, which had swollen into angry red lumps in the heat, and looking decidedly the worse for wear after my spell of incarceration.

I'd managed to maintain my British stiff upper lip through the weeks in the makeshift prison at Santa Verdiana. But I have to admit that now, without the company of the other girls to help buoy my spirits, a worm of self-pity began to eat away at my resolve. The reality of my situation – stranded in an unfriendly land, without access to money, a passport and a roof over my head – came home to roost very forcibly as I trudged along the hot, empty streets. With the egocentricity of youth, I imagined the city I'd so grown to love had turned its back on me. Silly, of course – it was nothing to do with me personally. The city had turned in on itself out of a sense of dread for what would come next, terrified for the young men – like Luca – who would be sent to fight in a war in which no one really believed.

My suitcase – which now represented everything I owned in the world – seemed to grow heavier and heavier and it banged painfully against my shins when I tried to hold it in front of me so I could grip the handle with both my hands. My palms were reddened and sore and my heels were blistered but I limped on in what I hoped would be the direction of my salvation at the hands of the Red Cross.

The streets were deserted. I almost wept with gratitude when I saw a woman come out of her house and I hurried over to ask her for directions. As I approached, she recoiled, then looked at me pityingly, and I realised I must have looked the most awful fright, sweating profusely, covered in angry sores and most certainly giving off a pungent whiff of the prison conditions in which I'd recently been living. She told me the church where the Red Cross had set up a post was just a few streets away, pointing me in the right direction, and then hurried off, obviously terrified at being seen talking to someone like me.

The church door stood slightly ajar and pinned to it was a piece of paper with a cross scribbled on it in what, on closer examination, appeared to be scarlet lipstick. It's amazing how these tiny things come back to one, but that makeshift sign seemed to me to offer such hope. The fact that some Italian *signora* had put her precious cosmetics to such good use in the service of others made me smile. I gripped my suitcase a little more firmly and squared my shoulders before pushing open the heavy wooden door and stepping into the blessed coolness of the church.

A woman sat alone at a table at the top of the aisle and she lifted her head at the sound of my lopsided footsteps on the flagstones as I limped towards her. She stood and smiled, then hurried towards me and took the suitcase from my hands. She looked like an angel to me. I couldn't help myself – I sank into a pew and began to sob, overwhelmed by her simple act of kindness, in what I had suddenly and forcefully come to realise was a very unkind world indeed.

Once I'd managed to get a grip, she brought me a cup of water and a bowl of cold bread and bean soup. I knew what it was without asking. I'd seen *ribollita* on café menus but it was cheap peasant food and it had never actually occurred to me to order it. I thought it was the most delicious thing I'd ever tasted.

While I ate, she asked me some questions and wrote down my responses in a large ledger balanced on her knee. She sat close, not flinching from the strong smells of prison and despair that were all too evident now I was no longer in the open air. I observed her as she worked. She was small and svelte, her neat figure dressed in an elegantly tailored skirt and blouse, the matching jacket draped across the back of her chair at the little table. Her dark hair was tied back, although the curls looked as though they might be keen to escape if given any leeway, and her face was as serene as the Madonna's in the fresco on the wall behind her. She made no comment, but I noticed how she raised her eyebrows when I mentioned the loss of my passport in the prison and jotted another note next to my name. Then she pushed back the cuff of her blouse and glanced at her wristwatch.

'*Allora*. We have some work to do. I'm expecting a friend any minute and perhaps you will be so kind as to help me when she arrives? But first,' she said with the utmost tact, 'perhaps you would like to freshen up a little?' She showed me to the vestry where there was a small basin in one corner, a hairbrush, and a clean hand towel. Best of all, there was a sliver of soap and I put the facilities to good use, trying to make myself a little more presentable. It's amazing how little one needs sometimes to feel a lot more human.

I heard voices, so I quickly finished brushing my hair and repinning it and then hurried back into the body of the church. Another woman had arrived and straggling behind her was a small and bedraggled band of children. I suppose they must have ranged from about five to twelve years old. The thing that struck me most was the look of bewilderment in their eyes.

We sat them in the pews and I helped serve them bowls of *ribollita*. Once they'd eaten – as ravenously as I had done – I did what I could to tidy them up and make them a little more comfortable, tying shoelaces and wiping noses. The two women retired to the table and spent quite a while writing in the ledger, speaking quietly and only glancing up occasionally to check on their charges, while I attempted to keep the children amused by playing I-spy.

I think we all jumped a little when the church door was pushed open and three more women appeared.

Then my Madonna came over to speak to the children. She hitched up her skirt so that she could crouch down to their eye level, and spoke in a low, gentle voice that nonetheless held their unwavering attention. She told them that they had been very brave already and that now they were going to go on an even bigger adventure together. They should follow the ladies and listen very carefully to the instructions they would be given. They were going to go on a long journey in a boat, to a place where they would be safe. She knew how hard it was, leaving their parents like this – at this point I put my arm around the little one beside me, who had begun to sob silently, as if instinctively knowing not to make a noise – but one day their families would all be together again. In the meantime, their mammas wanted them to make this journey because they loved them so very much. They should always remember that.

With reassuring smiles, the women gathered their small charges around them and ushered them out of the church, back into the glare of the afternoon sun. I glimpsed a row of cars parked at the kerb just before the door swung closed again, leaving the church filled with a silence that seemed even more profound than it had been before.

I watched as the woman reread what she'd written in the ledger, her features clouded with a deep sadness. Then she closed it with a sigh. She seemed lost in thought as she picked up her jacket from the chair and pulled it on. I stood to one side, unsure what to do next. Had she forgotten about me? Was I about to be turned back out on to the streets? But then she came over and took my hand in hers. She said my name as if trying it on for size. 'Beatrice Crane.' Then she smiled and the sorrow was replaced with warmth, like a candle being lit in the darkness. 'I am Francesca Robbia. Would you do me the honour of coming home with me while we work out how best to help you?'

I had no idea, as I picked up my suitcase again and lugged it out to the rather grand Lancia convertible parked in a side street behind the church, how that moment and those words had just changed my life.

Chapter 6

Tess – 2015

Beatrice's car is a tiny Fiat, somewhat battered and still bearing the scars from the recent altercation with a municipal bin that led to her licence being confiscated. After our first outing to the shops in it, I realise it needs a bit of work. The passenger door won't close properly until a couple of dents are beaten out, and two new tyres wouldn't go amiss either. So I drop it off at the local *carrozzeria* just outside Pienza, and spend a few hours wandering the little town's streets while the cheerful mechanic attends to the car.

After exploring the shops, crammed with delicious-smelling cheeses and bewildering arrays of different types of pasta (*why do they need so many?* you say), I settle down at one of the tables beneath a parasol in the piazza, across from the cathedral. As I sip my coffee, I think about what Beatrice has told me of how she came to the Villa delle Colombe. It's a reminder of how life – and everything you thought you knew about it – can change in a moment. For her, it was the war. For you and me, it was the day we walked into the doctor's consulting room at the hospital and I saw the look on her face.

A year before that, we'd moved to the flat in Southampton when you got your dream job at the Ordnance Survey. It was the culmination of all that time you'd spent gaining your qualifications in cartography, the natural next step on the path of your life that you'd plotted out so clearly and navigated so logically and methodically. Your love of mapping the world around you, of interpreting and making sense of it, had always been leading you here. As a freelance photographer, my more haphazard career path meant I was happy to pick up jobs anywhere and was used to travelling wherever my work might take me.

Even on our combined income, it was a stretch to buy the flat. It may have been shabby and a bit cramped, but it was ours and we loved it. At the weekends we painted the walls and ceilings, bringing light into rooms that badly needed it, and we filled it with furniture given to us by our families or bought from charity shops. That was the first time I noticed how tired you were. I put it down to the move and starting your new job and the never-ending list of chores to do in our new home. And when you dropped that tin of paint, spattering the kitchen floor with white gloss, we thought nothing of it. *It was just an accident*, you said, kneeling to wipe up the mess. *My own clumsiness.*

But you were never clumsy. You were meticulous and methodical in everything you did, your dependability the counterbalance to my creative scattiness. We laughed it off though, and I thought nothing more of it at the time. Looking back, I think you already must have known something wasn't quite right.

There were more signs, too, after that. I should have been paying more attention. You spilled your glass of water over the supper table; you flexed your fingers – looking a little puzzled when they wouldn't do exactly what you wanted; you missed your footing on the bottom step: every single one of those mishaps was a warning. But you continued to laugh them off or explain them away, protecting me from the shadow that had started to creep over you, its progress so subtle as to be almost imperceptible as with each day that passed it blotted out a fraction more of your body's ability to function.

You tripped again, on a perfectly even stretch of path, when we were in the park. We'd taken time off from working on the flat to go out and soak up some sunshine. I thought it would do us both good and help lift the pallor from your cheeks. Once we'd picked you up and you'd assured all the passers-by who'd rushed to help that you were fine, I watched you walk over to the nearby bench to sit and regain your composure for a few moments. That was when I realised your right foot had dropped. The toe of your trainer had almost totally worn through where it had been dragging for months.

When I pointed it out to you, you didn't seem surprised. You just nodded and said, *I'll go and see the doctor next week – get it checked.*

The GP referred you for some physio. But when the physiotherapist realised the muscle pads of your thumbs had wasted away – your grip growing weaker despite all the DIY we'd been doing – she referred you to a neurologist. *She thinks it might be a trapped nerve in my neck*, you told me. *Nothing very serious and it should be operable. And she's given me some splints to put in my shoe to stop the foot dropping – they've helped already.* You were your usual dependable, calm, rational self. And because I so wanted to believe you, I did.

I went with you to the hospital for your appointment with the neurologist. She checked you over thoroughly and said she'd like to carry out a nerve conduction study. Even when she phoned to say she'd looked at the results and would like us both to come in for another appointment, we were still making light of it, hoping she'd identified a pinched nerve or some inflammation from a long-forgotten injury that would just go away given enough time and patience. But when we walked into her office and I saw the expression on her face, I knew.

I'd vaguely heard of Motor Neurone Disease. It was what Stephen Hawking had, wasn't it? And there was a rugby player, too, who'd been diagnosed with it – you'd pointed out the story in the Sunday paper a while back, saying, *What a dreadful thing to happen to someone who's always been so fit and strong*. But it wasn't something that could ever happen to people like us, was it? Not to someone as young and fit as you?

'I've asked the MND consultant and a specialist nurse to join us,' the neurologist said gently. 'They'll be your points of contact going forward and will be able to answer any questions you may have.'

They meant well, I know. They were our team now and they only wanted to help. But I was so distraught I couldn't take in much of what they said. The nurse handed me a white lever arch folder containing all sorts of leaflets. 'I'll give these to you, shall I, Tess?' she said. 'You can both take your time having a read through once you get home.'

When we stood up to leave, numb with shock, I left that white folder sitting on the table. I didn't want to read those leaflets. I didn't want to know what the future held for us now. I didn't want the diagnosis you'd been given. I didn't want to let any of it into the home we were building together: not the doctors' words, nor the feeling of sick dread in the pit of my stomach, nor those useless leaflets – a whole folder full of them! – that could only tell us how little could be done to slow the inexorable deterioration of your body.

A bell chimes the hour and I blink, realising my thoughts have taken me miles away from the café in the piazza in Pienza. The sun has moved overhead, and I'm no longer in the shade of the canvas parasol. The bare skin of my shoulders feels tight and hot, the burning sensation tugging me back to the present. I glance at my watch, then drain the last dregs of coffee from my cup. It's nearly lunchtime and the car should be ready. But as I walk back down the hill to the garage, my chest feels taut, my breathing shallow. I still carry with me the desperate anger I felt when we were given the diagnosis and it cuts into me as tightly as the straps on a straitjacket.

It was your diagnosis, but in a way it was mine as well. Neither of our lives would be the same again.

◆ ◆ ◆

In the gardens at the villa, Beatrice is teaching me the names of plants and how to distinguish them from weeds. It's a slow process. I resort to using my camera to record my lessons and each evening, when I'm not typing up Beatrice's story, I load the photos on to my laptop and label each one with the names I've learned that day. Potentilla. Erigeron. Salvia. I'm beginning to be able to tell my nepeta from my nigella. It's the names of the roses I like the best. They're so very British: Lady Sylvia; Mrs Oakley Fisher; Dainty Bess. I can just imagine how this English garden – as Marco had called it – would have helped Beatrice feel a sense of home here at the villa.

It's strange that she stayed on, even when the war ended, you muse. *You'd have thought she'd have gone back.*

Part of her story, I suppose, I reply. *We'll have to wait and see. Oh look*, I continue. *This rose is called Peace. It must have given Beatrice and Francesca such pleasure to plant it.*

Earlier, I'd asked Beatrice where they'd managed to find all those plants for the English garden. 'Francesca was always very resourceful,' she'd replied, with a smile. 'And very persuasive – she cadged seedlings and cuttings from everyone she could think of. But the roses had to be sent from a specialist supplier outside Florence. He was shutting up shop as the war started to bite. He could no longer get the bare-root plants, which mostly came from France, and with all the young men leaving in their droves he couldn't manage the workload any more. We took a lot of stock off his hands and gave it a home here.'

All those English roses, transplanted here. Just as Beatrice had been transplanted by the war. *Weren't they lucky Francesca gave them a home?* I say to you, shutting down my computer for the night. *When the war took away all other options.*

I don't hear any reply. I wonder whether you're thinking of your own war, the one that was declared on your body by MND. It was a war of attrition. A war we had no hope of winning. No matter how determined we were to fight it, the outcome of that war was never in doubt.

Chapter 7

BEATRICE'S STORY – 1940

The very first thing I did when I arrived at the Villa delle Colombe with Francesca was to have a bath, gladly acquiescing to her gentle suggestion that it might be a good idea. I didn't linger in it for too long – there was far too much to explore, and I didn't want my charming new hosts to think I was an idle laggard – but I jolly well made the most of the heavenly soap and warm water and scrubbed every last vestige of the prison and the hot Florence streets from my body and my hair. Then I changed into the cleanest dress I managed to find among the crumpled, grubby things in my suitcase and, smoothing out the creases as best I could, descended to the parterre.

I remember everything about that first evening as vividly as if it were yesterday. The way the light danced on cut crystal glasses; the little dishes of gold-green olives and salted almonds – it still makes my mouth water now, just thinking about them. The wine, poured from a bottle with no label, seemed to cool my blood and relax my limbs, which had been tight with fear for so many long days and nights.

The surroundings were as beautiful as anything I'd seen at the Pitti Palace or the Boboli Gardens and I think I must have gawped in wonder at the orderly beauty of the terrace, the views across the valley, the horses grazing quietly in the paddocks below the villa. But, above all, it was the company of Francesca and her husband, Edoardo, that made me feel I'd tumbled headfirst into paradise. The easy courtesy of their manners and the way they seemed to accept my presence at their table as a natural, everyday occurrence quickly made me feel comfortable. Edoardo didn't ask me any personal questions that evening – I suppose Francesca must have briefed him on her acquisition of this lost waif while I was having my bath – but he seemed as calm and wise as she was kind.

He was some years older than her, his hair liberally salted with grey, but his dark eyes shone with a youthful energy, especially when they settled upon her as she refilled our wine glasses and urged me to eat. When I admired the pair of horses in the neighbouring paddock, their glossy coats shining as they contentedly cropped the long grass along the fence line, Edoardo told me they were descendants of a long line of thoroughbreds, established by his grandfather a century before. 'The estate is one of the great stud farms of Italy. It's taken three generations and we've put in years of hard work to build the reputation it enjoys today. I'm especially grateful to that particular mare,' he said, nodding towards a fine-looking chestnut who tossed her mane as if she knew we were talking about her. 'She is responsible for introducing me to Francesca. Indeed, I strongly suspect my wife married the horses first and me second.'

Francesca laughed, shaking her head. 'Edoardo, you know that's not true. I love you all equally!' She turned to me and explained, 'We met at the Olympic Games in Berlin. I was there to support my friend, Ondina Valla, who was part of the Italian athletics team. We'd run together at school – I wasn't too bad in my day, but she was always way ahead of everyone in any race she ran. She became the first Italian woman ever to win an Olympic gold medal. Cheering her over the finish line for the 80 metres hurdles was one of the most thrilling days of my life. Then another friend invited me along to watch the showjumping in the *Olympiastadion* and the rest, as they say, is history.'

'I was part of the equestrian team,' Edoardo continued. 'Our riders may not have won anything that year – the German team swept the board, of course – but I certainly felt I'd been given the best prize of all when this beautiful woman agreed to have dinner with me in Florence when we returned home.'

He reached for her hand and squeezed it. Their closeness was evident. I supposed working together to manage the estate and continue the thoroughbred bloodlines Edoardo's grandfather had established must have helped bind them together in such a tight partnership in the four years since they'd met and married, but there seemed to be powerful currents of emotion there too, something deeper about their love – a meeting of souls, perhaps.

The housekeeper appeared then, bearing platters of cold meats and more little dishes of pickled vegetables. As she turned to go, Francesca caught her by the arm. 'Silvana,' she said, 'allow me to introduce you to Signorina Beatrice Crane. She will be with us for a while. Please would you go to the Yellow Room and collect her clothes? They will need to be washed tomorrow.'

Silvana gave me a glance that clearly told me what she thought of this imposition, but she bade me a brusque '*Benvenuto*' before stomping back into the villa to carry out her mistress's instructions. I tried to protest – I was mortified to think of anyone other than myself having to handle those filthy, torn pieces of clothing. 'Please, let me do my laundry in the morning,' I stammered, rising to my feet as I watched Silvana's retreating figure, which seemed to radiate disapproval even from behind.

Edoardo put a restraining hand on my arm. '*Prego, signorina*, sit down. Don't mind Silvana, she's always a bit suspicious whenever Francesca brings newcomers to the villa.' His tone, and the twinkle in his eye, seemed to imply that he quite enjoyed ruffling the feathers of the housekeeper.

'Does it happen often, then?'

He nodded and laughed. 'These days, yes. Increasingly so, in fact. Let's just say my wife is a renowned collector of people.' Francesca smiled serenely at this description and passed me one of the platters, urging me to help myself.

As I tucked into a large helping of *prosciutto crudo*, trying to maintain some semblance of good manners and not wolf it down too quickly, their conversation turned to the day's events.

'Did it all go smoothly with the children?' asked Edoardo.

Francesca nodded. 'All went well. Those poor little mites, having to leave their homes and their families. Beatrice was a great help with them though.' She turned to me, passing a basket of bread, urging me to eat some more. 'You will be wondering who they were and where they were going, perhaps?'

The sound of the woman weeping in the cell next to mine in Santa Verdiana came back to me. Had she been a mother? Had she lost her family? And where had she been taken on the day her weeping stopped and that terrible silence fell? I dabbed carefully at my lips with my napkin, composing myself, before replying. 'I think I may have guessed. Were they Jewish?'

'*Sì, claro.* It's so hard for their parents, having to let them go, but it will be much safer for them in England until this war is over. Ironically, at the moment it's been somewhat easier getting them out of Italy than it will be trying to get you home. I have friends in London and we've made arrangements for the children, you see. We've been trying to get as many of them out as possible before that line of escape is shut down too.'

Edoardo sighed. 'Time is not on your side, I'm afraid, *cara mia*. At the council meeting today, our Fascist friends were taking a far more strident tone. They sense their absolute power, now that they have the German Reich behind them. I'm glad you got those children out today, and the others before them, but I fear they may be the last ones we can help.'

Francesca's eyes flashed with anger. 'We must never stop trying to help those families. If we don't stand up against their persecution, then who will?'

He placed a hand on top of hers, which had clenched into a fist. 'Of course we will keep trying. I'm just saying that the risks are even greater now.' He hesitated. 'Umberto Ciccone stopped me after the meeting and asked me how your visits to Florence were going.'

She looked shocked. 'How did he know where I was?'

Edoardo shrugged. 'I don't know. But he was certainly insinuating he knew something. It would be wise to stay put for a while. If he's watching us, then it could put others at risk . . .' He tailed off and then suddenly changed the subject. I sensed he wasn't comfortable carrying on the conversation in front of me. When he continued, his tone was deliberately light. 'There is much to do in the gardens. You know you can't trust me to make the right decisions when it comes to telling what is a weed and what is one of your treasured plants. And I have an idea for a project that will require your planning. You always said you'd like to plant a maze, and since we have the manpower at the moment, I think we should do it.'

Francesca nodded slowly, the frown melting from her face as she took her cue from her husband. 'You're right, of course. I should focus on keeping everyone safe here at home.' Then she laughed. 'What a moment to choose to plant a maze! Don't you know there's a war on?'

He smiled. 'All the more reason. It will be an act of defiance. A sign that we believe in a tomorrow for our home and our country. That we still have hope for better days ahead. If we plan it and lay out the groundwork now, then we can plant it up in the winter. That will give it the best possible start.'

As I lay in my bed that night – the most comfortable bed I'd ever slept in, with its well-stuffed horsehair mattress and fine cotton sheets – my mind whirled with the day's events. Had I really only left the prison that morning? Had I spent the previous night lying on a hard floor with only a rough blanket beneath me, or was everything that had happened in the last month just a bad dream? The bites on my arms and the bruises on my shins were all too real, though. Was it only a few hours ago that I was trudging through the city streets in despair? And how on earth had I ended up in this heavenly place? All I could think was that a guardian angel must have been watching over me.

My last thought, as I drifted into the deepest of sleeps, was that I hoped – if such a thing existed – some guardian angel was watching over those children too.

Chapter 8

Tess – 2015

As I eat my breakfast on the little terrace in front of the cottage, I realise there's something missing. In the months since you left, I've felt as though all my most treasured memories of our lives together have been obscured by the images from those final weeks that play like a film on a continuous loop, cluttered with the paraphernalia of illness and peopled by the carers and nurses we didn't want but couldn't manage without. But now, the quiet promise of a new morning achieves what the pills and the counselling and the constant, anxious love of my family could not: the film in my head pauses.

In the quietness, I notice the little bunches of grapes, as hard and green as peas, forming on the vine above my head. I watch the swallows as they flit to and fro against the endless blue of the sky on silent wings. The sunlight dances with the wildflowers among the grasses along the edge of the woods and the air is cool and kind, the faint breeze a gentle caress against the bare skin of my arms.

Looking out over the valley with its patchwork of fields and woodlands, stitched together by lines of dark cypresses, my mind quietens. The clutter fades and a different memory materialises in that space.

A few days after your diagnosis, we took a trip to Pepperbox Hill. We used to love exploring the New Forest and its surroundings, walking the woods and heathlands for hours on end. You were at your most relaxed then, in your element striding through that landscape, mapping it in your mind's eye, making sense of the lines of escarpments and pointing out to me the difference between a river-sculpted hill and a Bronze Age barrow. That day, as we hiked up the trail to the viewpoint beside the folly that gives the hill its name, I think we both wondered how many more times we'd be able to make that journey. Your pace was a little slower, a bit more careful, and you fixed your gaze on the ground, studying where to place your feet so as not to risk a stumble.

We walked in silence for much of the way, each of us absorbed in our own thoughts, only commenting now and then at the glimpse of a herd of fallow deer in the distance, or the sight of a common blue butterfly whose wings matched the colour of the harebells growing on the chalk upland. I guess we were trying to distract ourselves by pretending everything was OK.

When we reached the viewpoint and stood looking out towards the spire of Salisbury Cathedral, just visible beyond the folds of hills before us, you turned to me and took my hand in yours.

Let's get married, Tess, you said. *Now . . . soon, at least. I want to walk down the aisle in my best suit. With you in a white dress and flowers in your hair. I want that for both of us.*

You didn't need to say those other words we were both thinking. *While I still can.*

And so we had our wedding a few weeks later, quickly arranged on a weekday to accommodate it at such short notice, the service squeezed in by the sympathetic vicar at our local church and the party in the garden of our local pub. We still hadn't told our families about your diagnosis.

They'll think we're in a hurry because I'm pregnant! I laughed.

And you replied, *Then let's let them think that. Give them all that gift of not knowing the truth, just for a little longer.*

You smiled at me as we walked down the aisle, wearing your best suit and the splints in your polished shoes to stop your foot from dropping. And to everyone who applauded and cheered, it probably looked like you were supporting me on your arm, when really we were clinging on to each other for dear life. You were hanging on to me so that you wouldn't trip and fall. And I was clutching your hand so that I wouldn't collapse, sobbing with rage and ranting at a God who could allow such a cruel illness to exist.

The thought of that anger jolts me back to the present, kick-starting the film in my head again, the more unwelcome images crowding out the snapshot of you standing on your own two feet, looking so proud and happy on our wedding day. It's hard to remember the version of you that could climb a hill so easily as I trotted beside you to keep up with your long, lanky stride. I try to reach for it, to bring it back in my mind's eye. But the memories are as ephemeral as butterflies, and I can't manage to conjure them again.

I get up from the table and begin collecting together my breakfast things. At least now I know the happier memories are still there. That, in itself, is something.

Chapter 9

Beatrice's Story – 1940

I remember waking up with a start on my first morning at the villa. I'd slept soundly, dreaming I was safely back home in Scotland, and for a moment I couldn't think where I was. The previous evening, sitting beneath the trees on the parterre with Francesca and Edoardo, seemed much like a dream too. And yet here I was, lying on a mattress as comfortable as a cloud, in a room with sienna-gold walls and curtains of yellow silk chinoiserie.

I jumped out of bed and threw on the dress I'd worn the night before, all my other clothes having been removed by Silvana. I still felt somewhat mortified at the thought of the housekeeper having to wash my filthy belongings and so I hurried downstairs to see if I could find the laundry and deal with them myself. But I was too late. She was just hanging the last of my blouses on the line in a little walled yard behind the kitchen when I found her.

'I'm sorry, *signora*, I wanted to help but I have slept too long. Thank you for washing my clothes. *Grazie mille.*'

She raised her eyebrows in the expressive way she had that managed to convey disdain, disapproval and exasperation all at the same time, although she seemed to thaw just a bit when she realised

I spoke pretty good Italian. That, at least, was a blessing. She picked up the empty laundry basket and swept back inside, with me trotting meekly in her wake. Then she broke her silence with a torrent of words: 'There's some breakfast for you in the dining room. Not that we have much to spare these days and I don't know how I can be expected to carry on feeding the five thousand, day in, day out, I'm not a miracle worker after all . . .' She broke off her grumbling in mid-sentence at the appearance of a tousle-headed boy in the kitchen doorway, and her face transformed itself with an angelic smile. 'Gio! *Carissimo!*' She reached out to stroke his hair but he ducked away, embarrassed. 'Signorina Crane,' his mother continued, unabashed, 'allow me to introduce my son, Giovanni.'

I shook his hand. 'Pleased to meet you.' He was about eight years old, I guessed, although even at that young age he had the compact, capable air of one already used to physical work.

'And what can we do for you, *bambino mio?*' said Silvana.

Her 'baby' blushed to the roots of his hair at being addressed this way in public by his mother. 'Edoardo has sent me to fetch a ball of string and a pair of scissors. We're working something out in the garden.'

'But he has those things in the shed, surely?'

'Yes, but we need more. Much more. Francesca has even raided her sewing basket to help.'

Grudgingly, Silvana opened a drawer in the vast wooden dresser that took up the whole of one wall in the kitchen, and handed him what he'd asked for. 'Don't you go losing them now,' she scolded. 'These things don't grow on trees, you know, and heaven knows how I'm to be expected to tie the *porchetta* if there's not a scrap of string left in the house.'

With a grin, Giovanni measured an arm's length of the twine and snipped it off with the scissors she'd given him. 'There you go, Mamma. I don't want to be blamed for ruining today's lunch. The others would never forgive me.' And with that he turned on his heels and ran.

After I'd had some bread and jam, I followed in the direction he'd taken and went to see what was happening in the garden.

I walked towards the sound of voices coming from beyond the hedge that marked the limit of the villa's formal gardens, then stopped in my tracks. I'd been expecting to find Francesca, Edoardo and Giovanni, but not the small army of strapping young men as well who were swarming over the knoll. There must have been about twenty of them, hammering stakes into the hard-baked earth and running assorted lengths of rope, twine, brightly coloured wool and Silvana's kitchen string between them, marking out what looked to be a tangled spider's web of lines.

They were in full Italian flow, talking, laughing, arguing, but when they noticed me standing gawping in the gap in the hedge, they became still and a wary silence fell over the group. Francesca turned to see what had stopped them in their tracks. She beckoned me forward with a smile and called to the men, 'It's OK. She's a friend from *Gran Bretagna*.' Their closed expressions dissolved into relief and, with a few cheery waves in my direction, they resumed their work.

'Good morning, Beatrice,' said Edoardo. 'I can see you have slept well. If I may be permitted to say so, you look a good deal more refreshed than you did yesterday evening.'

'Thank you, yes, I'm certainly feeling a lot better, thanks to you and your wife.'

'I'm glad to hear that. But please excuse me for one moment.' A heated argument seemed to have erupted on the knoll. Edoardo hurried over, accompanied by his small henchman, Giovanni, who carried a set of plans, in order to attempt to untangle a section of the spider's web that seemed to be the source of the altercation.

'He's in his element,' Francesca remarked, smiling fondly after him. 'He likes nothing better than a project, and preferably one involving many challenges. This maze is going to keep him happy for months.'

'It looks like it,' I nodded. 'And all those men too. But who are they?'

She shot me a sideways glance. 'Why, they are our gardeners, of course. But naturally, you may be wondering why there are so many of them and why they are all such strapping young men.'

'It had occurred to me to ask that, yes. Especially when there's a war on.'

Francesca turned to face me fully and her expression grew serious. 'They are here precisely *because* there's a war on. These are the sons and nephews and cousins of our farmworkers on the estate. The Fascists have issued a call-up to all men between the ages of twenty-one and thirty, to be put into their hated uniforms and sent to fight for their detestable cause. None of the young men you see here can stomach that. They'd rather join the partisans, becoming outlaws in their own land and fighting against *Il Duce* and his Nazi friends. They're risking staying on the estate for the time being, waiting for the day to come when they'll receive their conscription papers. But when they do, they will leave us and make their way to the mountains, where they'll join the ranks of other men and women who share the same beliefs in freedom and justice.'

I watched the team of 'gardeners' as I digested this. They appeared so carefree and yet they were living under the shadow of arrest, imprisonment and even execution if they were caught resisting the draft. And what of Francesca and Edoardo's role in this, too? They were putting their own lives at risk to help these young men. It brought home to me, with some force, just how serious a situation we were all in now. The setting might have been heavenly, but the war had created a hell for everyone in it.

For the past year, as a foreigner I'd skimmed across the surface of Italian politics, ignoring the grim reality of the Fascists' increasing strength while I thought I was being so cultured, immersing myself in the country's art and architecture and sitting around in cafés with my friends. I felt such a fool. What an ostrich I'd been, burying my head in the sand. And now I was another burden the Robbias had taken on, putting themselves at further risk. Well, I gave myself a jolly good dressing-down at that point and resolved that I would find ways to pull my weight. As long as I was their guest at the Villa delle Colombe, I would do everything I could to be a help. And I would start straight away.

Silvana's grumbling echoed in my ears. It made sense now – this was what she must have meant about being expected to feed the five thousand. 'What can I do?' I asked Francesca. 'Where can I be of most use?'

She watched as Edoardo paced out one side of the maze and then directed the work party to extend it further towards the woodland. 'I think we are surplus to requirements here. But we could go and pick some tomatoes. Silvana spoke of making *passata* this afternoon and I'm sure she'd appreciate a hand. Come with me – I'll show you the vegetable patch.'

And so began my apprenticeship in gardening. I knew nothing, really, at first. Back home in Scotland, my parents' house had a herbaceous border and a few ancient apple trees beyond it where we picked up the least worm-eaten of the windfalls in the autumn, but I'd been away at school mostly and had taken no interest whatsoever in my surroundings when I came home. My parents weren't gardeners, either. We had a man who came and cut the grass and pulled weeds out of the flowerbeds and occasionally my mother would suggest we take tea on the lawn (an enterprise frequently interrupted by wasps or midges or a very Scottish shower of rain). But here on the estate, gardening took on a whole new significance. We were growing the food that would keep us all alive.

Beyond the villa walls, behind the stable yard and the farm-house, in the same place it is today, was the vegetable garden, where a man in a broad-brimmed straw hat was quietly at work, hoeing the neat rows of greenery. Francesca introduced him: 'Carlo is our gardener – a permanent one, not one of those other ones who are passing through.' I noticed he walked with a pronounced limp and wore a boot with a built-up sole. Presumably that was why he'd escaped the draft. She continued, 'He's Silvana's husband, the father of little Gio whom you have already met. They run this place really. I don't know what we'd do without them. At the moment, we also have Danilo, Tommaso and Pietro here to help him. You met them up there with Edoardo's gang. Danilo is our head groom – he has such a way with even the most nervous horses, calming them with just a few words. Tommaso and Pietro help at the stables and in the gardens, wherever they're needed.'

'And all those other young men? Where do they live?' I asked.

'On farms scattered across the estate, with their families, but those three are our permanent workers here at the villa, as well as Carlo. Heaven only knows how long we'll have them with us.' She passed me the basket she'd been carrying and nodded towards the nearest bed of vegetables. 'Shall we?'

In Carlo's day, that garden was a cornucopia of produce. Onions, garlic and fragrant basil grew in orderly ranks, flanked by wigwams of flame-flowered beans. There were plum-coloured aubergines and scarlet peppers, tiny fiery chillies and the tall, silvered leaves of artichokes. Tomato vines scrambled up a trellis of wires in the centre of the plot. The fruits – little sweet ones and huge, lumpy *Cuore di Bue* – were beginning to blush scarlet where the sun had caught them and we picked the ripest, filling a trug to carry back to Silvana in the kitchen. As we worked, Francesca told me that the estate was self-sufficient in most things: the farms produced wheat, olives and wine and they had a few pigs and cattle.

'Other things, like wild mushrooms and truffles, we collect from the woods in the autumn. The Val d'Orcia used to be thought of as a barren place. Indeed, you can still see the landscape of the Crete Senesi along the sides of the main valley.' I nodded as I plucked another tomato from its stem, recalling the bare, clay-coloured hills, their surfaces deeply etched by erosion, that I'd noticed on the way to the villa.

Francesca continued, 'But here, Edoardo and I have tried to nurture this barren land. We are fortunate to have a natural spring, which provides water to the villa and the main *fattoria* and allows Carlo to work his magic here. And we've encouraged the farmers on the estate to cultivate different crops, those best suited to each farm's situation. The vines grow on the south-facing slopes, the animals graze where there is a little more shade, and the cereal crops do best along the floor of the valley.'

'You've created a Garden of Eden,' I said as we began to walk back up the track.

She smiled. 'Maybe. But remember, even the Garden of Eden had its darker side. Try as we'd like, we can't shut out the realities of the world from our little piece of paradise.'

As if to prove her point, as we rounded the corner of the villa a car came barrelling up the drive and stopped in a cloud of dust. She sighed, then said in a low voice and with a wry smile, 'Speak of the devil . . .'

A heavyset man with a thick moustache got out. Even from a distance, there was something arrogant and faintly belligerent about the way he stood there, waiting for us to approach. He wore a black shirt, its buttons straining across his barrel-like chest.

'Hello, Umberto,' said Francesca, her tone guarded but carefully polite.

'*Buongiorno*, Francesca,' he replied heartily. '*Come va?* And who is your charming young companion?' The glance he shot me was as sharp as a blade, belying the ersatz friendliness of his smile.

'This is Miss Beatrice Crane. She is a friend of the family, come to stay and help me with planning my English garden.' I blinked at these two untruths but managed to take his outstretched hand with composure. He shook mine, keeping hold of it a few moments too long.

'An English garden, hey? I hope you're not thinking of creating anything that might be considered unpatriotic, Signora Robbia?' His tone was at once mildly flirtatious and a little arch – on the surface at least.

She laughed lightly, as if his suggestion were a joke rather than a veiled threat. 'Of course not, Umberto. It's just a fashion. There are pictures of the style in all the magazines these days. Popular in Germany too, I believe. And now that all our young men have gone off to fight, I'm having to resort to recruiting this young woman to help me with the work. As you know, all our older farmers are pushed to their limits, keeping production up for the sake of the nation and with so many of their boys away, I can't look for help there. Now then, I suppose it's Edoardo you've come to see?'

He bowed slightly. 'Great though the pleasure is of seeing you, dear Francesca, I have indeed come to speak to him about a matter that arose at the council meeting yesterday. But please don't let me interrupt you in your duties.' He glanced at the trug of tomatoes she carried. 'I can go and find him myself if you just point me in the right direction.'

Without turning a hair, she handed the basket to me and smoothly took his arm. 'It's always a pleasure seeing you too, dear Umberto. Let us go and sit on the terrace and Beatrice will go and let Edoardo know you are here.' She smiled at me. 'Perhaps you would ask Silvana to bring us a nice cup of tea, too? That's one British custom that even Umberto enjoys when he comes to visit.'

I took my cue from her and hurried away to find Edoardo and warn him of the presence of our visitor. The team of 'gardeners' immediately melted away, disappearing into the woods with a surprising speed and stealth, while he rolled down his shirtsleeves and pulled on a jacket that he'd flung down on the grass earlier.

By the time I reappeared on the terrace, carrying the tray laden with a silver teapot and porcelain cups that Silvana had given me, Edoardo, Francesca and Umberto were sitting around the table beneath the trees.

Umberto took the cup and saucer I passed him, which looked far too fragile for his huge hands. '*Grazie, signorina*,' he said. 'Our gracious friends here have been trying to educate a simple peasant such as myself and I have discovered that this strange British tradition of drinking tea is surprisingly refreshing in the summer heat.' He'd leaned back in his chair, the thick trunks of his legs stretched out in front of him, a pose that seemed calculated to emphasise the threat of his presence at the villa. Every word he said, no matter how pleasantly delivered, seemed to contain a barb like a fish hook just below the surface, lurking there to trap unwary prey. Despite their apparent ease, I could sense that both Francesca and Edoardo were holding themselves carefully, choosing their words with deliberate caution, being sure to give nothing away.

I wanted nothing more than to retreat to the safety of the kitchen and thought of saying that I should really go and help Silvana prepare the lunch, but I realised I had to follow the example of the Robbias and play my part in this charade to make Umberto believe that we had nothing better to do than enjoy sitting in his company, listening to him hold forth on some petty matter of local administration. I was so intent on sipping my tea and trying to look natural that I didn't take in a word they were saying.

Finally, he set down his cup and saucer and got to his feet, mopping his moustache with a fine linen napkin. 'So I can count on you to back me in a vote if it comes to it at the next meeting, Edoardo?'

'Of course,' Edoardo replied. 'I agree with you on this matter entirely.'

'Well, that makes a nice change!' Umberto slapped Edoardo heartily on the back and I saw him try not to wince with the force of it. 'We don't often have many areas of common ground, you and I, do we, Signor Robbia?'

He took his leave with elaborate courtesy. 'Signorina Crane. Francesca. A great pleasure, as always, and thank you for the tea. Perhaps you'll make a marquis of me yet!' He roared with laughter at his own joke and then drove off, leaving us waving goodbye until he had safely disappeared. As we walked back to the villa, Francesca shot Edoardo an anxious look. 'He seems worse than ever,' she said.

'I know. What a slim pretext for turning up here unannounced. I'm sure he was trying to have a good snoop. All that talk about the vote at the next council meeting is complete nonsense, of course. As if any of us has a say in anything these days! He pretends to go through the motions of it still being a democratic process, knowing full well that no one would dare vote against the Fascists.'

'Does he suspect anything?'

Edoardo shook his head. 'I don't think he knows anything for certain. He's just always on the lookout for trouble. And if he can implicate those he thinks of as having airs and graces then it will give him even greater pleasure.'

'We must tell the boys to be careful, then,' Francesca replied. 'Even more than usual. Is there any word of when they might be moving on?'

'Not yet. But it could come any day. Don't worry, *cara mia*, they are safe as long as they stay hidden on the estate. Now, let's go and help Silvana serve them their lunch before she gets too cross at us for delaying it.'

We sat at long trestle tables, which the men set up in the shade, and ate thick slices of herb-infused pork, served with dishes of beans and tomato salad.

Afterwards, Francesca's 'gardeners' carefully cleared everything away and disappeared back to their hiding places in the farmhouses dotted around the estate. Only then did I feel the tension I'd been carrying in my neck and shoulders ever since Umberto's appearance begin to dissipate.

Francesca invited me to join her for a walk to look at the staked-out lines of the new maze. There was nothing up on that part of the land then, apart from dry grass. Gio was there, still doggedly digging away at the dirt despite the heat of the afternoon. 'Hey, look!' he shouted suddenly. 'Come and see what I've found!'

'Well,' said Francesca, 'that really is a find.' He'd unearthed a grubby-looking curved shard of glass and she rubbed the caked-on clay from it between her thumb and forefinger. 'It's a piece of an old jar, I think. And from the look of it, it could date back many centuries – perhaps to Roman or even Etruscan times.' She handed it back to him. 'Bravo, Gio, keep digging. See if you can find any more buried treasure.'

We walked to the edge of the slope, where the hillside fell away to the valley below. As she gazed at the view of the horses in their paddocks, watched over by Monte Amiata in the distance, Francesca grew thoughtful. 'You know,' she said, 'I think perhaps we really should plan an English-style garden up here. I've always wanted something a bit more relaxed than the formality of the *terrazza*. And this would be the perfect place to plant it. It would give the maze a softer setting too. By the time Edoardo and the boys have dug up half the cypresses in Tuscany and transplanted them here, it's going to be quite a bold statement. Some landscaping will help make more sense of this whole area.'

And so we began to plan a project of our own. I had no idea how much it would come to mean to me.

Chapter 10

Tess – 2015

In the evening, once I've helped Beatrice water the pots in the formal garden and she's settled down with a book, I take my camera and walk through the gap in the hedge to photograph the views beyond the cypress maze. The beginning and end of each day are when I'm able to find a few moments of peace and when your presence is strongest. Perhaps it's something to do with the light, the way it softens and suffuses everything with a gentle kindness. I try to capture that essence in my pictures – the night-scented stocks coaxed by the cooling air into surrendering their perfume, the luminous flowers of the tobacco plants glowing like stars against the fading silver of the lavender bushes – but it's as elusive and fleeting as the flittering bats and silent moths that emerge as night beckons them from their daytime hiding places. Walking beneath the arbour towards the viewpoint, I breathe in the heady scent of the wisteria whose cascades of blooms form a purple-blue canopy overhead. You walk there with me, watching as I pause to pick one of the white roses to put in a vase on my bedside table. You smile, and say, *Like the ones you had in your wedding bouquet, remember?*

You sit next to me on the bench at the edge of the garden, gazing out across the empty fields towards Monte Amiata, dressed in its evening garb of shades of faded lilac and grey. Across the valley, even the bare clay edges of the Crete Senesi look a little less barren in the evening light. But they're still a reminder of how fragile this landscape is beneath its cladding of crops and woodland. *I can't believe Marco's seriously thinking of making a golf course here*, I remark.

You shake your head sadly. *It'll destroy everything that years of careful nurturing have managed to achieve. All that water it'll need, and all those chemicals to keep the grass green and kill the weeds . . . It's grotesque.*

I think about how hard Gio and Beatrice work each day, tending the gardens, nurturing the delicate balance to maintain Francesca and Edoardo's vision. They're both old – Gio in his eighties, I imagine, and Beatrice in her nineties. These gardens have shaped them just as much as they have themselves been shaped over the years. Beatrice's hands are as twisted and gnarled as the stems of the wisteria plants and Gio seems as tough as the heartwood of the oaks in the woodland, his muscles still strong, forged by his daily work. He labours silently and sometimes when I watch him I get the impression he carries a weight of sadness, too, on those sturdy shoulders of his. It bows his body like the curve of a scythe.

Listening to Beatrice's memories of her arrival at the villa, I realise Silvana and Carlo would have been Gio's parents. If he grew up on the estate, then he must have some memories of those years as well. The gardens have been his life. How devastating it will be for him to watch them being bulldozed into the dust, if he and Vittoria are still around to see anything of it, of course. *Where will they go?* you say. *And where will Beatrice go?*

I shake my head, unable to imagine. *She seemed terrified when she said that instead of giving her back her freedom, Marco's taking over the estate would mean the complete opposite. It's understandable, of course. Any change must be a daunting prospect, at her age. Perhaps she's worried she'll be made homeless. Or have to move into a nursing home.*

The dusk envelops us, erasing the outline of the mountain as night falls, and you fade too, leaving me alone on the bench in the darkness, my camera in my lap.

Behind me, the bulk of the maze lurks, blacker than night. I think of Francesca, Edoardo and the men who worked on it, determined to build something in the shadow of the war. What was it Edoardo had said? . . . Creating the maze would be an act of defiance . . . that it would be a sign of hope for better days ahead.

I sigh, getting to my feet. I gave up on hope a long time ago. It was taken from me the day we were given your diagnosis.

Chapter 11

BEATRICE'S STORY – 1940

Looking back, I think I must have been rather spoiled and dreadfully naive when I first arrived at the Villa delle Colombe. My days in the cells at Santa Verdiana and the subsequent weeks of incarceration in the prison were the worst thing life had thrown at me up until that point. And my first few months in the safe haven of the estate did little to change that. It was only later that the realities of that war – and what they meant for all of us – began to hit home.

The rhythms of life at the villa were peaceful ones. Once Edoardo and his gang of 'gardeners' had finished laying out the maze, they dug deep ditches into the dry clay soil. Gio helped and unearthed a few more bits and pieces of ancient glass. Most of it was broken beyond recognition, but one day he came running to find us, triumphantly carrying a jug. It was small, the glass pitted and weathered, but the curves of the body and handle were elegant. Francesca consulted some of Edoardo's books in the library and found a drawing in one that looked very similar. 'Goodness me, Gio,' she exclaimed. 'I do believe it dates from Roman times. Possibly as far back as the first or second century AD!'

'I found this too,' he said, pulling from his pocket what looked like an irregular four-leafed clover. Francesca pored over it, leafing through more books, but was unable to find anything that looked similar. 'I don't know what it is,' she said. 'But I don't think it's broken off anything else. Look, the edges have been smoothed and shaped deliberately. Perhaps it was some sort of ornament or piece of jewellery.'

It was Silvana who solved the mystery. When Gio showed her his finds, she took the rounded shape in the palm of her hand. 'It's a dove,' she said. 'Look, it's exactly the same shape as the panettone mould I use to make the *Colomba Pasquale*.' She dug a baking tin out of one of the kitchen cupboards and it was indeed an identical shape.

'At Easter,' explained Francesca in response to my puzzled expression, 'we eat a sweetened bread, made with honey, almonds and crystallised fruit. And it is precisely this shape – a stylised dove. Gio, I do believe you may have found one of the original doves from which the villa takes its name. Perhaps it was part of a mosaic, used to decorate a house that stood here in Roman times.'

Gio carefully washed it in the sink, drying it almost reverentially on a tea towel. Once you knew what it was meant to represent, you could make out the head, the curves of the wings and the tapering tail of a swooping bird. 'I'm going to keep it in my bedroom,' he said. 'I'll take very good care of it. But, Francesca, please would you keep the little jug? It's a bit delicate and I'm afraid I might break it.'

'I'd be honoured to do so, Gio,' she said. '*Grazie mille*. It's very beautiful.'

There were no more archaeological finds from the ditches dug for the maze and so the 'gardeners' prepared them for planting, lining them with manure from a dung heap on one of the farms. They ran a system of drip irrigation into them so that the transplanted cypresses would quickly re-establish themselves.

When Edoardo had spoken of using cypresses to create the walls of the maze, I had thought he meant the structural needle-like trees that lined the driveway to the villa and punctuated the wider Tuscan landscape here and there with lines of zigzag stitches. But he explained they'd be using a broader, more spreading variety. They'd be topped to limit their vertical growth, encouraging their thick branches to grow horizontally and knit together, helping the maze take shape very quickly when it was planted up in the winter.

While Edoardo and his team dug the complex outline of the trenches, Francesca and I planned the informal garden. With enthusiastic help from Danilo, Tommaso and Petro, who seemed keen to enjoy the opportunity of a little female company, we marked out the meandering curves of the path and they dug out the flowerbeds. The clay was fairly easy to work, dry and crumbling, but without added nourishment it was barren land. We dug in quantities of well-rotted horse manure, which the lads brought up in wheelbarrows from the stable yard, to enrich the soil.

With help from Gio, who passed screws and held hammers for his father while he worked, Carlo constructed the wooden pergola leading to the viewpoint and the arbour at its end.

The whole project – the maze and the new garden – kept all of us busy for months and was a very happy distraction from the news of the war that filtered through from beyond the estate's wrought-iron gates.

Occasionally, Francesca would ask Danilo to saddle up a couple of the horses for us and she'd take me on a ride. I was a nervous beginner, but they put me on Clarice, an elderly carthorse whose pace was as languid as her temperament, and I soon grew to enjoy exploring the tracks that criss-crossed the valley, meandering through the woodlands and skirting the fields belonging to the dozen or so farms that comprised the estate. Danilo often accompanied us, exercising one or other of the thoroughbreds. His skill with the horses was impressive. He seemed most at home in the saddle, and I loved watching him gallop across a meadow filled with wildflowers, hair streaming in the wind as he urged his mount onwards. He was as sure-footed as the horses he rode and knew every inch of the estate. I learned from him that most of the other labourers had grown up on the farms we circled, and they were utterly devoted to Edoardo and Francesca, whom they regarded as part of the big, sprawling family of workers who called the place their home. They seemed a cheerful bunch, all those lads, despite the fact that they were living with the daily fear of conscription and would shortly make the dangerous journey into the mountains to join the partisans. Danilo told me they'd exchange their farmhouse bedrooms for cold forests and damp caves, living rough and fighting against their own countrymen as well as the might of the German army, not knowing when they'd see their families again. But they'd have each other, their camaraderie and their memories of their home in this secluded Tuscan valley. I hoped that would help give them the courage and resilience to see them through the uncertainties and hardships in their futures.

In our new garden, once the paths had been laid and the flowerbeds dug over for a second time with more farmyard manure, Francesca declared it was time we went to the market in Pienza to buy the plants we'd need. Carlo had done a good job of dividing and potting up as much as he'd been able to glean from elsewhere on the estate, and we'd dug up some wild jonquil bulbs from the edge of the woodland to transplant for spring colour, but we'd still need roses, wisteria and some of the larger shrubs to fill the beds and soften the edges of the paths.

I loved going to Pienza, one of the prettiest Tuscan towns I'd seen, perched on top of a high cliff with breath-taking views across the countryside. Its cobbled streets were lined with little shops, each one a treasure trove. There were sweet-smelling soaps and lotions, fine lace and linens, and displays of local produce – strings of dried *porcini* mushrooms, jars of artichoke hearts in gold-green olive oil, pungent pecorino cheeses and skeins of fresh pasta. The pale travertine façade of the Cathedral of Santa Maria Assunta presided over the main square, and its lofty interior always offered a cool, peaceful sanctuary from the heat and hustle of the piazza outside. That Saturday, Francesca drove us in the Lancia, its roof down and our hair tied back with silk scarves that fluttered in the wind. Edoardo came behind with Carlo in the farm truck. We made straight for the plant stall and soon delighted the nurseryman and his wife by buying up most of their stock. Edoardo also placed a sizeable order for as many young cypresses as they could provide by Christmas.

Once the plants were safely stowed in the back of the truck, we retired to the piazza for a refreshing glass of lemonade. We were sitting at one of the tables beneath a green awning, Francesca and Edoardo exchanging pleasantries with several friends and neighbours who had also come to see what they could buy or barter for in the market, when we heard the noise. I couldn't work out what it was at first, but as a wary silence fell over the gathered company it grew louder and louder. Then I realised. It was the sound of marching feet. Of steel-capped boots striking the cobblestones in unison, each synchronised step an ominous, brutal blow. And then they appeared. A cohort of *squadristi*: Mussolini's Blackshirts. The rifles on their shoulders, their unsmiling faces and the starkly distinctive insignia of flames emblazoned on their uniforms were sinister statements of their intent. They stopped in front of the steps of the cathedral, standing in neat ranks while the commanding officer addressed them, barking a series of harsh orders that served little purpose and seemed intended mainly for the benefit of the watching civilians. In the front row on the right, I recognised Umberto

Ciccone. And while he remained facing straight ahead, I got the impression that he knew we were there, that his part in the display was somehow directed solely at us.

When the officer had finished, his troops shouldered their guns once more, standing to attention. And then several people around us began to applaud. I was taken aback. Our pleasant morning at the market and the sociable camaraderie at the café had lulled me into a sense of complacency. It had all seemed so normal, so relaxed. But as the volume of applause grew around us, I was forcibly reminded that this was a country divided. The undercurrents of bitter political differences ran just beneath the surface. Unsure of myself, I glanced at Edoardo and Francesca, wanting to follow their lead. They sat still as statues, hands in their laps, not joining the applause. One or two others did the same, but we were the minority. It was suddenly a very uncomfortable place to be.

As the troop of Blackshirts turned with another loud stamp of those steel-capped boots and began to march away, Umberto's eyes slid towards our table, locking for a moment with those of Edoardo. That single look spoke volumes, crackling through the air like forked lightning. It was filled with a hatred so hot and bitter that my mouth turned dry with fear.

Once the militia had disappeared, an uncomfortable silence fell over the square once again. Francesca pretended to glance at her watch, as if remembering some appointment elsewhere. 'I think it's time we got those plants home, don't you?' she said, pushing her chair back from the table and getting to her feet. We left our drinks unfinished and walked away, with just a subdued nod towards the few others who, like us, had marked themselves out with their stillness.

◆　◆　◆

When the first rains of autumn fell on the garden, the young rose bushes we'd planted drank thirstily, pushing their roots deep into the earth and growing strong. We'd watered them diligently on the summer evenings when the sun's heat finally relented and allowed the air to cool just a little. All those hours spent lugging watering cans backwards and forwards paid off with a final flourish of late blooms before the plants began to die back, preparing themselves for their winter hibernation.

I spent my days helping Carlo, Tommaso and Pietro harvest the profusion of produce in the vegetable garden while Silvana and Francesca toiled in the kitchen, preserving as much as possible. Everything seemed determined to deliver up its bounty simultaneously as summer ended. We picked bushels of *zucchini*, peppers, aubergines, artichokes and tomatoes. Carlo showed me how to plait the drying leaves of onions and garlic bulbs, creating tresses that could be hung from the rafters in the kitchen alongside bunches of dried herbs, for use through the winter.

In the orchard, we gathered apples, plums and pears. Danilo hitched Clarice, who had spent the summer days grazing among the buttercups and searching for windfalls in the lush grass, to an old wooden cart and he and I made the rounds of the farms on the estate, distributing it all fairly. He would ask me questions about Scotland as we trundled through the Tuscan countryside, laughing in disbelief when I described a typical summer day back in my home country, paddling in the chilly waves that lapped the shore of the Firth of Forth beneath Edinburgh's stubbornly grey sky. We were close in age – he was just a couple of years older than me – and I was so comfortable in his company that he felt almost like a brother to me.

Some of the other workers had left by then, disappearing one by one as their call-up papers arrived. After that morning in the piazza when the cohort of Blackshirts had put on their display,

Edoardo became increasingly ill at ease. I overheard him talking to Francesca one day: 'Umberto's definitely taking more of an interest in us these days,' he said. 'And that puts others at risk. Perhaps I should stand down from the council. It's becoming more and more difficult, siding against him and his Fascist friends.'

She was quiet for a moment. 'I don't want you to do anything dangerous. But how else can we make our voices heard? We may be in a minority, but we have to at least try not to let them bulldoze their way over everything this country once stood for.'

It was Edoardo's turn to fall silent. And then he said, 'You're right, of course, my darling. We must keep going. But I think we should tell the rest of the lads it's time to prepare themselves for leaving,' He forced a smile, although not before I'd noticed the look of fear that passed across his face like a cloud.

Before the last of the labourers left, Edoardo asked for their help with one final piece of work on the maze. It was an adaptation to his original plan. In the middle of the complicated layout of pathways – still awaiting their cypress walls that would hide the way through – they dug a deep pit, excavating a chamber into the hill. They shored up the roof and walls, lining them with rough planks, and covered the opening in the ground with a trapdoor, creating a concealed space at the very heart of the maze. Once the grass grew back over it, no one would ever have known it was there.

I was reminded of something I'd heard Mr Churchill say on the wireless several months previously. He was talking about Russia's role in the war, and he said, 'It is a riddle, wrapped in a mystery, inside an enigma.' That was what I thought of when Edoardo showed us what he'd done. Francesca's smile was tinged with sadness as he explained that here was a place she and I could come if we needed a refuge.

I noticed he said 'you', not 'we', and I flinched at the thought of being trapped in that dark hole in the ground, the two of us hiding there, terrified and alone. It was as though he had a premonition of the dangers that were to come.

◆ ◆ ◆

Danilo, Tommaso and Pietro refused to leave with the others. 'My horses need me,' Danilo said with a shrug when I asked him why they were still here. 'And the other two won't go without me. We will leave when there's no other choice, but for now our loyalty lies here with Francesca and Edoardo.'

Less than a week later, the Blackshirts came for the horses. A truckload of them pulled into the yard early one morning as we were working in the vegetable garden. The men spilled out on to the cobblestones, the hammering of their boots making the horses start and whinny behind their stable doors. Francesca threw down her hoe and ran in their direction. I began to follow her, but she hissed at me to stay away. 'Don't let them see you!'

I ran into the woods at the side of the track, hiding in the undergrowth from where I could see the stables. Francesca strode into the yard, with Carlo hobbling behind as fast as he could.

Danilo had been doing his usual morning rounds, filling water troughs and replenishing hay nets. He made no attempt to flee when the Blackshirts arrived but stood facing them down, the broom in his hands a poor match for their rifles.

Francesca hurried forward. 'Who's in charge here?' she demanded.

One of the *squadristi* stepped forward and thrust a piece of paper at her. 'By order of the *Milizia Volontaria per la Sicurezza Nazionale*, we have orders to confiscate these horses. They are needed by the Transport Division.'

'Surely there must be some misunderstanding?' Francesca said, forcing her voice to sound calm, although I could detect a tremor of

84

fear. 'These are thoroughbreds, not suited for such duties in either build or temperament.'

As if reinforcing the truth of her words, a stallion whinnied angrily and kicked its hooves against the wall of its stable, the sound echoing around the yard and setting off panic among the other horses.

The *squadrista* ignored her. 'Saddle them up,' he shouted to his men.

They looked a little nervous as they approached the half-open doors, the animals within shying away from them, showing the whites of their eyes.

Danilo took a step forward, attempting to block the way of one of the men, and I had to clamp my hand over my mouth to stop myself from crying out as he was struck viciously with the butt of a rifle and fell to the ground. 'Arrest that man,' shouted the leader. 'What the hell is he doing here anyway? He looks old enough to have been called up by now.'

Two of the Blackshirts picked Danilo up and bundled him into the back of the truck. From my hiding place, I could see the blood gushing from his mouth, and I picked up my heels and ran through the undergrowth to try to find Edoardo. Surely he could make this right?

But it was too late. By the time he hurried to the stables, the horses were being led away. The militia hadn't been able to get saddles on to most of them, as they'd put up such a struggle, but they'd clipped on halters and roped them together. The last thing I saw as the truck pulled out of the yard was Danilo's face, pale against the darkness of the interior, as he held his head high and tried to call words of comfort to the terrified horses that followed behind.

I wasn't there when they executed Danilo in the square in Pienza. They did it to make an example of him to any other young men who might have been thinking of avoiding the draft. I sobbed into Francesca's lap when she told me. Edoardo had gone to the town and tried desperately to intercede on Danilo's behalf, swallowing his pride as he pleaded with Umberto to allow him to live. But they'd gone ahead and shot him anyway. Edoardo tried to comfort me and Francesca, telling us that Danilo had faced the firing squad with courage and dignity, refusing the blindfold they'd tried to put on him. 'You know, I think he preferred to die than to live without his horses,' he said quietly. 'They were his whole life.'

He was silent for a few moments and then he reached out and took Francesca's hand in his. He seemed to be struggling to speak, as if the words he was about to say were so tough it was hard to get them out.

She nodded, trying to smile through her tears. 'I know, Edoardo. I've known for a while that the day would come when I'd have to let them go. Tommaso. Pietro. All of them. And the horses too. After all, how could we have carried on looking after them with the boys all gone?'

We still had Clarice, though. The Blackshirts hadn't found the old carthorse, since Danilo had turned her out to graze alone in the orchard below the villa on the day they came. And when Tommaso and Pietro left a few days later, heartbroken at the loss of their friend, Clarice stood calmly among the buttercups as I buried my face in the solid softness of her neck and wept.

Chapter 12

Tess – 2015

'So is there still a hidden bunker at the heart of the maze?'

Beatrice's gaze slides away sideways, intent on our morning's work in the vegetable garden, as she replies. 'No, it was filled in many years ago. We don't go into the maze now. It hasn't been properly maintained. Gio's too old. We get a man who just tops the hedges to keep them looking neat from the garden. But the heart is impenetrable. It must be so overgrown by now that it would be impossible to find the way through.'

There's something evasive about her response but the brusqueness of her tone discourages further questions. She tucks the pair of scissors she's been using into the pocket of her gardening smock and picks up the trug of produce we've gathered – peppery leaves of rocket, sweet cherry tomatoes and handfuls of the little fiery chillies Vittoria uses to flavour her *arrabiata* pasta sauce. 'Let's take these inside and I'll show you how we preserve the peppers.'

We thread needles and pierce the stems of the *pepperoncini*, creating long strings of them that can be hung up to dry. As we work, sitting at the kitchen table, Beatrice tells me more about the estate in the war years.

'Most of the farms have been sold off now, but when I first arrived here pretty much everything you could see from the view-point at the end of the English garden was owned by Edoardo and Francesca. This whole section of the valley – the woods and fields, the farmhouses and barns – was part of the estate. The families who lived here had done so for generations and they had a real sense of belonging to this landscape. So those young men who helped create the maze had grown up here. Their parents and their grand-parents before them had worked the land and they would have been expected to carry on the tradition. The war changed everything, of course. It was heartbreaking for those lads to have to leave their homes and go off to fight in the mountains, living rough in caves and forests. The only consolation was that they knew how to live off the land, having been forged by it from birth.'

She reaches for another length of thread and begins a new string of chillies.

'The older men weren't conscripted at that time, so they managed to keep the farms running, at least at first. And Carlo couldn't be called up because of his bad leg. But all of us, the older men, the women and the children, chipped in and worked hard to keep it going. We knew we had to, in order to survive. I felt I'd been taken in not just by Francesca and Edoardo, but by the workers too. We were like a big, sprawling family, sustained by the estate.'

Once we've finished the strings of *pepperoncini*, I stand on a stool and Beatrice hands them up to me to hang from a hook beside the fireplace. We make a salad for our lunch and, when I've cleared everything away afterwards, I walk back to the cottage, leaving Beatrice to her afternoon nap.

You walk beside me down the lane with its views across the valley. *Imagine, the individual farms may have passed to different hands now, but this landscape probably hasn't changed all that much since those war years.*

I stop for a moment. I look out across this landscape every day, but never lose the sense of wonder I felt the first time I saw it. Even the fields seem to be a part of the natural wildness of the valley, respecting the delicate balance the land can naturally sustain. Then I can't help thinking of Marco and what a city slicker he is.

You agree. *Who would want to tame it? Why would anyone want to tidy away all the wild places?*

I sigh. *Nothing stays the same forever, though, does it? But what a tragedy it will be to lose that garden.*

I push open the door of the cottage, expecting you to follow me inside. But when I turn to look for you, all I see is the empty terrace beneath the *loggia*, with the dark shadows of the woods beyond.

Chapter 13

BEATRICE'S STORY – 1941

When the *tramontana* began to blow, scouring the bare ridges of the valley, Edoardo, Carlo and little Gio brought the lemon trees into the *limonaia*, hauling the heavy terracotta pots across the terrace on a wheeled trolley. The doves huddled in the dovecot overhead, fluffing up their feathers against the bitter wind, which cut through one's clothing like a knife.

We closed off many of the rooms in the villa for the winter too, their windows tightly shuttered, the furniture ghostly in the gloom in its shrouds of dust cloths. There were no more outings to Pienza or Florence – the car was parked up in its garage and we saved every available drop of petrol to keep the farm truck running when needed. The furthest we ventured was to the local hamlet of San Quirico, to barter supplies from the estate for things like shoe leather from the cobbler to mend our boots, or beeswax to make candles and polish the fine furniture in the villa. We were lucky that the estate was pretty much self-sufficient, so there was really no great need to go out and about. Edoardo fixed up an old bicycle that had been rusting in one of the sheds, and cycled to and from his council meetings or to check up on how our neighbours and the farmers on the estate were faring as winter and the war hemmed us all in.

I made the most of Edoardo's library, spending hours reading about Italian history, art and politics, while Francesca set up her easel and watercolours on the other side of the fire and painted the images of summer she'd captured in her sketchbook. We were comfortable in each other's company and no further mention was made of trying to sort out my official papers. Any approach to the authorities would only draw attention to my presence on the estate, and travel to England was nigh on impossible by then. I knew, from the reports we listened to on the wireless in the evenings, that the Italians were sending planes to fight alongside the Luftwaffe over the skies of Britain and that their navy had already established a submarine base on France's west coast as part of the German defences along the Atlantic, so it was clear that any doors to my escape had now slammed shut. I just hoped my parents had received my last letter home, telling them I was safe, before the postal services stopped.

I remember that February evening vividly. Francesca and I were sitting close to the fire in the drawing room, books on our laps and some dance music playing softly on the wireless. Edoardo came in, pulling on his coat. He threw another log on the fire for us, sending a fountain of sparks flying up the chimney.

'Do you really have to go to this meeting tonight?' Francesca lifted her face to receive his kiss. She raised a hand to stroke his hair and the gesture was filled with so much tenderness it made me smile. The two of them were illuminated in the halo of lamplight for a moment and it seemed to encapsulate their love, suspending it in a drop of amber for all eternity.

It was bitterly cold outside, the air biting and the stars bright with frost.

'You know I do, my love,' Edoardo replied. 'It's the vote tonight. Time to stand up and be counted.' Over the months, I'd heard him tell her more about the motion Umberto had proposed, restructuring the council and giving more of a say to the committee he headed up to oversee local land use. I'd overheard Francesca's querulous responses as well, when Edoardo told her he intended voting against it. It was a brave man who would take a stand against the Fascists, and even though the ballot would be anonymous, she worried it would be all too obvious where the voice of dissent lay.

'Please,' she said. 'Be careful.'

He pulled a pair of gloves from his coat pocket, deliberately cheerful, deflecting her anxiety. 'Don't worry, I'll wrap up well and pedal hard up the hill to keep warm.'

With that, he turned and left, closing the door quietly behind him, and we returned to our reading.

If only we'd known. If only we'd stopped him from going. If only it had been pouring with rain instead of cold and clear and still that evening.

We always know our firsts: the first faltering steps a child takes; a first day at school; a first kiss. But we rarely know our lasts until it's too late. For it turned out those were Edoardo's last words to Francesca.

When he still hadn't returned from his meeting by ten thirty, we were both worried.

'Maybe the debate has run on and on,' I suggested, trying to sound reassuring. By now, Francesca was pacing back and forth, unable to settle. 'Or maybe his bike has had a puncture. Let's take the truck and go and look for him.'

We knew we'd be in trouble if we were caught out on the roads at this time of night, but we couldn't just sit there fretting and wondering. We grabbed overcoats and ran to the shed where the truck was housed. I was shivering as I climbed into the passenger seat and I wasn't sure whether it was the cold or fear that made my teeth chatter so. We drove cautiously down the drive, the headlights picking out the dense black columns of the cypresses as we went. When we approached the road, Francesca slowed the truck so I could jump out and open the gates.

It was the bicycle I noticed first, in the shadows beyond the arc of the headlamps. Its front wheel was buckled, its battered frame twisted. And then I saw the huddled form, lifeless in the ditch at the side of the road, and I looked back towards the truck, not wanting what I'd seen to be true. Francesca saw the horror written on my face and she leaped from the driver's seat, pushing past me where I stood, frozen, beside the gates.

The sound she made is something I'll never forget. It was a howl of unbearable pain, which shattered the frosty silence as she stumbled towards Edoardo's broken body and gathered him in her arms.

❖ ❖ ❖

As is the custom, his coffin was laid out in the drawing room for all the estate workers and many of our neighbours to come and pay their last respects. We covered it with sweet-smelling cypress boughs and silver branches of olive.

The lid was closed, contrary to tradition, because his face was so battered and bruised as to be almost unrecognisable. We knew those injuries couldn't only have been inflicted in a hit-and-run road accident, which is what the police suggested. He may well have been hit by a car, causing massive internal bleeding, but his injuries suggested he must have been beaten too, as he returned from the meeting that night, having been one of the few council members to oppose Umberto in the vote.

Umberto was one of the last to come and pay his respects. He turned up at the villa the day before the funeral and asked me to extend his extravagant condolences to Francesca. On being informed by Silvana that he was at the door, she had retreated to her room, unable to countenance seeing him. We had no proof, of course, that he was behind Edoardo's murder, but she couldn't trust herself not to lose control and scream her accusations into his face. We both knew that would have dire consequences for us all. So I showed him to the drawing room and bit my lip, swallowing the bile that rose in my throat as he remarked to the other mourners standing by the coffin what a tragedy it was that we had lost such a respected member of our little community and how unfortunate it was that Edoardo had evidently been cycling on the road without lights on such a dark night.

The next morning, beneath a leaden sky, six farmworkers carried the coffin to the cart that waited at the door of the villa and we followed it in silence to the churchyard. Francesca was frozen in her grief, her face as white as the frost that encrusted every bare twig and each shivering blade of grass. She stood straight beside the grave and only swayed once when the priest threw the first handful of earth on to the pine lid. I slipped my arm through hers then, trying to give her strength, and helped her walk tall past the line of mourners. It was only later, once we were back at the villa, that she collapsed.

For the next month, Silvana and I cared for her day and night, worried that her grief might destroy her. It was devastating, seeing her in so much torment. We urged her to drink the broth Silvana brewed, and to try to eat a little. I slept on a chair in her room, keeping a nightlight burning so that each time she woke from the short snatches of fitful sleep her troubled mind allowed, the darkness couldn't overwhelm her.

Then one morning I went to fetch her breakfast tray and returned to find she was out of bed, standing at the window. I went and stood beside her.

'Look,' she said. From the upstairs window we could see a corner of the English garden beyond the hedge. A ray of spring sunshine fell across the curve of the path, illuminating a little patch of yellow stars. The jonquils we'd planted in the autumn had pushed their way through into the light. 'Remember what he used to say?' she murmured, half to herself. 'That planting the garden would be a sign that we believed in a tomorrow for our home and our country.'

I didn't need to ask who 'he' was. I nodded.

'Edoardo doesn't have any more tomorrows now,' she went on. 'But we do. I owe it to him to keep going, don't I? For your sake, Beatrice. For the sake of all our workers on the estate. And for the sake of their sons, off fighting in the mountains. We need to make sure there will be many more tomorrows that are better than today.'

She looked so weak and fragile, standing there with her feet bare, her nightgown hanging loose on her slight frame. But there was a thread of steel-like strength running through her even so. I was relieved to see that old spark of determination rekindle itself within her. I knew then that her spirit had not been completely broken. She would be all right.

Chapter 14

Tess – 2015

I reread the section of Beatrice's story I've just finished typing up. 'We always know our firsts . . . But we rarely know our lasts until it's too late,' she'd said.

I remember the first time you and I met. It was at a wedding. I was there to photograph it and you were one of the ushers. As we stood at the back of the church, waiting for the bride to arrive – she was the obligatory twenty minutes late, of course – you surprised me by asking where I'd come from and how long I'd been working as a photographer. Usually at such events, my role makes me invisible. The camera forms a barrier between me and the guests as I try to remain as unobtrusive as possible while I snap away, capturing hundreds of moments that will end up in silver frames and photo albums, on Facebook pages or as screensavers on people's laptops. Even during the formal photographs, no one pays much attention to the photographer, so I was used to being ignored. You were so tall in your tailcoat, with its coral-coloured rose in your buttonhole to co-ordinate with the bridesmaids' dresses, that I had to tilt my head back to see your face. I noticed how your smile was shy and a little lopsided, making the corner of your mouth lift more on one side than the other. It lent a quirkiness to your otherwise regular features that only added to your appeal.

Not only had you noticed me, lurking in the shadows in my working uniform of navy trousers and cream-coloured shirt, but you seemed genuinely interested to hear my replies to your questions. I was bunking on a friend's sofa for two nights, unable to afford a hotel room closer to the venue. Ordinarily I wouldn't let on about that to a wedding guest, but there was something about you that made me feel I didn't have to put on my usual act of professionalism. You laughed when I told you. 'The unglamorous reality of life as a freelance photographer,' I said with a grin. You smiled back, looking right into my eyes, and that glance silenced us both for a split second. You told me later that you knew, right then and there, you would fall in love with me.

But then the bridal car pulled up at the door of the church and I had to snap my attention back to the job in hand.

You caught up with me later, when I was taking the formal pictures at the hotel where the reception was being held. As I stood patiently, waiting for the excited chatter of bridesmaids and family members to settle down so I could take the photos, I became aware that you alone stood still amid the milling, fussing, laughing group. You were watching me and when you caught my eye, you smiled that lopsided smile again, distracting me from my work. Suddenly self-conscious, I ran my fingers through my hair, then pretended to check the settings on the camera, even though I knew full well that they were fine.

At last, the rest of the wedding guests went off to find more glasses of champagne and consult the seating plan for the meal, leaving only the bride and groom. I wanted to take a few more photographs of them standing beneath a rose-covered archway I'd found when scouting the hotel gardens the day before. You hung back, too, offering to give me a hand with the tripod and bag containing my lenses. It was entirely unnecessary – I was more than able to carry my own equipment – but I said yes.

A few months later, when we'd become a couple and were invited to supper with Max – your best mate – and Emma, who were the bride and groom that day, Emma told me they'd known there was an immediate connection between us as they posed beneath the stone arch and noticed how you couldn't take your eyes off me while I took those photos. She'd given you my number the next day and told you to get over your usual shyness and to give me a call and ask me out.

Our first date was a trip to the cinema. We watched the new version of *True Grit,* having discovered during our lengthy chats over the phone that we shared a passion for westerns. In the pub afterwards, we both agreed it was as good as the original. And then you walked me home and we had our first kiss on Waterloo Bridge as the lights of a London night shimmered in the dark water of the Thames beneath us.

All those firsts . . . And we never could have imagined then that there'd be so many lasts. The last time you could walk unaided; the last time you managed to dress yourself; the last time you could tell me, in your own voice, that you loved me.

And that last day, which we'd known about and planned for, so long in advance.

Chapter 15

Beatrice's Story – 1941

The cypress maze seemed to give Francesca comfort in the months following Edoardo's death. She would often go and walk there, picking her way through the labyrinthine paths to the very centre until she knew the way by heart. I suppose she felt closer to him there and the very act of walking those narrow green pathways allowed her to be alone with her memories of him. It was as if she was walking through her sorrow, moving forward into the unknown. But at least she was moving, rather than staying stuck inside the cage of grief that had imprisoned her at first.

While she walked in the maze, I would work quietly in the English garden, weeding the flowerbeds or tying the snaking tendrils of wisteria to the wooden pergola. It was the best way I could think of to keep her company while giving her the space she needed.

Everything we'd planted the previous autumn was reawakening after the dark days of winter. First those starry-eyed jonquils opened their petals to the gentle spring sunshine and the forget-me-not seeds that we'd scattered over the freshly dug earth wove a sky-blue carpet beneath the still-dormant roses. The twigs of each shrub still looked bare and brown, but if you looked more closely you saw they were covered in buds, as if they were impatient to follow suit and burst into flower.

I understood, then, what Edoardo had meant when he'd said planting the new garden would be an act of defiance. In the autumn, it had been an act of faith. That spring awakening embodied the rebirth of the hope we'd so very nearly lost during the long, dark months of winter after he'd gone.

Once there was no longer any danger of frosts, Carlo and Gio moved the lemon trees out of the *limonaia* to their places on the terrace and we dusted the cobwebs from the garden furniture and set it out again beneath the holm oaks. The wilder areas had their own beauty too. In the orchard, where the horse had been turned out of its stable to crop contentedly on the new grass, a blanket of buttercups appeared, as if by magic, beneath the trees whose branches were covered in a froth of blossom. There were scarlet poppies, too, which sprang up where the horse's hooves had disturbed the earth the season before. And in the sheltered spots along the fringes of the woodland, shy Etruscan crocuses and delicate pink orchids peeped through the grass.

We scarcely left the estate in those days. There was no need, and the world beyond wasn't one Francesca wanted to venture into – that place where a good man could be beaten to death and left abandoned at the side of the road. Edoardo was only one of the casualties of the increasingly bitter war that fomented and churned beyond the wrought-iron gates. We heard news of other atrocities – either on the wireless or via Silvana – and of the powers Mussolini had given his henchmen to stamp out any anti-Fascist activity. I often thought of the boys from the estate who'd gone to join the resistance in the mountains. Nazi retaliation was swift and merciless, and we just hoped and prayed none of them had been captured and killed. The wider news wasn't good either: in North Africa, the Nazis had joined forces with Italian troops fighting against the British, and the Blitz continued over London.

So there I was – officially an enemy alien, caught in the limbo of that war – and I realised again how lucky I was to be living quietly at the Villa delle Colombe. Silvana told us that any young men from the valley who hadn't left or joined the army were being sent to work camps in Germany to help with the war effort and I knew I could have faced a similar fate had Francesca not rescued me that day when I'd been released from the prison in Florence, and I was sure it was only her influence that kept me safe at the villa.

One morning, Silvana came to find Francesca. She was evidently in a state of some distress, her normally disgruntled expression replaced by one of anguish as she twisted her apron between her hands. Unable to get the words out, she burst into tears.

'Silvana, what is it?' Francesca asked, rising from the breakfast table to put an arm around her shoulders.

'My brother . . .' Silvana sobbed. 'He has received a letter from the *Fascisti* . . .'

I knew Silvana had grown up on one of the estate's farms and her elder brother Matteo was still the tenant there, having taken over the running of it after their parents died. She and Carlo would often visit on their days off, and she always spoke with pride and fondness of Matteo and his wife, Annunciata, as well as her nephew, their youngest and last remaining son, Alessandro. Their other three boys had left the farm the previous year to join the partisans.

She was sobbing so hard we couldn't make out what she was saying, so Francesca urged her to sit down and drink a little dandelion coffee until she could regain control a little. We'd heard the authorities had recently lowered the age of conscription from twenty-one to eighteen. She explained that Alessandro had recently had his eighteenth birthday and was therefore eligible to be called up to fight. He'd been sent his orders and had promptly packed up and headed off to join his brothers in the north of the country. But now Matteo had received a letter from the head of the local *squadristi* saying that, since his son had not presented himself for duty, Matteo was to be arrested and sent to jail. Apparently, this was a new tactic the Fascists had come up with to try to prevent the disappearance of so many conscripts.

'What are we to do?' Silvana sobbed again. 'Matteo is an old man. He's exhausted with all the extra work since the rest of the boys left and it's taken a toll on his health. This will kill him. And how can Annunciata keep the farm running on her own?'

Francesca tried to comfort her. 'I'm not sure there's anything we can do. But let's at least attempt to reason with the authorities. Tell Matteo to come here to the villa on the day of his arrest so that I can speak to the *squadristi* when they come for him. I'll explain to them how vital he is to the running of the estate. Perhaps we can appeal to their better nature.'

We all knew it was futile. Silvana told us several of the neighbours had been threatened with similar letters and a few of their sons had given themselves up rather than let their fathers be arrested.

Early the following Monday morning, Matteo arrived at the villa, having walked the three miles from his farm. He carried a battered suitcase and was dressed in his best Sunday suit. There was something even more heartbreaking about the fact he'd attempted to maintain those shreds of his dignity in the face of the jail sentence he was threatened with, in order to save his youngest son. We gave him some breakfast and settled down to await the arrival of the Fascists.

By lunchtime, no one had appeared. We were all so on edge we could hardly choke down the lunch Silvana brought out for us. She urged Matteo to eat, conscious this might be the last good meal he'd have in a long time. The hours stretched out and Francesca and I tried to occupy ourselves with a little gardening. Matteo sat staring into the middle distance, a look of hopeless resignation on his lined face.

But still no one came, and by the end of the day Francesca told him to go back to the farm. 'If they come for you, we'll send word. But it looks as if they're as disorganised as ever. Go home, Matteo, and may God protect you and your family.'

Although he still had to live with the dread of arrest hanging over him, they never did come for him, and slowly life returned to normal for Matteo and Annunciata as they struggled to keep the farm running without the help of any of their sons. The incident did nothing for Silvana's nerves, though, leaving her more angry than ever about the state of the world in which we lived and the *idioti* who were running it.

The local Fascists continued to threaten those of us left in the valley, posting their decrees on walls and lampposts in San Quirico and stopping anyone who ventured on to the roads to demand they show their papers and explain their business. Nationally, as if one war wasn't enough, Mussolini led Italian troops into Albania to attack Greece as well. In the spring, that operation failed. Despite being vastly outnumbered, the Greeks fought back in the barren mountain terrain with a fierceness and a determination that overwhelmed the Italians and *Il Duce* made no headway. Even the reports on Radio Roma reluctantly admitted that there had been thousands of Italian casualties in that particular attempt to expand Mussolini's control.

And so the war surged and seethed back and forth across Europe and we did our best to keep to ourselves in our own little world on the estate, in what we hoped was now a forgotten corner of Tuscany. Spring gave way to early summer and we tended our gardens every day, nurturing and watering the vegetable patch and the English garden. The wisteria bloomed and then scattered its purple petals like confetti beneath the pergola, and then the fat rosebuds opened, their fragrance another reminder of our small acts of defiance and hope in the face of war. Francesca continued to walk in the maze each afternoon, as if sleepwalking through her grief, once the heat had begun to relinquish its grip on the day and the growing branches of the cypresses cast their dark shadows across its paths. While the rhythm of the seasons continued, it felt as if we had become stuck in a sort of purgatory, going through the motions of our daily lives, still stunned by Edoardo's death and waiting for we-knew-not-what to come next.

One day, though, a letter arrived that would shake us out of our stupor.

It was hand delivered, left on the doorstep of the villa one night by some unknown courier, weighted down with a pebble. Silvana found it there when she arrived in the morning and placed it on the breakfast table, propped against a jar of cherry preserve. Francesca read it in silence and then folded it and put it back in the envelope. She seemed deep in thought as she spread jam on a slice of bread. Then she looked up and gave me a broad smile – something I hadn't seen for many months. 'Beatrice,' she said. 'We are going to have some visitors. We shall have to prepare.' She picked up the bread and took a large bite out of it, then reached for the teapot and topped up our cups. She hadn't shown much of an appetite at all since Edoardo's death, so all these little acts came as a huge relief to me. It was as if she was coming back to life, reawakening from the winter of her grief with a glint of the old light of passion and purpose shining in her eyes.

The letter was from one of her local Red Cross connections, who had been in contact with others in the north of the country. Turin had been bombed several times already. With the escalation of the war, and especially some of the more recent Italian attacks on British ships in the Mediterranean, further retaliation was expected against the factories in the north. They were looking for a place to house a dozen children, to evacuate them to the relative safety of the countryside further south, and Francesca's name had been mentioned by a colleague. Would she perhaps consider offering the children a home until it was safe for them to return to their families in Turin?

No consideration was needed. Over the remains of our breakfast, we made plans for which rooms to put them in and what we might need in the way of cots and clothes and toys, and then Francesca went off to leave a message at the café in San Quirico confirming she would take in the children.

A few days later, Carlo helped us load up the truck with a barrel of wine for our journey to Montepulciano, where we were to collect the children. The barrel was to be our cover story for our trip if we were stopped along the way by any member of the local militia – a delivery to a *commerciante di vini*, who would bottle the wine and sell it on. As Francesca explained, it wasn't that we were trying to hide the children's presence at the Villa delle Colombe – there was nothing wrong with having them there as refugees – it was just that she preferred to keep it quiet. It was nobody's business but ours and she was naturally cautious in those days, when we lived in the shadow of so much suspicion and distrust.

Once we'd offloaded the barrel at the wine merchant's shop, we parked the truck down a narrow alleyway at the side of the church of Santa Lucia. We slipped through the door beneath the soaring travertine portico into the central nave. Light streamed through the rose window above the main altar, illuminating the worn tiles on the floor and catching the dust motes that danced on incense-scented air. Francesca led the way to a small chapel, tucked into a dark corner to the right of the entrance. It took a moment for my eyes to adjust to the gloom. The first thing I saw was the painting by Signorelli of the Madonna and her child, her simple red dress glowing richly in the darkness. And the second thing I saw was the children. They were huddled on two hard wooden pews, their faces as white as the marble walls of the church, and they looked a very sorry picture indeed, scared and exhausted as they were.

They must have been in a state of shock. Later, we learned their homes in Turin had been bombed and several of the families had been camping out in basements in the ruins for months. They had witnessed death and devastation, had lived with the constant fear of more bombing raids, and sickness and malnourishment had taken their toll too. By the time they were delivered into our care, they'd also been on a long journey from the north, negotiating roadblocks and passing through war-torn towns. For all they knew, they'd arrived at the very end of the Earth, separated from their families and banished to live with strangers. It must have felt more like a punishment than a deliverance.

We helped them collect up their pitiful bundles of belongings – a few clothes, a treasured doll made of rags – and led them to the truck. They were mostly about five to ten years old, but there were one or two younger ones, who clung to their older siblings in terror and sobbed at the prospect of another journey in this strange place. I was glad that I could comfort them, telling them I understood, that I'd been through an ordeal of my own before I ended up at the Villa delle Colombe, that all was well now. For a safe refuge awaited them just a short drive away.

Chapter 16

Tess – 2015

The Tuscan summer switches itself on all of a sudden. One day the temperature is still pleasantly warm as Beatrice and I work the whole day in the garden, the next the air is laden with heat, weighing down our limbs and draining our energy.

The nights are now thick and heavy, making my arms and legs prickle with irritation and keeping me awake for hours on end. When I do, at last, fall into a deep sleep, my dreams are troubled and troubling. Your daytime presence – the comforting one made up of mirages of happier times before your illness overwhelmed you – is obscured by more recent, vivid memories.

You are trapped in your body, your eyes pleading with me to help you find a way out of your living hell. I try to reach you, but stumble among the paraphernalia that enables us to keep you at home – the wheelchair, the hoist, the bottles of medicine and the bags and tubes that drain your poor, shrinking body. You speak, in those dreams, in the electronic monotone that replaced your own voice in your final year, further robbing you of your humanity and making your thoughts sound flat and emotionless. Sometimes I dream I'm walking down a long, dark corridor and there are cells like cages with steel bars on either side. In one of them, I find you slumped in your chair, unable to raise your head when I say your name. Then I hear another voice calling for me and I look into the next cell. Beatrice is there, clinging to the bars, begging me to unlock the door and help her get out. I begin to run, in that sickening slow-motion dream way where my legs won't work properly, searching frantically, looking for a key or for someone who can help me, but the corridor twists and turns, its walls becoming thick, knitted branches, and I realise I'm lost in the cypress maze.

I wake, gasping for air, lying among tangled, sweat-soaked sheets, my head and heart still pounding with the feeling of helpless terror, sick with a dream hangover.

The early mornings bring a little relief, each sunrise banishing my nightmares back to the dark corners of my mind with the promise of another day's work to distract me and the hope of your calm company once again. But the heat is still oppressive.

Beatrice must notice I'm struggling a bit because she often tells me to go and take a dip in the pool. The water is almost bath-like, heated by the blaze of the sun, but it's still a welcome way to cool down a little. 'Don't worry,' she says. 'In a few days there'll be a thunderstorm and this mugginess will break.'

One morning, she announces she'll be away for the day. Gio and Vittoria are taking her over towards Arezzo to visit an old friend. 'Would you like to come too, Tess? Or we could drop you in Montepulciano and pick you up on our way back? Otherwise you're free to take the car, of course, and go anywhere you'd like.'

I thank her but decline the invitation. It's too hot to think about driving anywhere, especially in Beatrice's old banger, whose air conditioning is long gone and would cost more to fix than the whole car is worth. It'll be a good opportunity to type up more of Beatrice's story inside, out of the heat of the day, and perhaps to take some more photographs of the garden and swim in the pool.

I wave the three of them off, then go back inside the villa. The old library is the coolest place to sit, I've discovered. Its thick walls are lined with books and antique prints and there's a framed collection of butterflies, too, their fleeting beauty preserved behind glass for posterity. When I'm on my laptop in that room, it connects me to the past, making it easy to picture Beatrice and Francesca there in those war years.

I stop for a swim at lunchtime, then drag one of the sun loungers over to the terrace and lie in the shade. The heat kills my appetite, but I pick at a plate of prosciutto with slices of melon, the perfumed juices sticky on my fingers, and gulp down glasses of iced water to slake my thirst.

All around, the hot air reverberates with the song of the cicadas and a thick drowsiness creeps over me like a blanket, my limbs and eyelids growing heavy . . .

I fall into a deep sleep and yet again I dream of finding you trapped in a prison cell and becoming lost in the cypress maze. I wake with a start, my own cry of anguish bringing me to my senses again. As the pounding of my heart begins to slow a little, I recall the words of Beatrice's story I'd been typing that morning. *The cypress maze seemed to give Francesca comfort in the months following Edoardo's death. She would often go and walk there, picking her way through the labyrinthine paths to the very centre until she knew the way by heart. I suppose she felt closer to him there and the very act of walking those narrow green pathways allowed her to be alone with her memories of him. It was as if she was walking through her sorrow, moving forward into the unknown. But at least she was moving, rather than staying stuck inside the cage of grief that had imprisoned her . . .*

I look across to the walls of the maze, just visible where they rise beyond the hedge. And suddenly I know I need to brave it, to try to penetrate its dense, dark heart, so that I too can move forward. If I can find a way to navigate it, maybe it will stop the dreams. Maybe it'll help me, as it helped Francesca. Maybe it will show me the way to navigate my grief.

But now I know the centre has been left to grow in on itself, I'll need some secateurs and the pair of strong, long-handled clippers that Gio uses to lop larger limbs when pruning trees. I remember the terror I felt the last time I stepped into those dark, twisting alleyways and how quickly I'd become disorientated, losing sight of the way out. And then I hear your voice, as clear as day. *Take the compass. Make a map*, you say. *Then you'll be able to make sense of where you are and be able to find your way back.*

I go back to the cottage to retrieve the compass. Dressed and armed with some sheets of paper and a pencil, too, as well as the gardening tools, I climb the knoll to the entrance to the maze. I slip off the shirt I'd put on over my vest top to protect me from the sun, realising I won't need it in the shaded pathways and it'll only make me even hotter. I let it fall to the ground in a heap and then, squaring my shoulders, I step into the dark embrace of its green walls and walk forwards to the first branch on the path. I stop, set down the tools, take a bearing and mark the first lines on my paper. Then I tuck the pencil behind my ear and carry on, choosing the right-hand fork. I have to retrace my steps several times, but the compass helps me keep track of the orientation of each pathway and the map does its job. I start to feel a little more confident in navigating the outer sections. You walk in the maze alongside me this time, nodding in approval each time I add another bit of the route to the map. *Be methodical*, you say. *It's best to plot the whole of the maze, even the paths you know lead to dead ends or loop back on themselves. That way you can make sense of the layout. Take your time.*

I've covered much of the ground when, at last, I come to the central section, which takes me round in a full circle, the entryways sealed shut by the overgrown branches. So intent have I been on my mapmaking that I've scarcely registered the distant rumbles of thunder accompanying my progress. But all of a sudden a much louder rever-beration shakes the air, bringing me to my senses. I look up at the sky between the cypress walls and see billows of angry black clouds. The humidity is suffocating and sweat drips from my face on to the map, making it difficult to draw. I set down the sheets of paper on the ground and wipe my forehead and hands with the hem of my T-shirt.

Just then, a gust of hot wind comes out of nowhere, heralding the storm that's about to break. It buffets the walls of the maze, forcing its way through them, catching the sheets of paper and blowing them in all directions. My map slips underneath the lower branches of two of the cypresses into an adjacent pathway. I stretch an arm through to try and reach it, but it flutters just beyond my grasp. *Never mind*, I say to you, *we'll just retrace our steps and then I'll be able to get it back. It's probably time to get out of here anyway. I can come back another day, now I've worked out how to get to the central section.* But there's no reply. I'm alone.

I try to swallow the panic rising in my throat, telling myself to stay calm. I walk back to the last gap I came through and turn into the pathway where the map should be. But by the time I get there, the pieces of paper have been scattered again, picked up and tossed into the air by the storm that's now closing in from all sides. I reach for one sheet that's pinned itself to a branch, praying it's the map, but it's blank. I try to take another bearing from the compass, but my hand is shaking so much the needle swings wildly, only increasing my sense of terror.

Hard pellets of rain begin to fall as I stand for a moment, try-ing to let the compass settle and to remember the lines I'd drawn. I think I'm going in the right direction but time after time I find myself back at the impenetrable centre.

I'm completely disorientated now, stumbling along random pathways, panicking as the sky above splits in two with a snake-tongued fork of lightning, followed almost immediately by an ear-splitting crack of thunder. Suddenly I'm acutely conscious that I'm on the highest piece of ground in the garden and I realise how stupid I've been. The next bolt of lightning could well strike the maze, with me trapped inside it. I'm running now, forcing my legs to carry me along the narrow, high-sided pathways, but it's like being back in my dream, unable to find a way out, and I begin to sob.

Then I hear something above the din of the storm. Someone is shouting my name. I wheel around and see Marco standing at the far end of the path. He's a good deal more dishevelled than the last time we met, his hair hanging in damp, bedraggled strands over the collar of his crumpled shirt. He's calling me, urgently motioning with his hands for me to come that way. As another flashbulb of lightning bursts overhead, my fear overcomes the antipathy I feel for the man and I run towards him. He grabs my hand and pulls me down two more pathways, turning back on ourselves so that for a moment, with another surge of alarm, I think he's leading me the wrong way. But then we emerge through the exit and into the full force of the storm.

I gasp as the rain spatters my head and shoulders and try to remove my hand from Marco's, but he's gripping it so tightly that I'm pulled along in his wake as we race to the villa. We stumble through the door and he slams it behind us, finally relinquishing his hold on me.

In the hall, with the noise of the storm outside muffled, we both stand for a moment, gasping for breath, stunned by the sudden quietness. He stares at me, his expression dark with fury, and I'm acutely aware of my bedraggled state, sweaty, storm-blown and soaked.

'What on earth did you think you were doing, getting yourself lost in that maze with a storm brewing?'

I disregard his question and ask one of my own. 'How did you know where I was?'

'I'd been at a meeting near Siena, seeing an architect who's a business partner of mine. It was so hot, on my way back to Pienza I thought I'd swing by the villa and have a swim. My hotel doesn't have a pool. And this one belongs to me, after all.'

I choose to ignore his barb.

'There was no one here, so I had a dip. I was just collecting my things, getting ready to go before the storm reached the villa, when this piece of paper fluttered at my feet.' He produces my map from his pocket, crumpled and soggy. 'I wondered what it was at first. And then I realised it was a plan of the maze. *Naturalmente*, I thought no one could possibly be stupid enough to actually venture in there in a thunderstorm, but I thought I'd better check just in case. I saw your shirt on the ground beside the entrance just as the storm hit.' I realise he must have picked it up, as he's holding it in his other hand – a limp, bedraggled rag. 'I used your map to find my way in and then I saw you and shouted. You know you could have been killed in there if the lightning had struck?'

I suppose I should thank him, but he's so self-righteous and arrogant I can't bring myself to say the words.

'What *did* you think you were doing?' he asks again, refusing to let it drop, and all the adrenalin that's been pumping through my veins sparks my anger.

'If you must know, I was trying to find a way to stop hurting so much,' I retort. 'I don't suppose you'd understand, since other people's feelings obviously mean nothing to you.' My voice shakes with indignation and hatred as I get into my stride. 'OK! So there was a thunderstorm, but I didn't know that when I started! I haven't slept properly for weeks so I probably wasn't thinking very clearly. And you haven't helped, marching in here and upsetting everyone with your ultimatums and your hateful plans!'

My outburst seems to floor him momentarily. He doesn't reply straight away, as I'd expected him to, with some dismissive response of his own. As I stand there, dripping on the hall tiles and glaring at him, the expression on his face changes. His own anger seems to melt away and his eyes soften. It's as if he's looking at me for the first time and really seeing me for who I am.

'Why do you hurt so much?' he asks, and his voice is quiet and low. If I didn't know him better, I might think there was almost some compassion in his question.

I shake my head, suddenly unable to speak because I think if I open my mouth, everything will come spilling out in a torrent of rage and pain and despair.

'Here,' he says, passing me my sodden shirt. 'You'd better dry yourself off a bit. And then let's get a hot drink, shall we? I think we both need something to calm our nerves after dicing with death out there.'

I go to the downstairs bathroom to compose myself a little and by the time I return Marco has the kettle boiling. We sit at the kitchen table, cups of lemon verbena tea before us, and he says, '*Allora*, I'm sorry you are sad, Tess. Would you like to talk about it? I'm told it helps, although I'm no expert. Communication was never a strong point in my family.' His smile is kind, for once, and a little self-deprecating. I feel he's letting down his guard just a bit. Maybe it's the fact that English isn't his first language that contributes to this emotional directness, or perhaps it's the after-effects of the drama we've just shared, but I drop my guard too, suddenly feeling too exhausted to keep up the effort of holding those barriers in place. Once I start to talk, it all spills out. I tell him about you, about the past three years, about how watching your pain was so unbearable. I tell him about the hopelessness and the anguish of seeing the illness consume your body and not being able to do anything to help you.

And I say what I've never said to anyone before: when you left, that final day in the clinic in Switzerland, your pain was over. But I held your hand as you closed your eyes, and I took your pain from you and made it mine. It was all that was left – all I had to remember you by. And it became something I had to bear all alone.

The storm has passed by the time I finish talking, far-off rumbles of thunder sounding its retreat. Marco drains the final dregs from his cup and sets it down carefully on the scrubbed pine table. He's listened in silence to my outpouring, only prompting me now and then with a quiet question. I feel empty, as drained as the thunderclouds, the flood of emotion having washed through me. I'm not sure how much he's taken in, but then he says, very quietly, 'You are brave, Tess. I guess we all have our burdens to carry but yours is an especially heavy one.' He's silent again for a moment, then continues, 'You gave him such a gift. Staying with him all through that final bit of his journey. Letting him go when all you wanted to do was make him stay. Even though it broke your heart, you gave him the greatest gift of all.'

I raise my eyes to his, my face wet with the angry, despairing, helpless tears I've cried as I've talked, and am surprised to find his expression has softened and he seems to observe me with a kinder gaze. In that look, I sense a spark of connection between us – a recognition of something shared. He hesitates, then reaches out a hand and squeezes mine. I sit there, frozen, looking at our intertwined fingers, scarcely breathing. But then the moment passes, and he withdraws his hand, glancing at his watch.

'I must be going,' he says. 'You'll be all right now?'

I nod. 'The others will be back soon. I should go and get changed. And Marco . . . thank you. For listening. And for coming to find me in the maze.'

'I'm glad I was here,' he says. 'And I'm glad your guardian angel sent that map flying to me so I could come and find you. I think you and I are not people who find it easy to ask for help. But sometimes we can't do everything alone.'

We let ourselves out of the villa and he walks with me as far as the stable yard. '*Arrivederci*,' he says. 'Look after yourself, Tess.'

And as I walk down the lane to the cottage, I glance back and see him still standing beneath the stone arch, gazing out across the valley as the dark clouds part and a ray of sunlight breaks through.

Chapter 17

BEATRICE'S STORY – 1941

The children soon settled in at Villa delle Colombe. There were a few bad dreams and wet beds to contend with at first, but the safe haven of the estate provided the best medicine for such ills. They had all had their heads shaved before their journey, their scalps having been crawling with lice, and the little girls cried when they saw themselves in the mirror in the room we'd allocated to them. 'We look like boys,' one of them wailed through inconsolable sobs. Francesca left me to help them settle in and unpack their few belongings into a fine mahogany chest of drawers, hurrying back a few minutes later with a fistful of gaily coloured ribbons.

'Here you go,' she said, tying a red velvet one round the head of the little girl who'd been so very upset. 'You don't look at all like a boy now.'

'Where did you get these?' I murmured as I helped tie bows for the others, who clamoured for pretty embellishments of their own.

'I took them from my hats and dresses. That red one was on my opera glasses. I think we've found a far better use for them, don't you?' And I completely agreed as the little girls twirled and danced, laughing and clapping their hands as they admired their new accessories in the mirror.

Over the next weeks, their hair began to grow back, although the girls kept their ribbons and wore them every day. The children's memories of their traumatic experiences began to fade, replaced by a garden filled with flowers and summer days filled with good food and kindness.

Their cheeks turned rosy and their skin took on a golden glow, and slowly their characters began to emerge too as we got to know them better. Elisabetta was the oldest at the grand old age of ten, and the self-appointed mother to the group. It took her a while to allow herself to be a child again, to know that it was our role, not hers, to care for the others – and to care for her as well. Her father was in a camp in Germany, she told us, and her mother worked on the production line at the Fiat factory in Turin, where they were making armoured vehicles these days, rather than cars. Most of the other children's parents worked there too and many of the families had made their homes in the Mirafiori district close to the factory. They were no strangers to British bombing raids targeting the plant that was turning out military vehicles and aircraft in support of the German war machine. When they found out I was British, some of the children were wary of me to begin with, but when Francesca reassured them that I was a friend and a refugee just like them, unable to return to my home, they quickly dropped their defences and accepted me as one of their own.

Silvana grumbled about the extra work at first, and my time in the garden was curtailed as I tried to help her out in the kitchen, preparing meals for so many extra mouths. My cooking skills have never been up to much – and Silvana said that was only to be expected from an *Inglese* as everyone knew English food was an abomination. I didn't feel it was the time to argue the point that I was Scottish since I was sure her opinion of my homeland's cuisine was probably even lower. She set me to the simplest of tasks – pinching off pieces of dough and rolling them into long, thin worms to make a local pasta known as *pici*. It was while I was struggling one morning to get the pasta even enough for Silvana's liking that Elisabetta wandered into the kitchen. She knelt on a chair beside me at the table and began to show me how it was done. '*Brava*!' Silvana cried. '*Perfetto*! Well done, Elisabetta.'

'My mamma makes this for us sometimes. She was born in the south, so my *nonna* taught her this way of making pasta,' Elisabetta said as she reached for another piece of the dough and deftly rolled it into the desired size and shape. Once cooked, the *pici* was satisfyingly filling, served up in bowls with a rich *ragù*.

After that, Silvana took the girl under her wing and she quickly replaced me in my role as cook's assistant, happy to relinquish the care of the others to Francesca and me. I was equally happy to be released back into the garden, working with Carlo and his new team of little 'helpers' in the vegetable patch. Gio was in his element, too, delighted to have so many friends his own age all of a sudden, and he led them in their games, splashing in the swimming pool and playing hide-and-seek in the maze. They mastered its layout quickly, once he'd shown them how to navigate its twists and turns. The sound of their laughter helped banish some of Francesca's sadness. She took up her painting again, and occasionally the lines of grief that had been etched on to her face would dissolve a little as she captured their joy in her sketchbooks.

Most of the children grew plump and strong, losing the pallor of city life as they swam in the pool, and ran and jumped and laughed in the gardens. But one of them failed to thrive. Little Alfredo Verlucci stood apart from the start, with his sallow cheeks and huge eyes. He was just five years old, and while the other children had formed a tight-knit group, he always seemed to hover on the edge of any games they played and sat awkwardly to one side while they frolicked in the swimming pool. He was as skinny as a rake, his knees as knobbly as oak galls, and some days, when the wind whisked the dust from the paths in little spirals, his lungs wheezed and his breathlessness turned his face a greenish white. We couldn't work out why he pushed the food around his plate until one day Elisabetta explained it to Silvana as she scraped his leftovers into the pail for the pigs.

'It's because of his religion,' she said. 'He doesn't go to church, like the rest of us. He's one of those ones who doesn't believe in eating pork. And he can't eat his Bolognese *ragù* if it has cheese on it either.'

Many Jewish families had left Italy a year or two earlier, knowing they would not be welcome in their own land any longer when the Fascists put their anti-Semitic laws in place. But a few had stayed, unable to leave a secure job or a beloved home, or perhaps unable to imagine such cruel discrimination to be humanly possible. Once we realised Alfredo was from a Jewish background, we were easily able to adjust the food we served up for him, and he began to enjoy his meals far more once we stopped expecting him to eat the *prosciutto* and *Luganega* sausage that the others devoured with such gusto, and with only a little extra grumbling from Silvana.

Francesca took him under her wing and encouraged him to join in the games with the others instead of hanging back on the edges. And Gio quickly took his lead from her and made a point of including Alfredo, the pair of them soon becoming firm friends. Alfredo's shorn hair grew back in a mass of glossy curls and, although he still suffered from his asthma, his general well-being began to improve. We fed him extra eggs and cheese and made sure he sat in the sunshine each day to help cure the rickets that had made his leg bones soft and lumpy. He was still reluctant to join in the games in the swimming pool, though, too scared of the water to learn to swim despite my offers to teach him.

One night I awoke to the sound of footsteps padding along the corridor outside my room. I pulled on my dressing gown and went to see what was happening, following the soft glow of candlelight that emanated from Francesca's bedroom two doors along. She was there with Alfredo, holding him in her arms as he gasped for breath, his eyes huge in the whiteness of his terrified face. She rocked him and sang to him quietly, all the while smoothing his curls back from his forehead.

I went to stand beside her and asked, 'What can I do?'

'It's all right,' she said, with a calmness that belied the anxiety she must surely have been feeling. He looked so fragile and those asthma attacks of his could be terrifying in their suddenness and severity. 'Alfredo has taken one of his pills and we're just waiting for it to work, aren't we, my darling? That's right, try to relax and take some normal breaths and it will soon pass.'

I sat with her until his breathing gradually began to steady and deepen. Eventually, his eyelids closed and he fell into a deep sleep in her arms.

'Shall I carry him back to his own bed?' I asked.

She shook her head. 'I'll keep him with me a while longer. Just to make sure the attack has passed.' She stroked his pale cheek with one forefinger, gazing down at him. I was reminded of Signorelli's painting of the Madonna and Child in the church in Montepulciano that day when we went to collect the children, and my heart tightened at the look of adoration she gave the sleeping boy. Then she raised her head and smiled at me. 'He reminds me so much of my own son. We lost little Edo to scarlet fever when he was just a year old. You might have noticed his gravestone when we buried Edoardo – his father lies beside him now.'

I shook my head. I hadn't been able to take in anything much on that dreadful day, other than Francesca's grief and the pain in my own heart. I had noticed, though, that she often took flowers from the garden and set off in the direction of the churchyard. I now realised there were two graves, not just one, where they would be left to lie as a token of her love.

'Having all the children here – and this *poverino* in particular, who so needs our love and help – has been a lifeline for me,' Francesca whispered. 'I understand now that grief is love that has nowhere to go. Alfredo has given my love a new purpose. I'd do anything to protect him. To protect any of them, come to that. It feels as if I've been given another chance.'

I smiled at her, understanding now just how much the youngsters were helping her to heal wounds that went far, far deeper than I'd known. And then I tiptoed from the room and left Alfredo sleeping soundly in her arms while Francesca softly sang to him, a long-remembered lullaby from years gone by.

Chapter 18

Tess – 2015

Beatrice insists we have an outing to Montepulciano. She wants to show me the church with the painting by Signorelli. 'You should really visit the cathedral in Orvieto too, though, if you want to see his best work,' she says. 'His frescoes of the Last Judgement are breath-taking.'

After we've wandered around the little church, we emerge from its muted dusk and squint into the glare of the sunlight outside. Beatrice leads me round the little town, which looks down on the plain below from its lofty perch. The medieval buildings cluster around the crest of the hilltop, forming a maze of steep, narrow streets that remind me with a slight shiver of how easy it was to get lost in the cypress maze. I haven't told Beatrice about that particular escapade, thinking she'd be angry that I'd tried to navigate it when she'd told me – so firmly and with such finality – that no one goes into it any more.

She's not aware, either, that Marco came to the villa that day. It would only upset her even more, I reason, knowing I've confided in him in a way that I haven't done with her. If I'm being honest, I also have to admit to feeling a bit guilty. Opening up to him about my pain feels like a betrayal of Beatrice, Gio and Vittoria: we ought to be united in our hatred of the man who's about to turn them out of their homes before razing the gardens to bare earth. But I'd glimpsed another side to him as my grief spilled out in that torrent of anger and raw anguish and he just listened carefully and let me talk. Something had shifted between us.

And that felt like another betrayal – this time I was betraying *you* by talking about those last months and weeks and days, admitting to the overwhelming mixture of emotions I experienced.

Even thinking about it makes me flush with another pang of guilt as Beatrice suggests we find a table at a nearby café and have some lunch. It's one o'clock and everywhere is packed with summer tourists. We stand, uncertainly, while the waiter shakes his head and gestures at the busy tables, all occupied. I'm about to suggest we call it a day and go home when I realise someone is waving at us. As if I've conjured him up with my guilty thoughts, Marco gets up from the table where he's been sitting and beckons us over. Before we can protest, the waiter ushers us across and pulls up an extra chair from an adjacent table.

'*Buongiorno*, Signorina Crane, Tess,' Marco says. 'Please, do join me. As you can see, I've nearly finished my meal.'

Beatrice raises her eyebrows in surprise. I can't tell whether it's because he's being so polite for a change, or whether she's noted his use of my first name, or perhaps it's just because she can't quite believe we're actually going to sit down with the man who's bringing such misery to her life. After just a moment's hesitation she takes a seat, sinking into the chair the waiter proffers and then fanning herself with the menu he hands her.

Marco doesn't mention the incident in the maze. Once we've ordered the spaghetti with truffles – which he highly recommends, having just consumed a bowlful himself – and he's poured us each a glass of iced water, he asks us, pleasantly, what brings us to Montepulciano.

Beatrice tells him about the church and can't resist adding, with just a faint hint of sarcasm, 'You might like to go and see it for yourself. After all, it was there that I first met your father, when he was just five years old.'

Marco smiles and says smoothly, 'I will certainly do so. The paintings sound wonderful.' Then he changes the subject, telling us he's come to buy a few bottles of the *Vino Nobile* to take back with him to Rome. 'Have you visited the *città sotterranea* below the Ercolani wine shop? I can highly recommend it. Did you know, there is a veritable labyrinth buried beneath this very street, where some of the wines are aged? *È incredibile!* The tunnels go on for several kilometres and there is this huge cavern with stone arches. I felt I was in a cathedral, but an underground one dedicated to the creation of Montepulciano's famous wines. Speaking of places to go and visit, you should see it, Tess.'

'It sounds fascinating,' I reply, as the waiter sets our bowls of fragrant pasta before us and Marco asks him to bring an espresso and his bill.

Beatrice busies herself with her food. Her head is bowed and I can't quite see her expression. But when she looks up again, I see she looks tired and strained, her features set in a mask of tension, lined with grief. Perhaps it was a mistake to come and join Marco. I've underestimated how difficult it must be for her.

I smile at Marco. 'Perhaps we'll do that another day.'

He nods, drains his cup of coffee in one gulp and slides some euros into the leather folder containing his bill that the waiter's brought. 'Well, I must be getting off,' he says, pushing back his chair and hooking a finger through the loop of his linen jacket, which he drapes nonchalantly over one shoulder. 'It was a pleasure meeting you so unexpectedly. Tomorrow I'm heading back to Rome for a while. But I'll be in touch.'

We say goodbye and wish him a safe journey. Beatrice watches his back as he walks away. She watches me as I turn my attention back to twirling another little nest of spaghetti on to my fork. 'He was a bit more civil than usual,' she remarks. 'One would hardly have known he had it in him.'

I feel that twinge of guilty betrayal again. 'Perhaps he's just glad to be heading back to the city,' I say, reaching for my glass of water. Then I change the subject, not wanting to dwell on Marco any longer. 'Tell me more about these tunnels. Are they worth a visit?'

I immediately regret asking. Her face looks drawn again as she replies. 'You should go and have a look sometime. But I'd prefer not to accompany you.' She's silent for a few moments, lost in a private memory, then continues, 'This town was the scene of bitter fighting during the war as the Germans retreated. You'd hardly believe it now, would you?'

I look around at the pretty medieval buildings, the terracotta rooftops spilling down the steep hillside before us, nesting swallows flitting in and out beneath the eaves as tourists stroll through the narrow streets, pausing to read the prices in the windows of the wine shops. She's right, it's peaceful and beautiful. And yet, for Beatrice, perhaps these same streets and the maze of tunnels beneath them conjure up far more complicated emotions . . . ones I hope I may come to understand better as her story unfolds.

We finish our meal, discovering upon calling for the bill that Marco has paid for our lunches as well as his own, and drive home in silence. I steal a look at her face, reflected in the car's wing mirror, and notice the sadness that's settled over her again, like a shutter closing out the light. Today's been too much for her, I think. Perhaps it was walking up and down the steep cobbled streets in the heat or maybe it was bumping into Marco, but I get the impression it's something more . . . she seems lost in memories of times long gone, slipping back down paths she once trod with others, scarcely aware of her surroundings as I drive her back to the villa.

When we reach home, she goes to the library. I follow, wanting to make sure she's OK. I pretend to busy myself looking through the notes I'd taken the day before of her reminiscences about Francesca and Alfredo. I imagine she must be thinking about those times again too, because she opens one of Francesca's sketchbooks and turns the pages until she comes to the painting she's showed me before, the one of the doves, with the children playing by the *limonaia*. We sit in silence for a while, each wrapped up in our own thoughts, and then Beatrice gets up and goes over to a rosewood bureau that sits in one corner of the room. She turns the little brass key in its lid and opens it, taking out a smaller, leather-bound sketchbook. She brings it over to show me.

Every page of the book is filled with paintings of a child. He's been painted asleep, long dark lashes resting on plump, rose-flushed cheeks, and wide awake, his brown eyes lively and laughing, his glossy black curls bringing alive the tilt of his head and the curve of his neck. There's love in every brushstroke.

'These are Francesca's paintings of little Edo,' Beatrice explains. 'After his death, she kept them locked away in her desk. They were never intended for public view, you see.'

I nod, sensing how personal and precious this little book of paintings must have been to her.

'She never painted a picture of him again, of course, after he went. Indeed, it was a few years before she was able to pick up her pencils and brushes again, when Alfredo and the others arrived. They were the ones who helped her heart to thaw when it had been frozen with grief for so long.'

Once I've looked through all the paintings, I close the cover gently and hand the sketchbook back to Beatrice. She locks it away safely in the desk once more and turns to me.

'What do you think will become of it when we have to leave the villa, Tess? I doubt Marco will be the slightest bit interested in it, so I suppose it'll simply be thrown away. Along with so much more of the estate's history.'

I demur, but I know how feeble it must sound. Despite his courtesy earlier today, Marco is, at heart, a businessman. I don't think he'll allow sentiment to enter into any of his decisions when it comes to disposing of what remains of the lives of the villa's previous inhabitants.

I realise Beatrice looks dead on her feet. It's already been a long day for her, and the late afternoon heat is draining. I insist on helping her to her room.

'I'm fine,' she reassures me, although her face is grey with exhaustion. 'Just a bit tired.'

I leave her to have a nap and take my camera into the gardens. I hope perhaps you'll join me there again, but you don't materialise.

I sit alone on the bench at the viewpoint. The only sounds are the hum of the cicadas and the faint echoes of children's voices from long ago.

Chapter 19

Through their first winter at the Villa delle Colombe, the children continued to grow in strength and confidence. Once the summer was over and they could no longer spend all their days playing outside and helping in the garden, we established a new routine, with lessons indoors in the mornings. We turned the library into a schoolroom, and I taught them geography, history and some English. Initially, they were reluctant to learn the language of the enemy who continued to bomb the cities in the north, but I pointed out that the war wouldn't last forever and that they might want to travel to Britain or even America one day, when the words would come in handy. I also did my best to remember the mathematics I'd learned at school and to teach them their sums. I was very grateful they were so young and therefore only required the most basic of groundings, which was about my own personal limit.

They loved looking at the globe on Edoardo's old desk and examining a collection of butterflies mounted in glass cases on the walls, which Edoardo and Francesca had inherited with the villa. I dug out leather-bound copies of *Treasure Island* and *The Wind in the Willows*, translated into Italian, to read to them on wet afternoons when they couldn't get out to play. I realised those books must have been bought by Edoardo and Francesca for the son they lost so young. I think she was pleased that they were being put to good use.

We had the *limonaia*, too, which we sometimes used as a studio for more creative pursuits. We covered the floor between the lemon trees with lengths of oilcloth to protect the tiles from the worst splatters and drips as the children enthusiastically painted pictures or coiled clay to make little pots and ornaments under Francesca's supervision. Gio was by now inseparable from his friend Alfredo and joined in the lessons with great gusto. Even Silvana grudgingly admitted that having the children there had its benefits, despite the extra work involved.

Our days were taken up from sunrise to sunset with the children's needs, and when we weren't teaching them we spent the time helping Silvana with washing their clothes and bedding, or cooking up vast cauldrons of pasta, soup or stew in the kitchen. We'd harvested everything we could from the vegetable garden and the orchard in the autumn and carefully preserved as much as possible to see us through the winter without having to rely on getting extra supplies in from the shops in San Quirico. The farms on the estate continued to supply us with eggs and milk and, with a bit of careful management and Silvana's wealth of culinary experience, we ate well and the children thrived. It was amazing how the most basic of ingredients – stale bread, a cup or two of cannellini beans, a few handfuls of rice or the brown wheat I learned was called *farro* – could be transformed by the addition of a few fresh herbs, a clove or two of garlic or some thin shavings of the coal-black truffles that Carlo dug up from a secret spot in the woods.

Of course, some of the children still had occasional bad dreams, or fretted for the safety of their parents back in Turin, but mostly we managed to find distractions to help them through those anxious times. We only listened to the wireless at night, once our charges were safely tucked up in their beds, protecting them from the reports of the battles and bombardments that continued to rage beyond the walls of the estate. Italian troops had been sent to fight alongside the Germans in Russia and we could only imagine how terrible the conditions must be for them there, as the winter wind buffeted the villa, scouring the bare valley walls and making the tall cypresses lining the driveway sway and bow to its bombastic force.

All the children succumbed to occasional ailments: colds, sniffles, cuts and grazes were all common. There were severe shortages of medicine in the area now, so Francesca spent hours poring over ancient medical tomes in the library, searching for traditional remedies. She appropriated the scullery and turned it into her apothecary, crushing, boiling and distilling roots, seeds and leaves and filling the air with the scents of lavender and liquorice. It was a favourite pastime of the children's to forage through the hedgerows and woodlands and come back with baskets filled with the ingredients for Francesca's potions. They quickly became adept at identifying wild plants and avoiding anything toxic. With our improvised pharmacy, we managed as best we could to keep everyone happy and healthy.

The one we still worried about most, though, was little Alfredo. His asthma attacks grew more frequent as the weather got colder, bringing chill winds and days of rain to the valley. Francesca dosed him with liquorice root to try to ease his cough and put drops of lavender oil on his pillow to help him sleep at night. Even so, he often had to be excused from lessons as he wheezed and gasped, and Francesca would take him to sit beside the fire in the drawing room, reading to him or letting him look through her sketchbooks. Gio would beg a little extra treat from his mamma in the kitchen – Silvana could never resist the charm of her son – and smuggle it to Alfredo to help bolster his friend's strength so that he could return to their games on the terrace or kicking a football in the orchard if the weather was dry enough. Often, I would come through once lessons were over and find the three of them curled on the sofa – Francesca in the middle with an arm round each of the boys – deep in a story. The lines of her face held a deep contentment at those moments, a peace I hadn't witnessed since Edoardo's death. Through Alfredo, Francesca found an outlet for her love. His presence at the villa gave her life meaning again. She adored that child.

We nursed Alfredo carefully through the winter, but it was a great relief when spring returned, bringing the warm sunshine to ease the labouring of his lungs.

'At least he's better off here than in the north,' Francesca commented. 'It must be doing him some good.' We were gathering the new growth from a patch of stinging nettles to make soup for lunch that day, filling a bucket with the fresh green tips, which, according to Francesca's research into herbal remedies, were filled with vitamins and good for us all. She also made Alfredo cups of nettle tea, which seemed to be helping relieve his asthma. He hadn't had a severe attack for a few weeks now and was sleeping better at night.

The spring sunshine was warm on our backs that day as we stooped to pluck the leaves from their stems, and it was good to be outdoors again after several days of rain. The children seemed energised by the warmth too and they ran in and out of the maze, filling the air with the sound of their laughter.

We were summoned back to the terrace by a wail from Alfredo. By the time we reached him, he was sobbing his heart out, holding the crushed remains of a butterfly in the palm of his hand. '*Caro*, what happened?' Francesca asked him, sinking to her knees beside him and enveloping him in her arms.

Gio stood to one side, looking a little sheepish as he kicked at the gravel. 'We didn't mean to hurt it,' he said. 'We thought we were helping.'

When we were able to piece their story together, it turned out they'd found a chrysalis hanging from a branch on one of the oak trees. In a recent class, I'd told the children about the life cycle of butterflies, using the framed specimens in the library to illustrate the lesson. 'So we thought we'd give it a helping hand,' explained Gio. 'We only wanted to let the butterfly come out and spread its wings in the sunshine. We wanted to save it the struggle and keep its strength for flying.'

Francesca took the dead butterfly – so nearly fully formed – from Alfredo's hand and gently opened its wings with her fingertip. 'But you see, my darlings, you can't do the work for it. The butterfly has to struggle to release itself from the cocoon in order to become strong enough to fly. See how its wings were fully formed? But nature still needed it to go through a little more so it could develop its strength. You meant well, I know. You wanted to help it, to save it from the hard work. But now you understand, it's the struggle itself that gives the butterfly the strength to survive.'

She handed the remains of the insect back to Alfredo, who sniffed back his tears. 'I'm sorry, butterfly,' he said. 'I'm sorry I didn't understand.'

Then Gio gave him a pat on the back. 'I know,' he said, 'let's give it a proper funeral. We can bury it in the garden, where the flowers are. It would like that.'

The two of them ran off to fetch a trowel and to call the others so that the proper formalities could be observed, shaking off their grief as children so quickly can.

Francesca stood watching them for a moment, one hand pressing her back as she stretched out the ache from our morning's labours. 'You know,' she said, 'I think we should plan an outing. We've all been cooped up at the villa for so long, I've almost forgotten what the outside world looks like. For a while now, I've been thinking it would do Alfredo good to bathe in the hot springs at

Bagni San Filippo. It might help his chest. And it would probably do the rest of them the world of good as well.'

'But how will we get there?' I asked, ever the pragmatist. It was virtually impossible to get fuel for the truck by then.

'We'll use the horse and cart. If the weather is fine, we can take our time. We'll pack a picnic and make a day of it.'

It was decided, and so the next two days were a bustle of organisation and preparation. As Silvana said, anyone would think we were going on an expedition to the ends of the earth. The children were abuzz with excitement, and I struggled to get them to concentrate on their lessons. Secretly, I think I was just as excited as they were and readily allowed them to finish a little early and run outside to play. Francesca searched out sun hats for everyone and washed their summer clothes. Carlo cleaned the cart, scrubbing straw and every last trace of manure from the wooden boards, and we lined it with blankets and bath towels to make it more comfortable and protect its passengers from splinters. Silvana got into the spirit of our adventure too, and baked loaves of the flattened bread known as *schiacciata*, which she studded with walnuts and sprigs of rosemary, and a golden *torta di ricotta* flavoured with lemon zest, big enough for everyone to have a slice.

The day arrived and we set off after breakfast, our thirteen small charges (the twelve children, plus Gio of course) crammed into the back of the cart, with Francesca driving Clarice, and me beside her where I could turn at frequent intervals and check everyone was behaving and no one had fallen out. The cart lumbered down the drive and through the gates. The children cheered as one when we turned on to the road and the horse plodded steadily southwards. We skirted the town of Bagno Vignoni, giving a wide berth to the bathing pools there, which Francesca was keen to avoid. She worried that they were too public for our party and was still wary of drawing attention to the number of children we were sheltering at the villa. Persecution of Jews was still rife, and with the Fascists enthusiastically backing the Nazis' approach to removing them, we'd become all the more wary in order to protect Alfredo.

The sloping hulk of Monte Amiata was a constant, reassuring presence in the distance as we journeyed onwards, past cows grazing placidly on the spring grass along the valley floor and swathes of bright poppies whose petals stained the edges of the wheatfields scarlet. I glanced across at Francesca as she held the reins. She looked the happiest I'd seen her in ages, joining in as the children began to sing an English song I'd taught them about going to Strawberry Fair, and although the vestiges of sadness lingered in the lines around her eyes, it was as if the arrival of spring had cast away the darkest shadows of her grief.

We arrived at Bagni San Filippo by mid-morning and unhitched Clarice, tethering her to a tree beside a cool stream where she'd be shaded from the midday heat. By the time we'd unloaded children, towels and baskets of food from the cart and set off along the path to the springs, the old horse was cropping contentedly on a patch of clover. I saw why Francesca had chosen this place as we wound our way beneath the trees into the deeply incised valley. It was wonderfully secluded, and we had it to ourselves. The way grew steeper and some of the children were beginning to flag a little, but Gio danced ahead, urging them on as he knew what lay before us. 'It's worth it,' he said to Alfredo, taking the towel his friend was carrying and draping it over his own shoulders. 'Just a little bit further . . . Look, see that steam rising over there? The water in the stream is hot now. *Non è incredible?*

We all stopped and stared in amazement at the sight that awaited us around the final corner. It was as though we'd stepped into another world. The trees thinned and opened on to a large clearing where steam rose from a series of pools, flanked by strangely sculpted formations like frozen waterfalls made of rock.

Our surroundings were other-worldly enough, but it was the colours that were most extraordinary of all. It looked as if someone had emptied Francesca's paints on to the canvas of the landscape. The milky water cleared to a vivid turquoise in places and the rims of the pools were dazzling white or encrusted with bright, sulphurous yellow. Dark green algae dripped from the rocks and mineral deposits had stained the walls of the canyon here and there with splashes of carmine and burnt sienna. Water trickled everywhere, breathing more wisps of steam into the air, cascading down an expanse of tiered deposits that sloped above the pools and were capped by a vast mound of bone-white rock so high that we had to tip our heads back to see the top.

Gio capered with excitement and joy at everyone's astonishment. 'I told you it was worth it!' he crowed. '*Guarda!* It's the *balena bianca*.' The billowing deposits did look a little like a vast whale, its mouth agape.

The children stood in open-mouthed silence too for a moment as they took it all in, and then Gio let out a whoop and began pulling off his clothes. 'Last one in's a rotten tomato!' he shouted, galvanising the others into action, and soon they were all wallowing happily in the warm waters.

Francesca and I were a little more circumspect, changing into our swimming things behind a screen of ferns before plunging in too. It was bliss to be out in the world again and to feel the soft caress of those warm springs on our flesh as the sunshine filtered through the trees on either side. The children soon grew in confidence, scrambling over the calcareous deposits and climbing on to the flanks of the whale to explore the grottoes and caves there. Alfredo was a little more cautious than the others and stood at the edge of a small pool, gingerly dipping a toe into the milky water. I took his hand. 'Shall we go in together?' He nodded and I went first to show him that it wasn't too deep. He breathed a deep sigh of bliss as he finally relaxed, surrendering his knobbly limbs to the soothing effects of the warmth. Francesca and I exchanged a smile as his expression melted into a look of wonder at the sensation of relief from his aches and pains and the breathlessness that dogged him wherever he went. After a while, at the urging of Gio, he too became brave enough to climb up to the white whale's mouth and join the others as they giggled and played there.

By lunchtime, we had to insist that the children get out of the water and come and sit on the blankets we'd spread on a little beach of white pebbles in the shade of an oak's generous branches. After their morning in the springs, they were full of beans, their skin as rosy as a lobster's carapace. Their adventures had certainly given them an appetite and they devoured the food Silvana had prepared for our picnic. After we'd all licked the last crumbs of *torta di ricotta* from our fingers, I read to them for a while. One or two of the children fell asleep, lulled by the shush of the water and the light dancing over them as it dappled through the leaves, but Alfredo and Gio lay side by side on their towels, chins propped in their hands, captivated as they listened to the adventures of Robinson Crusoe on his desert island.

We stirred ourselves an hour or so later, the children refreshed and eager to swim again before it was time to pack up and leave. Alfredo finally plucked up his courage and asked me if I would help him learn to swim in the deeper part of the pool. I happily obliged, glad that he was finally gaining in confidence and might be able to join in the games in the swimming pool back at the villa with the others at last. Francesca busied herself, packing up the picnic things and shaking out the blankets before folding them, ready for our return. Alfredo and I had waded into the deepest water, beyond his depth, and I was holding his hands as he determinedly kicked his skinny legs, when suddenly I heard her say my name. It was her tone that made me look up. Her voice was deliberately low and calm, but there was an urgency in it too. 'Beatrice. It's time to get out of the water,' she said.

'Look, Francesca, I'm swimming!' Alfredo called, oblivious to the note of warning I'd detected.

'Beatrice,' she said again levelly. 'Get out of the pool. Now.'

Her eyes flickered to the clear turquoise water beyond where I stood and I followed her glance. A lithe black shape had slipped into the pool behind us and was making its way in deliberate, sinuous curves towards where Alfredo splashed in the depths. Grabbing his hands, I pulled him to me and turned away from the snake. I must have made it across the pool in about three strides. Francesca later told me she couldn't believe how fast I'd moved, encumbered as I was by the water and the child I carried. She reached for us as we neared the beach and pulled us to safety.

We said nothing of the snake to Alfredo, who chattered happily about his achievement in being able to swim three whole strokes without holding my hands as Francesca wrapped him in a towel and hugged him. At the far side of the pool, the dark shape slipped back through the water and silently disappeared into the bushes on the far bank.

'Sit there for a minute and get your breath back,' Francesca told me, once Alfredo had run off to tell the others of his achievement. 'That was a close call: another one of those serpents in paradise.'

'Was it a poisonous one?' I asked quietly as my heart rate began to settle a little.

She shrugged. 'Probably not – they mostly aren't around here, but you can't risk it. A big one like that could certainly deliver a nasty bite to a little scrap like our Alfredo. He's only just stopped having those terrible nightmares, too. We don't want to give him any new ones.' She shook out the damp towel and began to fold it. 'Time to go home now, I think,' she said.

I nodded, still shaken. 'I'll go and tell the others to get themselves dry and put their clothes on.'

It took a while to get everyone rounded up and dressed again and the shadows were lengthening as we made our way back down the path. The children were a little tired now after their hours playing in the water, but their cheeks were as rosy as cherries – even Alfredo's. We rounded a bend in the track and were surprised to see a figure walking towards us. Having seen no one all day, it was unexpected. Before we could stop them, the children called and waved, and then Francesca froze beside me, automatically reaching for my arm. 'It's Umberto.' Her voice shook as she spoke his name.

He walked towards us, raising a hand in recognition. 'What an unexpected pleasure! Signora Robbia, and her charming English companion.' His smile was disingenuous. Had someone told him we were here? Had he followed us?

He continued, 'I wondered who the wagon belonged to at the bottom of the valley. Never did I imagine the delight I would have of meeting you here. And accompanied by such an unexpected cohort of little soldiers too!'

'Signor Ciccone.' Francesca's tone was cool, her words stiff but carefully civil as she acknowledged him. 'Have you come to take the waters?'

'I have indeed, *cara* Francesca. Thought I'd take a trip back to my old childhood stomping ground. I grew up over there.' He pointed out a little hamlet just visible through the trees, clinging to the top of a small hill. 'I come back sometimes to pay my respects to my parents. They are buried in the graveyard here. And for the past few weeks, my back has been troubling me again, so I've not been sleeping. I thought a dip would do me the world of good. As, indeed, it appears has been the case for you. You are looking remarkably well, if I may say so.'

I glanced at my friend. Despite our day in the sun, she remained thin, pale and strained – indeed, all the more so in his presence. Umberto's unctuous flattery somehow brought to my mind the sinister movement of the snake through the water, intent on its prey.

Francesca stood silent, unable to reply, mesmerised by his loathsome manners and frozen with the fear of letting slip her hatred of this man.

'Well,' I said briskly. 'What a pleasure it's been to meet you so unexpectedly like this, Signor Ciccone. But we mustn't keep you from your swim, and the children are tired so we'd better get them home.'

His eyes flickered over me briefly before returning to Francesca. 'Staying with you at the villa, are they? How very gracious of you to take in refugees. I'm glad to know you're doing your bit for the war. I must call in one of these days. It's been far too long, and some of your delicious tea would no doubt do me the world of good.'

Francesca nodded abruptly, still unable to speak, and then I ushered the children onwards, flowing around him as he continued to stand in our way in the middle of the path. '*Arrivederci,* Francesca,' I heard him say softly as we passed him. 'I'll be seeing you soon.'

Chapter 20

Tess – 2015

I google 'poisonous snakes in Tuscany' and discover there are two types, both belonging to the viper family. Even though they seem to be pretty rare, I can't help drawing my feet up on to the chair I've been sitting on. I can hear you laughing at me for being so squeamish. *You probably won't see any around the villa*, you tell me. *And certainly not here in the library! They're shy creatures, and there are plenty of wilder places for them to live about these parts.*

It seems unlikely the snake that invaded the hot springs was one of those, as Beatrice described it as large and dark-coloured, but apparently even the non-venomous snakes in the region can grow up to two metres long and that sounds scary enough for me, never mind for a small child.

To distract myself from scrolling through more images of snakes, I look up some of the butterflies in the collection hanging on the wall behind me instead. *Look*, I tell you, *some of them are the ones we used to see on Pepperbox Hill.* From our walks, I recognise the common blue and the silver-washed fritillary, whose wings are a deceptively muted camouflage of pale green and silver-white when closed but open to reveal the hidden surprise of their vivid orange and black leopard-skin patterning.

It's a bit sad seeing them like this though, isn't it? Stuck through with pins and mounted behind glass? As if their lives weren't fleeting enough already, you say.

I think about the story Beatrice told me of Gio and Alfredo trying to help the butterfly break out of its chrysalis. *I think grief is a bit like that*, I tell you. *You become trapped in it and no one can really help you get out. Of course, other people can support you, keep you company, perhaps even distract you sometimes. But you have to go through the struggle yourself to become strong enough to survive life after loss.*

You smile. *How's that working for you, then? When do you think you're going to be able to spread your wings and fly again?*

Not sure, I say with a shrug. *Most days still seem like quite a struggle. I think I still need to build some more strength. How long does it take, do you think?*

It takes as long as it takes. But you do have some support here.

Beatrice? I suppose so, she certainly understands what it is to grieve.

You nod. *Not just Beatrice though. You can talk to Marco too, can't you?*

I feel that twinge of guilt again, that sense of having betrayed both you and Beatrice by confiding in him the other day. *He was surprisingly sympathetic*, I concede, *but I suppose it was just because I was in such a state after getting lost in the maze. I don't think he's going to be around much either, is he?*

I look round, expecting a reply from you, but all I see are the butterflies in their frames, frozen there forever in time and space.

A little gingerly, I stretch out my arms as wide as they'll go, as if pushing against the cocoon surrounding me. It's still there, the now familiar sense of despair wrapping itself around me, refusing to give. But I realise I have to be patient. Perhaps if I can just trust that it's there for a purpose, to help me grow stronger. Until one day I can emerge to face the world again, knowing that my grief has served its purpose and that perhaps it's even been an important part of my survival.

Chapter 21

Beatrice's Story – 1942

After encountering us on the path at the hot springs that day, Umberto began calling at the villa again, unannounced. The first time he appeared, just a couple of weeks later, one warm day in early May, I was in the schoolroom. I heard voices through the open window and looked out to see him there with Francesca. The set of her shoulders was tense, although she kept her expression carefully neutral.

'*Che piacere, cara* Francesca – it was such a pleasure to encounter you and your charming companions at Bagni San Filippo the other day, and to see you looking well.' He paused and surveyed the parterre, the buttons of his black shirt straining across his chest, its collar uncomfortably tight-looking around the rolls of fat at his neck. 'And your garden is just as beautiful as ever, I'm pleased to see. *Naturalmente*, my last visit here was on such a sad occasion, when I came to pay my last respects to our esteemed Edoardo.' Francesca flinched visibly at the mention of his name, but Umberto carried on regardless. 'Since I was passing this way, I thought I would call in, to make sure that you are coping and to see if there's anything

I can do to help provide for your small charges. It must be hard, now you don't have a man about the place.'

'Thank you, but we are managing very well,' she replied. 'I have the help of Carlo and Silvana, as you know. And Signorina Crane helps look after the children.'

He smiled indulgently. 'Ah, you have always been a most capable woman, Francesca. You know you have my utmost admiration.'

From my station at the window, Francesca looked to me as if the thought of Umberto's admiration was making her physically sick.

'And where are the dear little ones this fine morning?' he asked.

'They are having their lessons with Miss Crane.'

He glanced towards the villa and I hastily turned away, saying loudly, 'Right, children, let's see who can recite their times tables today,' hoping our sing-song chanting of *two twos are four* might help hasten him on his way.

But he was still there fifteen minutes later when I dismissed the children for their morning playtime, sitting at the little table beneath the oaks while Francesca poured him a cup of tea.

She glanced at me, her eyes filled with gratitude, fully aware I'd let the children out earlier than usual. 'Do join us, Beatrice,' she said. 'Signor Ciccone is paying us a visit.'

'*Buongiorno*, Signorina Crane. Our dear Francesca has very kindly offered me a little refreshment.' He picked up his teacup. 'And most welcome it is, too, on this warm day.' Patches of sweat darkened the fabric of his shirt and I caught a whiff of the acrid stink of it as I pulled up a chair. He continued, 'I was just saying how much I admire you ladies, doing your bit for the cause of our beloved country by giving these children a safe haven while our enemies threaten us on all sides.' He looked directly at me, but I pretended to busy myself with the milk jug. 'And while I appreciate you are managing well for yourselves, please do let me know if there's anything you need. Us men do have our uses, you know, especially ones like me who have a certain standing within the Party.'

Francesca had clearly had more than enough of his false fawning and his insufferable arrogance and she stood up abruptly. 'You'll have to excuse us, Umberto. I don't wish to seem rude, but the children need us. Please do take your time to finish your tea, though, and then perhaps you can see yourself out?'

He picked up his cup again and took another sip, in no hurry to leave. 'But of course. Don't mind me, I always feel so very much at home here. I don't want to keep you from your duties. Indeed, I have my own to see to and cannot stay long. But please rest assured, I will be back again soon to keep an eye on you. After all, it's the very least I can do, given what a close colleague Edoardo was.'

We left him sitting there and ushered the children through the hedge to the English garden. 'Everything he says sounds like a threat to me,' Francesca muttered once we were safely out of his earshot.

'That's because it is,' I said. 'You are right to be careful. He's like a cat playing games with a mouse. But we can play games too. And we're a lot more intelligent than he is.' I glanced back and saw that the chairs on the terrace were all empty now, the tea things sitting abandoned on the table. 'He's gone.' And we felt we could breathe freely again as we led the children in a game of hide-and-seek, their laughter helping dispel the suffocating odour of his presence.

◆ ◆ ◆

Our summer was taken up with the routine of lessons, games, and – in every spare minute – gathering and preserving the food that would see us through the next winter. In autumn, once the last of the harvest was in, a bitter chill settled over the valley, filling it each night with a dense, dank fog that surrounded the hilltop estate. We felt safer then. The fog gave us the impression of being completely cut off from the outside world, although the daytime still brought the occasional unwelcome visit from Umberto.

One autumn day he turned up with a large sack over his shoulder. 'Look, Francesca,' he said, 'I've brought you all a gift.' It was a haunch of wild boar and Umberto proudly explained how he'd led the hunt a few days earlier and shot the beast himself. 'I got the head and liver, of course, but also this piece of excellent meat. And I thought, it's too much for a lonely bachelor like me to consume alone. So I will share it with those who need it most. Naturally, my thoughts turned to you and the children. We'll give it to Silvana to prepare, shall we, and I'll come back on Sunday for a feast of a lunch with you all.' It was a statement, not a question.

How could we turn down such an offer? It would have been too obvious a snub and, to be honest, we needed all the food we could lay our hands on. So the next Sunday he arrived wearing his best suit – the same one he'd worn at Edoardo's funeral, I realised – and sat himself at the head of the table. Fortunately, that meant Francesca could place herself at the other end, as far away from him as possible. I sat in the middle, helping the younger children cut up their food, and noticed she was scarcely able to choke down a single morsel of the meat. The children, however, devoured the rich *cinghiale alla cacciatora* that Silvana had prepared, stewing the meat in red wine and adding garlic and herbs. All, that is, except Alfredo. Silvana brought a small dish of rabbit stew for him and set it at his place. And Umberto noticed.

'Not eating my delicious boar, son?' he asked. 'What's the matter with you?'

Alfredo shook his head, unable to lift his eyes from his plate as he pushed a piece of carrot on to his fork and chewed it carefully.

'He doesn't eat pigs, even wild ones,' piped up Gio cheerily. 'But that means there's all the more for the rest of us. Delicious stew, Mamma.' Silvana and Carlo had joined us at the table and she gave her son a severe look, shaking her head very slightly as an admonition to him not to say more.

'I see,' said Umberto. He chewed a chunk of meat noisily, them washed it down with a gulp of red wine, all the while watching Alfredo through narrowed eyes. '*Ah si, ho capito.*'

Francesca quickly changed the subject, asking Umberto to recount for us all the story of the boar hunt. But we knew he had realised exactly why Alfredo wasn't eating the *cinghiale*, and that he had stashed the fact away in case it might be of use to him in the future. Carlo reached over and topped up Umberto's wine glass and I smiled at him knowingly. Perhaps if we got him drunk enough, he'd forget.

At last Silvana brought out the *cantucci* she'd made to round off the meal, along with cups of chicory coffee and tiny glasses of *Vin Santo* for the grown-ups from Francesca's precious supply in the cellar. Raising his glass, Umberto called the assembled company to attention and made a little speech. 'Today we give thanks for this wonderful bounty. So let us bow our heads and recite the grace in order that our Lord may know we are proper Catholics . . . Father of mercy, we praise you and give you glory for the wonderful gifts you have given us: for life and health, for faith and love, and for this meal we have shared together. Father, we thank you through Christ our Lord. Amen.' I watched him surreptitiously, keeping my head bowed, and saw his eyes slide towards Alfredo, who sat looking straight ahead, a single tear sliding down his cheek. I was furious at Umberto. He'd done it deliberately to humiliate the child. But there was also something menacing in the way he'd delivered each word of the grace. It was as though he was using it to threaten us all.

In October, the British began area bombing Turin. We heard the news on the radio. The calm tones of the BBC as it reported the targeting of the Fiat plants and the weapons factories were a stark contrast to the outrage of Radio Roma, which described the destruction of a psychiatric hospital and several residential areas. Hundreds were killed and injured. I was tormented by the news of the attacks. It would have been far easier to listen to the reports from my parents' home in Scotland, at a safe emotional and geographical distance. As it was, I felt a muddled mix of shame, fear and grief alongside the hope that these latest blows might change the course of the war. One evening, I confided in Francesca about the internal conflict I was struggling with. Her expression was at once tender and sad as she told me that many Italians felt the same way. Their country was being bombed by an enemy with whom they felt more affinity than they did with their ally.

'All we can do,' she said, 'is carry on with what seems to us to be right, minute by minute, day by day, step by step. That is how we will get through this. Edoardo used to say that when a storm howls around us, the best thing to do is to sit very still in the middle of it all and wait for it to pass.'

We were lucky to have the sanctuary of the villa to protect us from those storms. The people of Turin were a lot less fortunate, facing the devastation of wave after wave of bombing.

One November evening, just after we'd got the children into their beds, the silence of the winter night was disturbed by the sound of a heavy vehicle coming up the drive. Francesca and I exchanged a terrified glance. 'Germans?' I whispered, not wanting the children to hear if any of them were still awake.

She shrugged. 'Only one way to find out.' Her face was pale, but her jaw was set with determination as she marched to the front door and drew back the bolts. I stood at her side and, as we watched, a rather rickety-looking charabanc drew into the courtyard.

'What on earth . . . ?' I said.

A woman got out from behind the steering wheel and stood for a moment, her hands clasped into fists as though ready for a fight. She swayed, appearing half dead on her feet, and Francesca stepped quickly towards her to give her an arm.

'Please, *signora*,' the woman said. Her voice was scarcely more than a hoarse whisper. 'Take our children.'

It was then that I realised a dozen faces, pale with fear and exhaustion, were pressed against the windows of the bus, watching us warily.

'Come inside.' Francesca supported the woman, helping her up the steps. 'Beatrice, would you bring the others? Let's get some food into them, the poor things must be starving.'

Once they were seated around the big kitchen table and began to thaw out in the warmth from the stove, the woman was able to talk. 'I'm sorry, *signora*, arriving like this without warning. But we heard you took in some of our children already and we didn't know what else to do.'

'Did you drive down from Torino today?' Francesca asked, pouring tea into cups to warm our unexpected guests.

The woman nodded, licking her lips, which were cracked and raw. 'It's been terrible. The bombing. Our homes are destroyed. Many of us are living on the streets or trying to find shelter in the ruins. We live with the constant fear of another raid. It's no place for these kids. They've seen things no child should ever see . . . their friends and neighbours – sometimes even their parents – maimed or killed. There are corpses piled up in the streets. There's nothing to eat, no clean water, no way to keep the kids warm, nowhere for them to be safe. Please,' she begged again. 'Will you take them for us?'

Francesca and I exchanged a glance. Our winter supplies were already stretched thin and it wasn't even December. How would we cope with even more mouths to feed? I did a quick head count . . .

fifteen more children. But there was no choice. We couldn't turn them away.

'Of course we will,' Francesca said. 'We'll keep them safe for you here.' Then she ladled soup into bowls and urged them all to eat. We'd have to find something else to give the children for their lunch the next day and I, for one, wasn't looking forward to the wrath of Silvana when she found out. But, as Francesca had said, we were simply doing what seemed right, minute by minute and day by day, step by step. We'd face tomorrow when it came.

The new children were shell-shocked and traumatised. They'd lost their homes and spent sleepless nights in bombed-out cellars, kept awake by the scuttling of the rats and the strain of listening for the next wave of bombers approaching overhead. We went through a period of bad dreams, wet beds, temper tantrums, fear and suspicion all over again during the first few weeks. But Gio, Alfredo and the others helped them learn to adapt, to see that the estate was a safe place and that they were among friends.

When two of the new arrivals started to pick on Alfredo, sensing his vulnerability and his different background as children so often do, Elisabetta and Gio quickly put them back in their place. I heard their raised voices one December afternoon, coming from the maze, and hurried over to see what was going on. Evidently, the two newcomers had thought it a good game to trap Alfredo in the maze and refuse to let him out. Elisabetta was giving them a dressing-down, wagging a finger beneath their noses with the air of an indignant hen, her feathers ruffled. 'You want to be as bad as the Germans? Then go back to Torino! While you are living here, under the wing of Signora Francesca, you respect everyone.'

Gio had an arm around his friend's shoulders and turned his back on the boys. 'Come on, 'Fredo,' he said. 'Forget those idiots. We'll go and finish making our den in the woods.'

Seeing that there was no need for me to intervene, I went back to turn a skipping rope on the *terrazza* for some of the others. But I kept an eye on the two potential bullies and, half an hour later, was pleased to see them collecting fallen branches to help Gio and Alfredo build a thatch over their woodland den.

After a few more protestations and much throwing up of her hands, Silvana rose to the challenge of catering for our newly swelled ranks. But it did take a great deal more effort, finding and preparing food for all those extra hungry mouths and taking care of their practical daily needs. Francesca and I tried to continue the established routine of morning lessons, but soon had to concede that the children's schooling would need to become a lot more flexible if we were all to eat. I taught them indoors when I could, but we also rallied our army of small helpers and spent more time foraging in the fields and woods for useful provisions, gathering sacks of acorns to feed the pigs and filling baskets with pine cones and bundles of twigs to light the fires. One of my favourite pastimes was hunting for edible fungi in the woods and, with the help of Silvana's expert knowledge, my little tribe of mushroom hunters soon became adept at telling edible *porcini* from the red-tinged devil's variety.

When not out on our foraging expeditions, we helped Carlo tend the vegetable garden, which we'd had to extend as our needs grew. We dug new beds, ready for planting additional supplies of the fast-growing crops like radishes, beans and salad leaves that would take their places alongside the ranks of tomatoes, *zucchini* and aubergines in the spring. Carlo put in more potatoes, onions and garlic to help see us through the winter, and with his calm air and patient kindness he soon gained a band of devoted followers, city kids who forged a new-found love of the land and became keen gardeners themselves. And so the newcomers were soon absorbed into the life of the estate and we adapted our routines to make sure every child was safe and well and every belly was full by the time the villa fell silent each night.

◆ ◆ ◆

The approach of Christmas was a welcome distraction from the bitterly cold weather, and we were determined to try to make it a happy time for the children, aware that their thoughts would quite naturally turn to their families in the north. We thought carefully about how best to mark it, not wishing to exclude Alfredo, and determined to make it a celebration of light and friendship at a dark time in the year. Francesca helped the children make decorations out of pine cones gathered from the woods, tied with strands of coloured wool and painted. We wove branches into wreaths and swags and put them around the doorways inside the villa, and we collected leaves and berries to tuck along the top of picture frames, filling the rooms with their resinous scent.

We'd been living on meagre rations, eking out the supplies we'd carefully stored away in the autumn. Now we had double the number of children to feed, we were worried that the food would run out long before spring arrived. The farms on the estate continued to supply us with eggs and milk and Silvana used turnips – originally intended for cattle feed – to help bulk out stews made with rabbits that Carlo shot. Apart from that, we ate scarcely any meat, but Silvana continued to conjure up tasty bean stews and dishes of pasta flavoured with garlic and the herbs we'd hung in bunches to dry.

A few days before Christmas, Francesca hitched up the cart and she and Carlo disappeared off to Pienza, returning triumphant that evening laden with two sacks of chestnut flour, a wheel of pecorino cheese, a bushel basket of carrots and – best of all – four plump geese. I later learned that she'd taken what remained of her jewellery and bartered it for the supplies.

On Christmas Eve, the children were fractious and over-excited, having been cooped up inside for two days while the bitter wind drove volleys of cold rain down the valley, rattling against the shuttered windows like hails of bullets. That morning, a calmer chill settled over the hills, dusting the tops with frost, and the clouds parted to allow the watery winter sunlight to trickle through. Bundled up in their threadbare coats and wrapped in as many woollen scarves as we could muster, the children went outside to play. I was standing on the terrace, cradling a cup of camomile tea in my hands to warm them, when Gio and Alfredo came running from the direction of the *limonaia,* their eyes wide with a mixture of excitement and fear.

'Beatrice, we found a man! Come and see! He's sleeping behind the lemon trees. We couldn't wake him up.' Gio was full of the importance of their discovery, his words pouring out.

'Maybe he's dead,' Alfredo said, a little more timidly.

'No, I'm sure I saw his chest move so he must be breathing. But he looks in a bad way.'

They raced back to the glasshouse, and I followed a little more slowly. Maybe it was one of the partisans returned home after many months spent fighting in the north. But I was already thinking that if it was someone on the run from the Blackshirts, then it meant danger.

I caught up with Gio and Alfredo as they reached the door of the *limonaia* and grabbed their arms, stopping them in their tracks. 'Wait here while I go and have a look,' I told them. 'Where is he?'

'Over there, behind the big pots.' Gio pointed.

I crossed the tiled floor, picking my way between the glossy leaves of the lemon trees. Outside, beyond the glass walls, the voices of the other children were clear as bells on the still winter air as

153

they played. But it seemed to me that the sounds faded away and a silence fell when I saw the man lying there. His cheeks were as pale as wax beneath their shadow of rough stubble and his body was curled in on itself, huddled beneath the thick overcoat he wore. His hair was covered by a black woollen cap, but a single sandy curl escaped at his temple. Something about his features – the chiselled line of his nose, the blue shadows underlining his closed eyelids – didn't look Italian to me. Was he a German soldier, perhaps? But then surely he'd be in uniform?

Gingerly, I nudged the toe of his muddy boot with my foot. No response. I did it again, a little more firmly this time. '*Mi sente, signore?* Can you hear me?' I said in Italian.

His eyes fluttered open and he looked up at me, his expression dazed. The low sun was streaming in behind me, turning my hair into a fiery halo, as he licked his cracked lips. Then he said politely, with impeccable manners and a soft Scottish accent at once so familiar and so out of place that it made my heart somersault beneath my ribcage, 'I'm so sorry. I appear to have bled all over your beautiful floor,' before passing out again.

As soon as Gio and Alfredo heard him speak, as he lay bleeding to death on the floor of the *limonaia*, they ran off to tell the others of their find before I could stop them. I was more intent on stemming the flow of blood that I'd now realised was pooling beneath him, staining his heavy overcoat with its ooze. I managed to roll him on to his back so that I could see his wound more clearly. In his side, just beneath his ribcage, a dark hole had been torn in his clothes and the flesh beneath them where a bullet had passed clean through him. He must have been there for much of the night and had lost a great deal of blood. I wadded up my scarf and pressed it against the wound, fearing it was too little too late by the look of his waxy pallor and the shallowness of his breathing.

The children clustered around the doorway, summoned by Gio's excited shouts, and I called over to them. 'Don't come in. Go and get Francesca. And fetch Carlo too. *Presto!*'

As I waited for help to arrive, I drew the man's head into my lap, cradling it there as his life seemed to ebb away before my eyes.

'Hold on,' I whispered to him. 'Please, stay with me.' I reached down to put more pressure against my scarf to try to stem the flow of the blood that continued to seep through it, staining it scarlet.

And then, without opening his eyes, he placed his own hand over mine and the corner of his mouth seemed to lift with the ghost of a smile, so faint I thought I must have imagined it.

Chapter 22

Tess – 2015

Next time I'm by the pool, I check out the floor of the *limonaia*. Its black and white tiles are clean, apart from the odd dead fly and a dried leaf that's been blown into one corner. But when I look a little more closely, I can see that a patch of the grouting, alongside the back wall, is very faintly stained.

Sometimes, when Beatrice is telling her story and I'm jotting down notes, her memory meanders. She frequently stops and has to go off to look up the name of a particular plant or rose, or she loses the thread of what she's telling me and I have to prompt her gently to bring her back to what she was saying. Often, she consults Francesca's sketchbooks. The pencil drawings and watercolour paintings of the garden and the children spark reminiscences of little incidents or dramas – the usual ups and downs of life. She talks about the day Gio tried to learn how to whittle, having borrowed his father's penknife (without his knowledge), and sliced the top off one of his fingers. Or the time Elisabetta made a cake in secret as a surprise for Silvana's birthday, reducing Silvana to tears. It was the only time anyone had ever seen her cry. It was a sour, tasteless thing, made out of chestnut flour and lemons, without enough sugar to sweeten it, but it was devoured as though it were the most delicious treat anyone had ever tasted.

But when she told me about finding the injured Scottish soldier in the *limonaia* that day, her eyes shone like those of a young woman, as if she were seeing his face all over again.

'His name was Harry Priestley,' she told me, 'and he was the love of my life.'

When her memories meander, Beatrice also talks, frequently, about Alfredo, pointing him out in Francesca's drawings. Her eyes fill with tenderness when she does so. He was clearly very much loved by the women who'd taken him in. I still don't know what could have happened to turn him against them as vehemently as Marco would have me believe. But I've learned to be patient. There's no point trying to force Beatrice to go at a faster pace, she just gets muddled and loses her train of thought all the more often. Her story unfolds at its own tempo. My job is not to edit her memories but to set it all down, in the hope that I can finally understand what happened, and make Marco understand too.

I know only too well, from my own experience, how fickle memories can be. Like my photographs, they're snapshots of moments in time and space, but they rarely tell the whole story. Some memories dominate and obscure others. I've tried so hard to remember the good times, the days when you could still talk and eat and our lives were reasonably normal. But the more I grasp at them, the more elusive they become. Your appearances by my side since my arrival in Italy only occur when I'm not trying to remember you.

I hate the fact that my memories of that final day have blotted out so many of the others I'd stashed away over our years together. I used to hold on to them, knowing each one would be even more precious to me after you'd gone. But now, no matter how hard I try to picture you striding over the hills or smiling up at me from your chair when I brought you a cup of tea, all I can see is the room in the bland apartment on the outskirts of Zurich, with its magnolia walls and the table on which sat the two syringes containing the drugs. The attendants – two women whose faces I can scarcely recall – repeated the instructions we'd been given over and over in the few days since arriving in Zurich. Firstly, they stressed again that you could change your mind at any point. Even after you'd administered the anti-nausea drug in the first of the syringes, via the gastrostomy tube leading directly to your stomach, you could stop the whole process in its tracks. We could leave the apartment, buy a return plane ticket for you, go home together. But once you'd administered the second drug there would be no going back. You would fall asleep within moments, first into a normal sleep, then a deeper one and finally you'd slip into a coma. Your breathing would stop, and you would die.

I remember every word they said. I remember the fake leather chairs and the recliner in one corner. You stayed in your wheelchair, unable to move to the recliner without the hoist we'd used at home to transfer you from your adapted bed to your wheelchair and back again. I pulled up one of the plastic-covered chairs and sat down beside you.

I'm angry at my memory of that room. It's hidden all the other memories like a thick grey cloud. I know they're there somewhere, but I just can't find them when I want to. It's only when you appear and talk to me that the cloud evaporates for a while and things become clearer.

I've had to learn not to try to hold on to you when you're here with me. Your presence is always fleeting, as ephemeral and fragile as a butterfly. You join me in those in-between times at dawn and dusk, the subtler moments of transition that bookend the certainty of day and night, when my camera allows me to detach from the world as I photograph the sunrise catching the face of

Monte Amiata, or the evening light slanting through the cypresses lining the drive. I hear your voice in the sigh of the wind through the oaks and I catch a glimpse of your smile in the sunshine that filters through the silvered leaves of the olive trees that encircle the orchard.

But, far more often, I remember the two women leaving us alone in the room in the Swiss apartment. We sat in silence, and you looked at me as if you were imprinting my face on your memory. I told you I loved you. You blinked slowly, telling me you loved me too.

I remember that. And the look in your eyes as you let go of my hand and reached for the first syringe.

Chapter 23

BEATRICE'S STORY – 1942

We installed the wounded Scotsman in the empty cottage below Carlo and Silvana's farmhouse, safely away from the inquisitive pestering of the children and any chance visit by Umberto.

Francesca had cleaned his bullet wound and treated it with some antiseptic ointment she'd made from marigold petals. She bound it tightly to stem the bleeding. Fortunately, he remained out for the count while she did so, because otherwise the pain would probably have been unbearable. Luckily for him, as the bullet had passed right through him, it had by some miracle missed his vital organs. The wound was badly infected though. All through that afternoon and night, I sat at his bedside, pressing cool, damp cloths to his forehead as he burned with fever. It was all we could do. Francesca made a tincture from willow bark, which was the best resource we had in the way of medicine, and I tried to get him to take a few drops every hour. He seemed lost to the world, slipping beyond my reach as I tried to draw him back from the brink, and I despaired that we were too late to help him.

I must have fallen asleep sometime just before dawn because I woke with a start, my head jerking painfully as I came to. The room was quiet, the candle that I'd kept burning through the night guttering low on the bedside table as the first light of Christmas Day stole through the window.

He was watching me.

'Hello,' I said. 'So you've decided to stick around for a bit after all, have you?'

At the sound of my voice, his eyes widened in surprise. 'You're Scottish?' he asked, his voice a hoarse whisper.

'As are you, apparently,' I replied, smiling with the relief of knowing he might pull through.

He made a sudden movement, trying to sit up, but gasped with pain, his hand going to the swathes of bandaging around his midriff.

'Don't move,' I said. 'You'll only start bleeding all over everything again.'

'My things . . . ?'

'Don't worry, they're here, safe and sound.' I gestured towards his bloodstained coat, which hung on the back of the bedroom door. 'Heaven only knows how we'll get those stains out. Your clothes are soaking in the sink downstairs. I'll wash them properly later.'

He looked at me warily.

'Yes,' I said. 'I found the gun in the pocket, if that's what you're wondering. I've hidden it for safekeeping. And your pack is over there in the corner.'

Seeming a little reassured, he slumped back against his pillows. I held a spoonful of tincture to his lips, and he grimaced at its bitter taste as he swallowed it dutifully.

'What is this place?' he asked, glancing about at his surroundings as the daylight began to reveal the room's bare floorboards and raftered ceiling.

'You're in a cottage on the Villa delle Colombe estate. We found you in the glasshouse yesterday.'

He blinked, trying to remember. 'I'm afraid I was rather out of it. I have no recollection of that at all.'

'Hardly surprising, given the state you were in. What happened?' I gestured in the direction of his gunshot wound beneath its clean dressing.

His hand went to his side again, automatically. He looked at my face, appraising me, and then seemed to decide I was trustworthy. 'I had a bit of a run-in with a sentry at a roadblock just outside Grosseto,' he replied.

'I see. And how did you come to arrive on the floor of our *limonaia* then? Did someone bring you here?'

He shook his head. 'I walked,' he said. 'I kept to the back roads, travelling after dark, and slept in the woods in the daytime. Once I found a derelict barn. But mostly I stayed away from farms. I was trying to get to Siena, where I was supposed to be meeting someone. But I suspect I've missed my deadline now. What day is it?'

'It's the twenty-fifth of December,' I smiled. 'Merry Christmas.'

'Oh.' He looked crestfallen. 'I'm too late then.' He was silent for a few moments, then composed his features again, regaining his manners. 'Merry Christmas to you, too. May I ask your name?'

'I'm Beatrice. Beatrice Crane.'

He extended his hand, wincing slightly at the pain in his side caused by the movement. 'Pleased to meet you, Miss Crane. Harry Priestley.' He smiled up at me and I couldn't help noticing how his eyes crinkled in a rather attractive way when he did so. 'Jolly nice to make your acquaintance. And thank you for saving my life.' His tone was so prosaic, so utterly British, and it made me realise how used I'd become to the heightened emotion of the Italians.

I nodded. 'What is your rank, Mr Priestley? I assume you are here courtesy of the British Army.'

He raised his eyebrows, a little taken aback by my bluntness, I suppose. 'Captain,' he replied. 'The Black Watch regiment. But please don't let us stand on formality. Under the circumstances, I think perhaps we can dispense with titles, don't you?'

'Very well.' I was trying to remain businesslike. Captain Priestley may have been a guest under Francesca's roof, but I reasoned that he wouldn't be staying long. So there was no point in becoming too friendly, despite the fact that I warmed to him and was surprised to find how much I had missed having a fellow compatriot to talk to after more than four years as an outsider in a foreign land. I glanced at my watch. 'I'll bring you something to eat. And then I'd better get back to the villa. It's nearly breakfast time.' I knew the children would be buzzing with excitement at the prospect of our Christmas feast later in the day, and that Francesca and Silvana would need my help keeping the younger ones distracted while those who could be of help lent a hand in the kitchen.

I brought Harry a cup of nettle tea and a slice of polenta that Silvana had left for me on the table downstairs the previous evening. The cake, made of ground chestnuts, was staple fare for us by then. It was stodgy and rather tasteless, but he devoured it hungrily. 'When did you last eat?' I asked him.

He shrugged. 'Can't remember, I'm afraid. My rations ran out a few days ago. Although I did find a cache of hazelnuts in the forest. I suspect there's a rather disgruntled squirrel looking for me too, now, as well as the Italian Army.'

I laughed. 'Don't worry, you're safe from both here. You'll live, I think. Now get some rest. I'll be back later.'

I went to take his heavy worsted coat down from where it hung on the door, intending to leave it downstairs so I could have a good go at cleaning it later on.

'Wait!' His command was so abrupt it made me jump. Then, a little more gently, he said, 'Please don't bother yourself with that. I'll sort it out myself another time.'

I looked at him a little quizzically. I'd gone through the pockets earlier, discovering the pistol concealed there, which I'd hidden in an empty flour crock in the kitchen. But apart from a rather grubby handkerchief and a slightly damp box of matches, I'd found nothing else. 'Very well,' I said. 'Suit yourself.'

'Thank you, Beatrice. Might I trouble you to pass over that pack of mine before you go?'

I placed the canvas rucksack on the bed beside him. It didn't seem to have much in it, judging by its lightness, but I noticed how tightly he gripped it as he watched me leave the room. Captain Priestley was evidently keeping a few secrets, but perhaps it was best not to be a party to them.

Up at the villa, the children were already awake, the sound of excited voices ringing through the house as brightly as any Christmas carillon.

'How is our patient doing?' Francesca asked quietly, as we followed the noisy gaggle of children to the breakfast table once we'd tied the last hair bow, found the final stray sock and fastened up the last pair of boots.

'Much improved. The wound is responding well to your ointment. He's going to need a good deal more rest before we can send him on his way, though. He's still very weak.'

She nodded. 'We'll keep him hidden at the cottage. But I think we should tell the children he's left. They've been asking about the man in the *limonaia* and I've told them we've made him well again so that he can go home. The fewer people who know he's still here, the better.'

Later that day, once we'd eaten our fill of roast goose and rounded off the Christmas feast with several *struffoli*, little honey-dipped doughnuts, which Silvana carried in heaped on to a broad platter to rapturous applause, I prepared a basket of food to take to the cottage for Harry. I waited until the children were safely gathered in the sitting room, listening to Francesca read the next chapter of *Alice's Adventures in Wonderland,* and then slipped out of the back door and down the track to the cottage.

Its windows were in darkness, the shutters drawn. Quietly, I lifted the latch on the door and stepped into the kitchen, setting my basket down on the table. There wasn't a sound from upstairs and I thought Harry must be sleeping. I lit a candle, then climbed the stairs and gave a gentle tap on the bedroom door. 'It's me, Beatrice,' I said softly, not wanting to wake him. As I pushed open the door and the candlelight flooded the darkness within, there was a swift movement in the shadows, something being hastily pushed beneath the whiteness of the pillow. I pretended not to have noticed. 'You're awake then?' I said.

'Hello. Yes, I am, and jolly pleased to see you again. I've been mouldering away here all day, bored out of my wits.'

I laughed. 'In that case, you're certainly on the mend. Once patients begin to complain, it's always a sign they're getting better.'

'Sorry, I didn't mean to sound ungrateful. And actually I think I probably slept for most of it. But I am truly pleased to see you again.'

I tilted the candle so that a few drops of melted wax fell on the saucer at his bedside to hold it in place. I laid my hand against his forehead, checking his temperature and trying to ignore the way my heart beat faster at the touch of my skin against his. 'That's good, your fever seems to have broken now. May I have a look at your wound? It needs to be cleaned again and re-dressed.' Although he was practically a stranger, a peculiar intimacy enveloped us, so I spoke briskly to dispel it, filling the silence that seemed to thicken the air between us.

A little blood had seeped through the bandages at his waist, but as I unwrapped the layers I was glad to see it was a clean red colour, healthier than the dark, yellow-streaked ooze of yesterday. He suffered my ministrations stoically, only wincing once or twice when I pressed a little too hard as I cleaned the wound.

'Sorry,' I said. 'I have to make sure we get rid of all the infection.'

'Please don't apologise,' he said. 'You make an excellent nurse.'

I packed the wound with a pad of gauze smeared with some more of the calendula ointment and then wound a clean length of bandage around his waist to hold it in place. He had to sit forward so that I could pass the bandaging behind his back as I unrolled it, but he was too weak to do so on his own. I propped him up so that he was leaning against my shoulder and completed my task as quickly as I could, my arms encircling him, pretending to ignore the fact that the bare skin of his chest was closer to mine than any man's had ever been before.

'Now then,' I said, 'just another spoonful of this delicious medicine and then you can have your Christmas dinner.'

He grimaced again as he swallowed the bitter willow bark tincture. Then, as I started to draw my hand away, he took it in his own. 'Beatrice,' he said. 'Thank you. For all of this.'

I sat there with my hand in his for a minute that seemed to stretch into an eternity. It was as if everything in my life so far had been leading up to that moment, sitting there like that, with my hand in his. As if, in those times of uncertainty, we had stumbled across something so certain that it filled my heart and soul with a peace I'd never known before. My eyes were fixed on our two hands, clasped there on the white sheet, but then I slowly raised them and met his steady gaze. His features creased into a smile and my heart turned a somersault. I'd only ever kissed one man before, during those heady days in Florence. Luca and I would meet in the Boboli Gardens at dusk and steal kisses beneath the frescoes of the Buontalenti Grotto in snatched moments when we found ourselves alone there. I'd fancied myself in love then, with all the blissful ignorance of youthful inexperience. But this was something else. Something far more profound. A meeting of souls.

From the orchard beyond the cottage, an owl hooted in the darkness, bringing me to my senses. 'You must be starving.' I drew my hand away and got to my feet. 'I've brought you the remnants of our Christmas feast.' I smiled. 'Don't think you can get used to it though – our usual fare is a lot more basic.'

I brought him a plate of food and sat at his bedside as he ate. We talked and talked, exchanging our life stories. I told him all about Francesca, about Edoardo's death and about the estate where she gave shelter to so many waifs and strays (myself included). He was a little more wary. I noticed he avoided saying anything much about how he'd come to be in Italy, but he told me he'd been at university in Edinburgh, so he knew the city well. He talked about his upbringing on a farm in the Highlands and we both sympathised about being sent away to boarding school. His had been Eton, though. Despite that life of privilege, he'd missed Scotland terribly and had wanted to return home as quickly as he could, choosing a Scottish university and joining a Scottish regiment as soon as he'd graduated. Finding ourselves washed up in an enemy land and discovering we shared our Scots roots helped forge the deep connection between us so swiftly, I think.

I told him about my spell in the prison in Florence, but when I asked him how he'd ended up in the *limonaia* at the Villa delle Colombe, he became evasive again. He simply said he'd been aiming to travel north and that he'd been stopped at a roadblock and shot. With his injury – ('although the sentry came off worse than I did,' he said with a rueful frown) – he'd been unable to make good progress. He'd realised he was in trouble as he reached our remote valley beneath the slopes of Monte Amiata. Suffering from the infection that had flared in his wound, he'd stumbled through our woods and found the *limonaia*. 'It seemed like a good place to hide at the time,' he said, 'although I probably wasn't thinking very clearly by then. Perhaps I just thought it would be a good place to die . . .'

His eyes met mine in the flicker of the candlelight and he reached for my hand again. 'I've remembered something about yesterday,' he said. 'At first I thought it must have been a hallucination or a fever dream I'd had. But I think it was real. I was lying on a tiled floor and an angel stood over me with flaming hair. She was surrounded by a blaze of light. And she seemed so strong. I thought my time had come, that she brought death. But I was wrong. She brought life, didn't she? She was you.'

I nodded, my eyes not leaving his, not wanting to break the spell of that moment when we both knew we'd fallen in love. It was the best Christmas gift I'd ever had.

Chapter 24

Tess – 2015

You come and walk beside me as I wander through the gardens. It's evening and I've offered to water the more tender plants that need a little help through these scorching summer days. The heat seems to make Beatrice wilt too and she's retired to her room with a headache.

I fill the watering can from a brass tap alongside the stone basin and take it over to the first urn, snapping off one or two dead geranium heads and tucking them into my pocket. As I lift the can and let the water flow over the thirsty plants, I sense your presence behind me, but I know better than to turn and look. So I just say, softly, *You know, writing Beatrice's story helps me remember things about us that I'd forgotten.*

Like what? you ask.

Like falling in love. Her memories of discovering Harry in the *limonaia* and tending to him in the attic bedroom of the cottage have reminded me that you and I, too, once had something akin to that meeting of souls.

Before you lost the ability to speak or swallow, before we knew anything much about MND, and before a whole host of other medical acronyms became part of our daily vocabulary . . . before all of that, we met and fell in love. We walked and danced, we laughed, and sang along with the radio in the car as we drove to lunches with family and dinners with friends. We complained about the daily awfulness of the news, and we binge-watched old westerns on TV on winter weekends when it was too wet to go out for a walk. And you understood me. You laughed at my jokes and listened to my anecdotes about the dramas and cringe-worthy wedding speeches from my latest work assignment. You shared your passion for mapping the world around us and you brought home bars of chocolate on Friday nights and sometimes a bunch of flowers, just because. I used to look at you in wonder sometimes, overawed at how much I loved you, and sometimes I'd catch that same look in your eyes as you watched me.

I go back to the tap to refill the watering can, and you say, *Do you think you'll try to find the centre of the maze again? After all, Marco gave you back the map and you'd almost finished plotting the outer sections when the storm hit.*

Focusing on watering the final urn, so that I won't scare you away, I shrug. *Maybe*, I say. But I know I won't. At least, not on my own. I can't ask Beatrice again, and I don't want to ask Marco. I presume he's back in Rome by now, anyway. I glance up at the green-black cypress walls and can't help feeling I'll never really be able to work out how to escape. I wanted to master the maze, to be able to walk through its twists and turns as Francesca did, navigating a way through my grief. But failing so ignominiously has only made things worse. I feel more trapped than ever, going round and round in circles and never finding a way through. Even though I can experience the beauty of the garden and feel the warmth of the evening light, the dark walls pressing in on me seem more real.

Despite the vagaries of her memory, I think Beatrice does a better job than I do of keeping her thoughts in order and being able to recount her memories in a logical order. I'm trapped right in the centre, on the day of your death, and I know I need to try to retrace the steps that got me there so I can escape. If only I could find the way.

Chapter 25

Beatrice's Story – 1943

In the weeks following Christmas, thanks to Francesca's homemade medicaments and Silvana's nourishing food, Harry's wound continued to heal well. By the time the new year was a month old, he was able to get up and dress himself, and even to sit in the weak winter sunshine on the terrace outside the cottage, when we thought it was safe for him to do so. Once my teaching duties with the children were fulfilled, I spent precious, snatched hours with him, sitting talking in the cottage or foraging in hidden woodland glades for *porcini* mushrooms and winter purslane. He was still weak and tired easily, so we walked slowly, arm in arm, his closeness a daily joy to me as I described our lives at the villa, telling him about Francesca and the children, the ways we struggled to provide for everyone, the ever-present threat of another unannounced visit from Umberto.

'I wish I could do more,' he said one afternoon as we wandered through the woods. 'I feel such a burden being here and not lifting a finger to help.'

'It's better if we keep you hidden. If anyone saw you, it would take some explaining. Silvana and Carlo know about you, of course, but they're as discreet as anything. If the children saw you, they might let something slip, and God forbid Umberto should find out about you. It's not only your life that would be in danger then.'

He nodded. 'I know. It's a huge risk having me here. Don't worry, though, I'll be strong enough to move on soon.'

'You won't be leaving before spring. Francesca and I have discussed it. At least that'll give you the best possible chance of escape, once it's warmer.' We walked on in silence for a while, neither of us wanting to face the inevitability of our parting.

I wished, more than anything, that we could keep Harry safe on the estate; but although we seldom went out into the neighbouring towns now, and we had few visitors from the world beyond the villa's gates, Umberto continued to drop in unannounced every now and then. He seemed to think he had the right to court Francesca, turning up with little gifts of honey or sugared almonds, which he presented to her with a flourish, even though she was repelled by his presence. She was too afraid to rebuff his advances, knowing he could make more trouble for us all. Without discussing it, I knew she was doing it to protect me, as well as Alfredo. His knowledge of my presence at the Villa delle Colombe was just one of the bargaining chips he held. He certainly knew Alfredo was Jewish, and if he suspected we were sheltering an enemy soldier too, then all our lives would be at risk.

◆ ◆ ◆

One bitterly cold night in February, when the garden lay embalmed beneath a covering of frost, Francesca invited Harry up to the villa. 'The children are all safely asleep,' she said. 'We thought you might like to come and sit by the fire for a couple of hours and listen to the news on the wireless.' He couldn't light a fire in the cottage as the smoke would have been visible from the valley and drawn attention to his presence.

To date, Umberto had never called by after dark, preferring to time his impromptu visits for morning or afternoon when he could make the excuse that he was just passing and thought he'd stop in for a cup of tea. We sat by the fire, Francesca in an armchair and Harry and I on the sofa, and it felt so very comfortable and normal that I had to pinch myself to remember how extraordinary it was that the three of us were sitting there together. For a moment, I allowed myself to imagine a time after the war was over, when we might legitimately spend evenings together without the shadows of fear and persecution from the outside world hanging over us.

Francesca reached across and switched on the wireless. It was tuned to the BBC, the sound turned low, and we listened in silence to the day's reports. There was some hopeful news. American forces were engaged in a battle against Italian and German troops in Tunisia as the struggle to control North Africa continued. And on the Eastern Front, after a long and bitter siege, the Russians had finally defeated the German army occupying Stalingrad. At that news, Harry sat up and leaned forward to listen intently. When the report was over, he turned to me with new hope in his eyes. 'That's good news for the Allies – could be a turning point, I think. I shall need to try and get a message out to my lot, let them know I'm still alive and kicking. There may be useful things I can do, now we're making some progress.'

Panic rose in my chest at the thought of him leaving the safety of the estate and going back out into the hostile countryside where he'd already almost lost his life. 'You're not nearly strong enough yet,' I protested. 'You know how exhausted you get.'

'But, Bea, I have to do something. What sort of a man would I be if I just sat here enjoying your kind hospitality? Don't you understand, I'd be doing it for you. For all of us here.'

Of course I understood. I just didn't want him to leave.

Francesca, though, listened with her usual equanimity as he asked whether she might be able to get a message out through the Red Cross.

'I can probably arrange a meeting with my contact in Montepulciano,' she said. 'But to travel any further afield would be dangerous and arouse suspicion.'

'That would be fine,' Harry replied. 'If they can deliver a letter to Siena for me, there's a cell that can take it from there. Might you have a pen and a piece of paper I could use?'

He scribbled a brief message, then folded it and pushed it into the envelope Francesca gave him. She put it in her pocket for safekeeping. 'I'll drop it off next time I go to town.'

Then Harry stood, reluctantly tearing himself away from the warmth of the fireside and preparing to return to the chilly cottage.

'Hang on a sec, I'll come with you,' I offered. 'I could do with a breath of fresh air before bedtime.'

As we tramped down the lane, lit only by starlight, our breath hung in clouds on the frosty air. Harry shivered. 'You should have worn your coat,' I chided him, tying my woollen scarf around his neck.

He shrugged. 'But then I wouldn't have an excuse to do this.' He wrapped his arms around me, drawing me close, and kissed me, the warmth of our bodies mingling to shut out the cold. We carried on, arm in arm, past the darkened farmhouse where Silvana and Carlo were presumably already asleep.

As we approached the cottage, he froze.

'What is it?' I asked.

'Shh. I think I saw something.' His voice was a whisper.

Then I saw it too. A tiny glint of light wavering unsteadily, just visible through a broken slat in one of the shutters covering the kitchen window of the cottage. Someone was inside.

'Wait here!' he hissed. I shrunk back against one of the stone pillars of the *loggia* as he approached the door. I wondered whether his pistol was still in the flour crock, or had he hidden it somewhere else? Stealthily, he lifted the latch and pushed the door open. My whole body tensed, anticipating a shout or a gunshot.

Instead, he said levelly, '*Cosa ci fate lì ragazzi?* What are you boys doing there?'

I stepped forward, craning my neck to see over his shoulder.

'Gio! Alfredo!' I gasped at the sight of the two small reprobates, guilt written all over their faces, illuminated by the torch that Gio carried. They looked up from the drawer in the kitchen table, which they'd pulled open. The barrel of Harry's pistol glinted there.

'We're sorry, Beatrice,' Alfredo said. 'Gio said he'd seen a man coming out of the cottage earlier. We waited until everyone else was asleep and then came down to have a look.'

Gio gazed up at Harry and shone his torch into his face. 'It's you, isn't it? The man from the *limonaia*. They said you'd gone. I'm glad you're still alive. When our old dog died, Mamma told me it had gone to live on another farm but then I saw my pappa burying it in the woods. I thought maybe they'd done the same with you.'

Harry laughed. 'No. I'm still here. But you have to keep it a secret. Not a word to anyone else, all right? You've done a very good job spying on me. But spies have to know how to keep information to themselves. Do you think you can do that?'

The two nodded, giving their solemn promise.

Harry lit a candle and set it on the table, glancing into the open drawer as he did so. I put an arm round each of the boys. 'Come on, you two. It's way past your bedtime. I'll walk you back to the farmhouse.'

'Hang on a tick,' Harry said. 'I think you may have something that belongs to me?' He held out his hand. Gio and Alfredo exchanged a glance and then Gio fished a small capsule out of the pocket of his trousers, handing it over with evident reluctance.

'We thought it was a sweet. We were going to share it when we got home,' said Alfredo.

Harry's face was grim in the flickering light. 'It's certainly not a sweet,' he said. 'In fact, if you'd eaten it, you'd be dead. It's poison.' His eyes met mine and I thought I detected a flicker of apology that he'd kept this from me and inadvertently exposed the children to such danger.

I drew the boys close, shivering at the thought. 'Right, you two.' I kept my voice brisk and matter-of-fact, covering up the fear I felt at the thought of what had so nearly just happened. 'That's more than enough adventuring for one night. Let's get you home.'

As I hurried them back up the track, I whispered to them that they mustn't tell a soul about anything they'd seen that night. 'If you want to protect all of us – Carlo and Silvana, Francesca, all the other children – then you have to keep quiet about Harry being here, all right?'

'We promise,' they chorused, and I watched as they slipped through the farmhouse door and closed it quietly behind them so as not to wake Carlo and Silvana.

Of course, despite their promise, Gio and Alfredo couldn't keep Harry's presence a secret for long. The temptation to steal down to the cottage and visit him again was too strong and the other children soon noticed something was up. I only realised it had become general knowledge when Elisabetta came across me putting food into a basket in the kitchen one day and said casually, 'The English soldier might like some jam on his bread. Silvana found three jars hidden behind the preserved peppers in the larder yesterday.'

I discussed with Francesca what was best and we agreed that if all the children now knew of Harry's existence he might as well come out of hiding and make himself useful around the place. As his strength slowly grew, so did his frustration at being cooped up and unable to contribute. We decided he should continue to live in the cottage, away from the prying eyes of Umberto or any other neighbours who might chance to call in, but he gladly set to work in the garden. Although some days he was still overcome by his weakness and grew tired quickly, he won Carlo's approval as well as an entourage of small followers, who became his willing helpers.

There was one thing that preyed on my mind: that capsule of cyanide the boys had found. I asked Harry one day where it was. 'Don't worry, Beatrice,' he said. 'I've made sure it's safely out of the way of the children.' He showed me how he'd wrapped it in a hanky and pushed it into the lining of his greatcoat through a small hole he'd made. When he wasn't wearing it, he kept the coat hanging on the inside of his bedroom door, out of the way of prying eyes and exploring fingers and I was satisfied it was well hidden.

I'd realised, of course, that poison wasn't something an ordinary soldier would carry with him. I suppose Harry had decided by then that he was able to trust me. One evening, without any probing from me, he opened up about his mission and the tortuous journey that had brought him to the Villa delle Colombe. He'd joined a unit known as the Special Operations Executive, selected because he could speak Italian, having studied languages at Edinburgh University. He'd been sent to Italy to reconnoitre what he called 'the potential for dropping in'. In his understated way – which I'd come to learn was typical of him – he made it sound as if the British Army were contemplating making a social visit for afternoon tea. He'd reached the coast via a submarine, which had deposited him a mile offshore in the middle of the night, along with a collapsible canvas kayak in which he paddled to a hidden cove. He was supposed to have made his way cross-country to a rendezvous point in Siena, mapping the terrain along the way. But his plans had gone awry when he stumbled across the roadblock on a back road just outside Grosseto.

'And that's how I ended up in the *limonaia* and at your mercy,' he smiled, taking my hand in his. 'The Fates truly were smiling down on me on Christmas Eve.'

I didn't tell Francesca that Harry was not just an ordinary soldier but a spy. We were already risking enough, keeping him hidden away on the estate.

◆ ◆ ◆

That spring seemed to me to be enchanted. I was in love, and I was loved. And so every unfurling leaf in the woods, every tiny violet in the hedgerows, every new bud on the rose bushes seemed to hold more promise than ever before. That spring, I learned that love heightens the senses and enhances each tiny moment of every day, so that even the most mundane of chores becomes filled with joy. Digging the beds in the vegetable garden, pulling the first weeds from the flowerbeds, manoeuvring the lemon trees on to the parterre – each task spoke of the months ahead, filled with the promise of a summer to come.

By the time Easter came around, the wisteria was just beginning to open its first purple petals over the pergola and the roses we'd planted were covered in tight buds. Some days were warm enough to shed a few layers of the makeshift clothes we wore, but other days a bitterly cold east wind would funnel down the valley, scouring the dust along the Crete Senesi and sending us running back inside to the shelter of the villa. Despite that, one morning Francesca found a single early bloom bravely shivering on one of the rose bushes. She cut it and brought it into the kitchen in triumph. 'Look!' she said. 'The white rose is the traditional flower of

Italy. And what's more, we give them in odd numbers for happy occasions. So this has to be a sign, *vero*?' She set the single flower in the centre of the kitchen table, in the Roman glass jug that Gio had given her, and its pure-white petals really did seem to glow in the shadows like a symbol of hope, that brave flower that had bloomed despite the cruel wind from the east.

Perhaps, too, the intensity of that magical spring was heightened by the ever-present threat that besieged us in our gated paradise. Francesca, Harry and I still listened intently to the nightly radio broadcasts, trying to interpret the truth behind the propaganda and work out what was really happening. According to the reports on Radio Roma – broadcasting snatches of impassioned speeches made by Hitler's propaganda minister, Joseph Goebbels – the Italians and their German partners were making excellent progress. A few weeks previously, they had vowed to wreak 'Total War' against the Allies, and German U-boats had sunk many convoys in the Atlantic as they attempted to carry supplies between America and Britain. But the BBC's more measured tones reported Allied victories in North Africa, driving back Rommel's battalions in Libya and Tunisia. At the end of March had come the news that American planes had bombed the oil refinery at Livorno, but even that attack – just a hundred miles away – couldn't encroach on our sense of sanctuary on the estate. In our minds and our hearts, we tried to keep the war firmly at bay, refusing to let it encroach into our domain. We needed to stay positive for the sake of the children and I believe we put on a good show, allaying their fears and helping strengthen their minds as well as their bodies. I knew Francesca was still worried about Umberto's visits, as well as about how to feed her multitude of dependants, but, protected as we were by the remoteness of the valley with its steep crenellations of bare clay, and fortified by Harry's love, I felt safe.

The orchard was a froth of blossom, the canopy of the ancient fruit trees forming a pink and white parasol overhead, and underfoot the lush grass was a tapestry of scarlet poppies and golden buttercups. It was the perfect place to take the children to play as they could run free there, so Harry and I were supervising a game of hide-and-seek one afternoon, giving Francesca some peace and quiet up at the villa where she was sorting out bills and filing paperwork. We sat beneath one of the ancient olive trees that encircled the orchard, leaning our backs against its gnarled trunk, as Alfredo counted to a hundred with his hands over his eyes and the others ran off across the carpet of red and gold flowers to go and hide. The soft spring air was good for him, his breathing relaxing and deepening as the cruel winter chill relaxed its grip on his chest.

The sound of birdsong filled the silence once Alfredo had triumphantly shouted '*Cento!* Ready or not, here I come!' Then, once we were alone, Harry took my hand in his.

'Bea, there's something I need to say to you.'

I reached a finger to his lips and said, 'No. You don't.'

He smiled at me quizzically, his eyebrows lifting in surprise.

Answering his unasked question, I went on, 'Because when you look at me like that, with such a serious expression, I know it must be something that might spoil all of this. Our time together. We both know it can't last forever, but can't we just let it last for now?' I let go of his hand and began picking buttercups and poppies from the grass, gathering a little posy of them by way of distraction.

He stilled my hand, taking the flowers from me and setting them on the ground beside us, then put a finger under my chin and raised it so I had to look at him again. The olive tree's silver leaves painted gentle shadows over his winter-pale face and his expression was so filled with love that it made my breath catch in my chest.

'Well, I'm going to say it anyway. Because this is really important. And the children will be back any second and it's impossible to get much time alone with you, so I need to seize the moment.' He took a deep breath. 'Beatrice Crane, will you marry me?'

I let out an involuntary yelp of laughter. Then clamped my lips shut when I saw the expression on his face change to one of hurt at my reaction. 'Sorry,' I said, and I leaned forward and kissed him to make his smile return. 'It's just that wasn't what I was expecting you to say. I thought you were going to make a speech about how uncertain the future is, that you'll be off again soon, that while there's a war on we can't make any firm plans, and that in any case our paths probably lie in different directions.'

It was his turn to laugh then. 'Well, all of that's true, I grant you – apart from maybe the last bit – but I still want to marry you. And then perhaps we can work out the direction thing together when the time comes? What do you think?'

I smiled at him, my joy overflowing. 'I think yes. I think it's exactly what I want too. You are the love of my life, Harry Priestley.'

And so Harry and I became engaged, with a buttercup that he wrapped around my finger for a ring, twisting the stem back on itself to keep it there.

One by one, the children drifted back, tired out from all their running around, and flopped down on the grass around us. We made them buttercup chains to hang around their necks, and crowns of poppies for their heads, and by the time we trooped back up to the villa to help get ready for supper they were bedecked in red and gold, which glowed where it caught the slanting rays of the afternoon sunlight.

The mood quickly changed when we neared the house though. We were almost at the gate when Silvana came hurrying through it towards us, her apron slightly awry, pressing a finger to her lips to tell us to be quiet. 'Umberto Ciccone is there. Hide yourself,' she hissed, shooing Harry back down the lane towards the cottage. She turned to me. 'You'd best keep the children in the garden for now.'

'Look, Mamma,' said Gio. 'We've got crowns.'

Her appraising glance took in the chains of flowers the children wore and I saw her notice the one twisted around my finger too. She sniffed disapprovingly and shot a look towards the retreating figure of Harry, then began to chivvy the children towards the garden, urging them to be quiet. '*Andiamo! Rapidamente!* Don't make a noise and disturb Signora Francesca and her guest.'

I led them to the edge of the English garden and sat them down to play a game of 'My Grandmother Went to Market', hoping to keep them away from the villa for as long as possible. But they were tired and hungry, and it was impossible to constrain them for long. The game soon deteriorated into a heated argument about who had missed out what from the list and I began to feel I was trying to herd twenty-eight frantic cats. 'All right,' I said with a sigh. 'We'd better go and start washing hands and faces and give Silvana some help getting supper on the table.' She was already in a bad mood and it wouldn't do to delay any longer, Umberto or no Umberto.

We filed through the gap in the hedge on to the parterre, where Umberto sat at the little iron table, his legs splayed wide, his fat thighs like overstuffed sausages straining against the fabric of his black trousers. Francesca looked drawn and tense.

'Well, well,' he said, not bothering to get to his feet as we approached. 'Signorina Crane and her band of little followers. And how very many there are nowadays! They seem to have been multiplying like rabbits.' He raised a fat forefinger and began counting heads. 'Twenty-seven in total. And little Giovanni here too, with so many new friends! How are your parents these days, my lad?' Without waiting for an answer from Gio, he continued, 'What a wonderful effort you ladies are making, protecting so many of our precious children from the terrible atrocities the foreigners are inflicting on our proud nation.' He beckoned Elisabetta forward. 'Come here.' She approached him warily. Instinctively, none of them liked him. 'Such a pretty young lady you are. And wearing a scarlet crown, I see. Now tell me, my dear, what is your British teacher telling you about the war? I hope she isn't putting any lies into your young heads.'

I clenched my fists in the folds of my skirt, inadvertently crushing the buttercup ring. It fell from my finger to lie on the gravel at my feet. I thought of Harry, safely hidden in the cottage, and prayed he would stay that way.

Elisabetta was more than a match for Umberto though. 'No, *signore*,' she said with a guileless smile. 'Signorina Crane teaches us our times tables and all about the great Italian artists whose work she has admired in the Uffizi museum in Florence. One day, when we have won the war, she is going to take us there to see the heritage of our proud nation for ourselves.' From the seemingly innocent way she repeated the phrase 'proud nation', I could tell she was mocking him, but Umberto didn't seem to notice.

Francesca's hand shook as she began putting the tea things back on to the tray, the rattle of the delicate porcelain cups against their saucers betraying her tension. 'I'm sorry, Umberto, I hadn't realised how late it is. We mustn't hold you back, and it's time to get the children's supper ready. Please excuse us.' She stood, a clear sign for him to leave, but he was in no hurry. He leaned forwards, his elbows on his knees, and fixed his eyes on me.

'Well, Signorina Crane had better make sure she sticks to teaching mathematics and art. We wouldn't want her straying into any more dangerous territory, would we?' His words appeared to be directed to Elisabetta, but his eyes never left my face. I lifted my chin, refusing to be cowed by his bullying.

'*Venite, bambini*,' I said. 'Come along, children. Into the house and wash your hands and faces.'

Slowly, Umberto heaved himself to his feet and settled his black cap over the bald patch on his head. The Fascist symbol of power pinned to it – an eagle perched on a bundle of sticks containing an axe blade – glinted in the last of the sunshine. I felt that our chains of buttercups and our crowns of poppies were quietly stronger than that cold metal emblem. He reached for Francesca's hand and raised it to his lips, the bristles of his moustache brushing her skin. '*Grazie*, Francesca. Thank you for the most refreshing cup of tea. As always, it has been a pleasure spending time in your company.'

Francesca surreptitiously wiped the back of her hand on her skirt and summoned up a sickly smile as she showed him to his car, making sure he drove away without snooping further. As I herded the children into the house, Alfredo smiled at me encouragingly. 'Don't listen to him, Signorina Beatrice,' he said. 'He's just an idiot who likes the sound of his own voice.'

I laughed, picking a blade of grass out of his dark curls. 'Oh, he doesn't frighten me one bit, Alfredo, don't you worry. Now hurry along and wash the dust off.' As he disappeared into the hall, I bent down and picked up the bruised buttercup from the gravel at my feet, slipping it carefully into my pocket. It was limp and a little crushed, but it was still my engagement ring. One of the most precious things I'd ever been given.

Chapter 26

Tess – 2015

Beatrice shows me the pressed buttercup. It's as fragile as a butter-fly's wing after all these years. She's kept it safe, between the pages of a leather-bound copy of Dante's *Divine Comedy* and as I carefully replace the flower, the words on the page catch my eye:

> That love was lit again within your womb;
> By whose warmth, in the everlasting peace,
> Was this flower allowed to bloom.
> For us above, you are a noonday blaze of love,
> And there below, on earth, among the
>   mortals,
> You are a living spring of hope.

'That's beautiful,' I say. '"*A living spring of hope*".'

Beatrice nods and looks out through the open window, across the lemon trees and geraniums on the terrace towards the English garden. She speaks quietly, as if talking half to me and half to herself, reading my mind. 'There are seasons of grief, Tess, just like there are in the garden . . . a frozen winter that it seems will never end; then a spring thaw, when hope returns, bringing with it the promise of summer. That's when the memories return – the good ones, the ones you thought had died.' She glances up at me, making sure I understand. 'But there's an autumn too. A letting go. A time when you start to forget again. I suppose without that ending there can be no new beginning. It's nature's way.'

She looks so sad, but the lines of sorrow on her face soften as she touches the flower that was once her engagement ring. 'In Italian, a buttercup is a *bottone d'oro* – a golden button. Funny, really, when we were so poor. Our clothes were shabby and makeshift by that point in the war. It was impossible to get hold of material to make anything new. Francesca ransacked her wardrobe of dresses and suits and we made them into skirts and trousers for the children. Edoardo's clothes were put to use as well. We adapted what we could for the older boys and made his shirts into smocks the little ones could wear. I could see how it pained Francesca to give up his things, but she never hesitated. She always put the children's needs first.'

'It was amazing how you managed to keep everyone clothed and fed.'

She laughs. 'You know, Tess, I think what I remember most vividly is the sound of our shoes. We had to put wooden soles on them when they wore through and the whole lot of us sounded like a troop of clopping horses as we moved around the stone flags indoors and up and down the stone steps outside the villa. Shoe leather was at an absolute premium. But sometimes Francesca managed to exchange olive oil and wine for hides in Montepulciano and we got the local cobbler in San Quirico to use them to make shoes and patch boots, which were handed down from one child to the next.'

She closes the book carefully, making sure the buttercup is held safe between its pages once again.

I ponder what she's just said about the seasons of grief. I seem to be so stuck in that frozen winter that even the heat of the Italian summer can't penetrate it. But perhaps there are a few subtle signs of a thaw. When you appear beside me and I can remember you as you were in happier times – is that the beginning of a change? Will I have my spring filled with hope and my summer when the good memories return? And does that mean, too, that there'll be an autumn some-time? A time when the memories will let go and fall like dying leaves?

I don't want to let you go. It already feels like a betrayal that my life has moved on without you. Getting on to the plane home from Switzerland, without you beside me, seemed such a cold-hearted thing to be doing. How could I go through the motions of life after watching you die? And then leaving your poor, wasted body in that room for the attendants to deal with the practicalities of calling the undertaker and organising the cremation?

There have been countless other betrayals since. Every time I mark an anniversary or birthday without you there, or go to watch a film I know you'd have wanted to see, or treat myself to a bar of chocolate to eat alone in front of the TV, I feel that sense of betrayal all over again. Even the daily headlines in the newspapers bring a pang of guilt that life goes on for the rest of us but not for you.

My life feels like it belongs to someone else, because my real life ended in that Swiss apartment when yours did. What I'm inhabit-ing now is the life of the woman I see, but don't recognise, when I look in the mirror. She has become a stranger to me, that woman who can keep on living.

Lost in my thoughts, I realise I'm rubbing my wedding ring with the thumb of my left hand. It brings me back to the task I'm supposed to be concentrating on – listening to Beatrice tell me more of her story.

A buttercup was her engagement ring. But she never married. So, I wonder, what happened to Harry?

Chapter 27

BEATRICE'S STORY – 1943

Everything changed that summer. The first cracks in Italy's defences began to show when Tunis was lost to the Allies in May. Then in June came the news the Allies had captured the island of Pantelleria, and while it was just a remote rocky outcrop barely raising its head from the Mediterranean Sea between Sicily and Tunisia, it was the first piece of Italian soil to fall. As we listened intently to the radio reports, we nurtured a tiny flicker of hope, and Francesca and I exchanged tentative smiles.

Harry nodded, although his expression was more serious. 'It's a start,' he said. I knew he was more frustrated than ever at having to stay hidden away in our remote valley. He wanted to be out there, doing something – anything – to make a difference to the wider war. But there had been no response to his letter, which Francesca had delivered to her Red Cross contact in Montepulciano. Perhaps it had got lost somewhere along the line between there and Siena. Conscious of the risks, none of us wanted to admit to the thought that perhaps the person carrying it had paid with their life for doing so. Or that it could have fallen into the wrong hands. Francesca said it was more likely that the partisan networks were simply too distracted by the latest developments, and it had got lost in the chaos as Italy's war began to unravel. She had heard, via an old friend of Edoardo's, who'd managed to maintain his secret political connections, that there was a lot going on behind the scenes. 'At the very highest level,' she told us, putting a heavy emphasis on the words. Knowing her as I did, and the circles she had moved in before the war, I suspected that meant the king himself.

As the summer heat grew to a crescendo, the news came in July that the Allies had captured Sicily.

Mussolini, though, was so blinded by his sense of power that he refused the offer from Hitler of more German troops on the ground in Italy to shore up the defence against an Allied invasion. Radio Roma rang with his words as he declared, in his bombastic way, that Italy would retain its independence and the only way Anglo-American forces would occupy the country was as corpses.

Francesca had been in Montepulciano to try to barter for another sack or two of chestnut flour, but I knew she would also use it as an opportunity to meet her Red Cross contacts and exchange letters. The children drew pictures to send back to their parents and occasionally a letter filtered through in return. We knew things were still bad in Turin and it remained a target for Allied bombing raids, but it still came as a terrible shock when we received a letter, addressed to Francesca, telling us that Alfredo's parents had been killed. Their apartment on the south side of the city had been hit by a bomb during one of the raids.

'Should we tell him?' I asked her. 'Or would it be better to keep it from him for now?'

Francesca thought deeply about what to do. 'Telling him now isn't going to do anything but cause him great distress,' she decided. 'There's nothing we can do, and their funerals have already taken place. Not that we could've got him there safely even if we'd known in time. While he's here with us, I think it will be better to say nothing. But I'll begin making enquiries about any relatives he might have. We should at least let them know where he is.'

We both knew tracking down Alfredo's relations would be a nigh on impossible task, the way things were in the country then. Most Jewish families had left, only to meet whatever dire fate awaited them at the hands of the Germans as the war hounded them across Europe. The only comfort we could give ourselves was that we were keeping him in a safe place and taking the best care of him we could. At least his parents had died knowing they had done that for their only son. But we both wept bitter tears in secret, for them and for him, as we continued to try to protect him.

◆ ◆ ◆

It was midnight and I was in the cottage with Harry, the hot velvet of the darkness blanketing us as we lay on the bed beneath the cottage eaves. Through the open window, the song of a nightingale drifted from the direction of the hedges forming the maze. But it stopped abruptly, replaced by the sound of a pair of wooden soles clopping rapidly down the track towards us, which made us sit up hastily. Then we heard Francesca calling my name. She was out of breath, her voice taut with urgent excitement. We pulled on our clothes and rushed downstairs.

'It's happened!' she said as I drew back the bolts and flung open the door. 'They've arrested him! *Il Duce*. After twenty-one years, we're finally free of Fascist rule!'

The three of us ran back up to the villa and into the drawing room, where the wireless chattered on excitedly. We learned that Mussolini had been arrested by order of King Victor Emmanuel III, and that the new President of the Council of Ministers was to be Marshal Badoglio, an army general who had held views opposed to those of *Il Duce*.

While Francesca and I hugged each other and laughed, Harry was less exuberant in his celebrations, sitting there as if glued to the wireless as more details were reported.

'Why so serious?' I asked him. 'This is good news, surely?'

'Of course it is,' he said, but his smile couldn't quite erase the look of caution in his eyes. 'It's just . . .' He hesitated, not wanting to put a dampener on our mood. 'The Germans aren't going to sit back and allow one of their strongest allies to be swept aside. I'm afraid there'll be a backlash.'

He was right. Nothing is ever straightforward. Things changed, rapidly, bringing the war right up to our gates. Within a couple of weeks, German tanks rolled into Italy and then were in our valley, and we watched as clouds of dust from their manoeuvres billowed from the parched earth below the estate, filling the air we breathed. We tasted it between our teeth and it got into Alfredo's lungs, making him wheeze and gasp for breath whenever he tried to run with the others. He would often be found sitting in the curve of Francesca's arm as she read to him in the library, where she kept the shutters closed to keep out as much of the heat and dust as possible.

One hot August night, Harry, Francesca and I were listening to the wireless when the reporter's voice was drowned out by the sudden roar of planes overhead. The children woke immediately, memories of that same roar over their homes in Turin triggering panic, and the darkness was ripped apart by their screams. The three of us ran to comfort them.

'Come now,' Francesca said. 'They're not going to bomb the Villa delle Colombe. But just to make us all feel safe, we'll go down to the cellar and I'll tell you a story about a mouse who was very brave, who helped a lion with a sore paw.'

Harry and I set to, helping the younger children tie their shoes and wiping away their frightened tears. Silvana and Carlo appeared, having run up to the villa from the farmhouse with Gio and Alfredo in their pyjamas.

The cellar beneath the kitchen was filled with racks to hold barrels of wine and olive oil and even though our supplies were running low, there wasn't enough space for all of us to crowd in. Another wave of panic began to spread again as the next plane flew overhead, lower and louder this time.

'Quick,' I said, making a split-second decision. 'Carlo and Silvana – take the little ones down the ladder with Francesca. Elisabetta and you four others, come with me and Harry.'

'Where are you going?' Francesca asked, keeping her voice low so the children wouldn't hear the tremble in it. We were trying to stay calm, but the children's panic was infectious.

'To the maze,' I replied. 'It's time to put Edoardo's hidden chamber to use.'

She hesitated, then nodded reluctantly, knowing it was our best option. 'OK. But go quickly and be careful.'

I gave her a brief hug and then led my little gang to the door, grabbing a couple of torches from the chest of drawers in the entrance hall and handing one to Harry. The sound of the planes was a distant rumble now, so we all held hands and made a run for it to the maze. The children led the way to the centre, navigating the twists and turns with ease even in the wavering torchlight, sure of the route from all the hours they'd spent playing there. I pulled the dry mat of grass off the trapdoor and, to my relief, Harry and I were able to open it without too much resistance. I shone the beam of my torch into the blackness below, lighting up the ladder Edoardo had installed. The children hung back. 'Who's going to go first?' I asked. But they shook their heads, reluctant to clamber into that dark hole.

'There might be spiders,' said Elisabetta, her tears drowning her voice. 'Or snakes.'

I shuddered at the thought, but the noise of another aircraft approaching reminded me the threat was greater above us than below. So I handed her my torch, hitched up my skirt and climbed down. Thankfully the chamber, lined with rough-hewn planks, was clean and dry and uninhabited by any wildlife. 'It's fine,' I called. 'Come down, quickly.'

Harry helped the children scuttle down the ladder and brought up the rear, closing the trapdoor above our heads, shutting out the thunder of the plane's engines. In the sudden quietness, we heard the distant thud of a bomb, then a second explosion and a third. The children's eyes were huge in the torchlight and I drew them to me in a tight huddle. 'Look,' I said. 'See how protected we are here? Nothing can harm us. And the others are safe with Francesca.'

'Are they bombing the villa?' asked one girl, her voice quivering.

'No, my darling, those explosions sounded much further away.' I sent up a quick prayer to anyone who might be listening that no stray bombs would fall any closer.

I drew two of the children to my side, encircling them in my arms, and their trembling slowly stopped as silence fell and they began to relax.

'Beatrice, do you know the story about the brave mouse and the lion too?' asked Elisabetta.

'Certainly I do, and I will tell it to you now. I'm proud of you, because you have all been as brave as the bravest mouse tonight – haven't they, Harry?'

He smiled at me above the children's heads, and I felt safer than ever before, knowing he was there beside me.

Once I'd finished recounting the fable, one or two of the children fell asleep. We stayed there for another hour or so, just to be certain there wouldn't be another wave of bombers. Then, at last, Harry looked at me and pointed upwards towards the trapdoor, his brows lifting as he asked a silent question. I nodded, and he carefully moved the sleeping child from his shoulder and gingerly made his way up the ladder. His feet disappeared above us, out into the night air, and I could see the pinpricks of stars in the rectangle of sky over our heads. After a few minutes, he reappeared. 'All clear,' he said quietly.

We roused the children and helped them climb out of the chamber. Back at the villa, I knocked gently on the cellar door before opening it. Francesca sat in the middle of the huddle of little ones, watching over them as they slept, her Madonna-like face pale with exhaustion.

'It's OK,' I whispered, not wanting to wake the children. 'They've gone.'

'Where did the bombs hit?' she asked. 'I heard the explosions.'

'There are fires on the mountainside across the valley, above Campiglia I think.'

They burned for hours and we watched them from the windows of the drawing room, once we'd got all the children safely back into their beds.

Although there were no more bombing raids, that night brought home to us forcefully the fact that Italy had now become a battlefield as the Germans and Allies – attacking from the south – arm-wrestled for control.

And then the pendulum swung again. On the eighth of September, an armistice was signed between the Kingdom of Italy and the Allies. That act, which one might have expected to bring peace in a country that wasn't so divided, sparked a civil war. The Fascist-backed National Republican Army clashed with the Italian Co-Belligerent Army, which sided with the Allies. So, instead of unifying Italy, the armistice and its ensuing tumult sparked a war within a war, which shattered the country into pieces.

A few days later, it was announced that the Germans had freed Benito Mussolini from his prison in the Apennine Mountains and restored him to power in the north of the country, where he would set up a new Fascist state, the Italian Socialist Republic. Nominally, now, there were four governing powers: the Germans in the north; the Allies in the south; the Fascists, led once more by Mussolini and backed by Hitler; and Marshal Badoglio, backed by the king and the Allies.

What that meant for us, in the hitherto peaceful paradise of our remote Tuscan valley, was that all at once we found ourselves in territory that fell under German martial law.

Chapter 28

Tess – 2015

When Beatrice fails to appear one morning, I go to look for her in her apartment. It's the first day of August and the heat has risen to a crescendo, the air resonating with the blare of the sunlight and the chorus of cicadas. The temperature saps the energy from us – even Gio and Vittoria take shelter in their farmhouse with the shutters closed for much of the day – and there's hardly a breath of cooler air at night, making sleep difficult. Still, I'm concerned not to find Beatrice outside on the terrace or dusting the shelves in the cool of the library when I walk up to the villa.

Her apartment consists of a couple of rooms at the end of one wing of the villa, with their own entrance. I knock on the door, but there's no reply. Worried now, I push it open – we never lock anything around here – and step over the threshold. This is Beatrice's private space and I hesitate to invade it. The air smells a little musty, as if it's grown stale from being trapped behind the tightly closed shutters. She always used to fling open the windows at least once a day, both here and in the rest of the villa, keeping the rooms aired. While she's still scrupulous about carrying out her duties in the main part of the house, I get the impression she seems to have neglected her own living quarters for a while.

I call her name, but there's still no reply, so I knock on the door of her bedroom and am relieved to hear a faint response.

'May I come in, Beatrice? Is everything all right?'

She's still in her bed and she seems a little disorientated. 'What's the time, dear?' she asks me. 'Oh my goodness, Tess, I've overslept. It was so hot last night, I lay awake for hours and then fell into a deep sleep when I should have been getting up.'

'Let me bring you some breakfast in bed,' I offer. 'And shall we open the windows for a while before it gets too hot again?' I'm not really expecting her to allow me to look after her. Ordinarily she makes a point of proving she's still determinedly independent. But today she seems exhausted and readily lets me plump up her pillows and bring her a tray of tea and toast.

I perch at the foot of her bed, making sure she eats a proper breakfast. I've flung the windows wide but angled the shutters to keep out the direct blaze of the sun's rays and in the diffused light the lines of her face are even more deeply incised, her expression bleak. It's as if the steely strength of will that kept her going for so many years as she determinedly watched over the villa, waiting for Alfredo's return, has finally failed her. And now here we are in the final month before she has to leave the villa. It's not what either of us had anticipated, but at least I can be of practical help to her, I think.

'Will you be needing a hand with packing up your things?' I ask.

I glance around the room, realising for the first time how little she seems to have in the way of personal belongings. Her bedroom is sparsely furnished, almost ascetic, with its single bed and just one ancient mahogany wardrobe in the corner containing her clothes. Apart from the book sitting by the lamp on her bedside table, the only ornament is a little jug containing a single white rose. It's made of glass, I realise, but it's so misted with age that it looks like pottery at first glance.

She sees me looking at it and smiles. 'That's the Roman jug Gio found when they were digging out the maze. I like to keep a flower or two in it, just as Francesca always did. It reminds me of our friendship.'

I reach out and trace the curves of its handle with my finger. Despite the stuffiness of the room, the glass feels smooth and cool. 'Amazing, isn't it, how something so fragile can have survived for – what? – two thousand years? I suppose Gio must still have the little glass dove?'

She shakes her head. 'Oh no, he gave that away a long time ago. It's long gone, like so much else.' I'm disappointed to hear that. I'd have loved to have seen it. It would have been another link to the villa's history and to the part the children played in it all those years ago.

I urge her to eat a little more of her breakfast. Hoping to distract her as she does so, I say, 'You mentioned Francesca tried to find Alfredo's surviving relations once you'd heard his parents had been killed in the Turin bombings. Did she ever manage to come up with anything?' I know I'm clutching at straws, but I wonder whether there might be anyone I could contact to help appeal to Marco's better nature, now that I've caught a glimpse of it beneath his cold exterior.

Beatrice shakes her head. 'There was no one. In fact, Francesca decided she would adopt him herself. He always was like a son to her. That's why it was so important to her to leave him the villa.'

A hundred more questions crowd into my head again – since he was so loved, why did he go away, and – more importantly – why did he never return?

But before I can think how to phrase them, Beatrice finishes her tea and places the cup back on its saucer, looking a little more like herself. With a bit of her more customary briskness, she says, 'And thank you for your kind offer of help with my packing, Tess, but there's really very little to do. Everything belongs with the villa – it's part of Marco's inheritance now. It'll only take me a day or two to pack my clothes.'

'Have you thought where you'll go?' I still can't bear to think of her having to leave what has been the only home she's known for most of her life.

She shrugs. 'Don't you worry about me. I shall be taken care of.' But there's nothing reassuring about the way she says this. In fact, her tone is slightly grim. A prickle of fear runs up my arms.

'Beatrice, I know this is incredibly hard for you. But you aren't thinking of doing anything . . . well, anything to harm yourself, are you?'

'Oh Tess,' she says, and her eyes fill with sudden tears. 'I'm so sorry – of course it's only natural you might think such a thing after everything you've been through. But I promise you, I'm not thinking about taking my own life. I'd never dream of doing that. And especially not when I know how much it would hurt you. Please don't worry about me. There are things I shall have to face, but let's not think about them until the time comes. After all, we have enough to do.' She fishes out a handkerchief from under her pillow and blows her nose loudly. Then she smiles at me, mustering her strength again. 'I need to finish telling you my story. Come what may, it will be good to have told the truth at last. I'll get up now.' She passes me the tray. 'Why don't you go and get yourself a cup of coffee and I'll come and meet you in the library, shall I?'

Chapter 29

BEATRICE'S STORY – 1944

We tried to keep a low profile through the winter that followed the September armistice and the ensuing chaos, now living as we were under German martial law in a country that was also at war with itself. On the wireless, we heard of the Allied landings at Naples, and then at Anzio in January. The southern part of the country was in their hands by then, and they continued to try to fight their way northwards, but progress was painfully slow.

For our part, under the German administration, we heard some of the locals had been rounded up and sent off to the so-called work camps in the north of Italy. According to Silvana – who was our main source of news from beyond the villa's gates – their names had been on a list of anti-Fascists, given to the Germans by spies from within the Fascist party. The danger was all too clear to us, but what could we do but continue to lie low, keeping Harry well hidden and praying Umberto wouldn't hand Alfredo and me over as well.

Through the winter and into spring, Umberto continued to drop in unannounced, although his visits were less frequent. He was too busy with his own puffed-up self-importance now that the Fascists and Germans were working together in the region. When he did appear, Francesca was careful to be as courteous as she could. His desire for a closer relationship with her was our only bargaining chip, and the children and I kept well out of the way.

One morning in early summer, Silvana told us she'd heard rumours in the valley that the Germans were visiting farms and taking everything they could find. As she clattered pots and pans in the kitchen, she complained loudly that we'd all soon be starved to death if we weren't shot first.

'Hush, Silvana,' Francesca admonished her gently. 'Don't scare the children. We'll make a plan. Right now, in fact, since there's no time to lose. Come on, let's gather together as much as we can and hide it in the chamber in the maze.' Although it was still early in the season, we'd already begun to harvest all we could, replenishing the store cupboards. Silvana had a point: the Germans were timing their raids cleverly, knowing this would be the case and not caring one bit about the fact that we'd all starve in the coming winter if they took our precious supplies now.

We called everyone together and soon even the youngest of the children were running back and forth between the house and the maze, carrying jars of preserves and tresses of garlic. Harry went down into the chamber and stashed everything around the walls as each item was passed to him. Carlo carried the heavier supplies – a side of ham and some flagons of olive oil – and Francesca and I lugged a sack of arborio rice between us. Gio and Alfredo managed to wrestle a large wheel of pecorino cheese into a wheelbarrow and pushed it triumphantly up the hill.

'Leave some room,' Francesca murmured quietly to Harry, as she and I were passing the last two bags of polenta down to him. 'You never know when we may need the space.'

As I hurried back to the villa to gather the last bundles of vegetables that Silvana had tied up in two tablecloths, I offered up a little prayer of thanks to Edoardo for his foresight. The secret chamber at the heart of the cypress maze – that riddle, wrapped in a mystery, inside an enigma – would hopefully be well hidden enough from the Germans, should they choose to raid the Villa delle Colombe.

◆ ◆ ◆

They arrived scarcely a week later. We were forewarned by Gio, who'd appointed himself and Alfredo as lookouts. He burst through the door and announced, breathlessly, that an armoured jeep and two trucks had stopped at the gates and a German soldier was opening them. We'd taken to keeping them bolted shut, knowing even the few extra seconds that would give us might be important.

'Go!' I said to Harry, and he returned my quick, fierce hug before dashing off through the gap in the hedge. We'd agreed he should hide in the maze if the Germans came. The cottage wouldn't be safe enough.

I ushered the children into the schoolroom and gestured to them to sit cross-legged on the floor. Then I picked up one of the storybooks we'd been reading and opened it at random. I put my finger to my lips to quieten their chatter and began to read, in Italian, focusing on making my accent as credible as possible.

Francesca appeared in the doorway, a German officer at her side. 'And here, you see, we teach the children who are staying with us until their homes are safe from the bombing.'

He replied in stilted, strongly accented Italian, I was relieved to hear, hoping he wouldn't detect the traces of a British accent in mine. 'Ah yes, *i poveri bambini*, whose homes have been destroyed by our mutual enemies.'

She ushered him away and I heard her telling him that now he could see why we didn't have much in the way of supplies.

His concern for the 'poor little children' didn't preclude him from ordering his troops to confiscate every scrap of food they could find in the kitchen, though, undeterred by Silvana, who stood glowering at them as they pulled the bunches of drying herbs from the beams and made off with what remained of her last precious sack of wheat flour. They clattered into the cellar and took all the wine they could carry. They decimated the vegetable patch and raided barns and storehouses across the estate, loading the squealing pigs into one of the trucks and chasing the chickens, grabbing as many as they could (although luckily several managed to flutter off into the orchard, where they cackled their disapproval from the branches of a cherry tree, just beyond the reach of the marauders).

We heard a revving of engines at last, and their cavalcade drove off down the drive. The children and I hurried to Francesca's side as she stood at the front door, watching the dust clouds settle. 'They've taken the truck. The Lancia too.' She sighed. 'Not that they were much use to us now there's so little fuel available. But that car was a gift to me from Edoardo. Still,' she said more briskly, as if giving herself a mental shake, 'they've left us Clarice. I suppose they thought she was too slow to be of any use to them. And we have the cart. And we are all safe, that's the most important thing. Thank God we hid those supplies in the maze. You'd better go and tell Harry he can come out now.'

A few days later, we hitched the horse up to the cart and Francesca and I made the short trip to San Quirico. We wanted to find out how our neighbours were faring under the presence of the Germans, and we needed to collect a dozen pairs of shoes and boots that we'd taken to the cobbler to have patched and mended before autumn came and the children could no longer run barefoot. Each season, as the children grew, we went through the ritual of reallocating clothes and footwear, letting down hems and sleeves and darning socks and sweaters. I knew Francesca would also take the opportunity to rendezvous with her contacts to hear the latest news – the sort that wasn't broadcast on the radio – and pass on messages for the children's parents to let them know they were thriving. I never knew exactly who her contacts were. At one time I'd suspected it might be the cobbler, but we simply picked up the pile of shoes from him and she handed over a fistful of lire and a canister of olive oil by way of payment, without anything more than an exchange of pleasantries. Then she suggested I get myself a cup of coffee while she went to speak to the pharmacist about a few minor health issues the children had, so I remained none the wiser. I'm sure it was deliberate. She was protecting my safety as well as that of her connections. We wound our way back down the hill, the horse's hooves clopping steadily along the road and the cart lurching here and there when we couldn't avoid the potholes left by German tanks and trucks. We didn't encounter any roadblocks between San Quirico and the villa that day, although Francesca told me she'd heard several had been put up on the more major routes. She'd also heard that some homeowners had been ordered to billet German officers. 'At least we seem to have escaped that particular challenge,' she said grimly. Then she laughed. 'Perhaps the thought of Silvana's scowls and of having to share with all those noisy children scared them away!'

Our journey was a rare opportunity for us to talk without company or interruptions. Francesca seemed loath to broach one subject that I thought was on both our minds, so I brought it up myself.

'We all know Harry's presence on the estate is putting us in even more danger. He's been talking about it too. It bothers him greatly, especially now he's so much stronger. He told me the other day he's thinking of finding a way to get to the south. He wants to try and meet up with the Allied forces and do his bit again, now they're so much closer.'

He'd sat up a little straighter the evening before when we heard the BBC reports of Allied troops having broken through the German lines, at last, at Monte Cassino, and I'd known what he was thinking even before he'd said anything to me about it afterwards. A few days before, he'd added his boots – the soles of which had worn right through – to the pile to go to the cobbler for mending and I knew that, too, was a sign he was preparing to go. I knew how much it meant to Harry to play his part in the war again, but whenever I thought of him leaving, my heart was gripped by an unbearable pain.

She nodded, pulling on the reins to steer the horse around one particularly bad pothole. 'I understand. But I think we've left it too late. We're completely surrounded by German forces now. It'll be riskier than ever for him to try and get out. My contact told me today that the roadblocks make it almost impossible for anyone to pass through undetected. If they catch him and trace him back to the estate, it'll put all of our lives in danger.'

The sudden roar of a plane's engine in the sky overhead startled the carthorse from her habitually sleepy pace and Francesca had to haul hard on the reins to stop Clarice from bolting. All around us, the air filled with what seemed to be a fluttering of wings, as if we were being engulfed by a flock of doves. But then we saw this was no message of peace – it had been a German plane and it was scattering leaflets across the valley. One fell into Francesca's lap. She read it in silence and then crumpled it into a ball, tossing it into the road.

'What does it say?' I asked.

Her mouth was set in a grim line as she replied. 'It was a warning. It says anyone supporting or sheltering rebels will be shot.'

We travelled the rest of the way in silence. Thoughts crowded my mind and my emotions were turbulent and very mixed. There was fear, certainly, and those fluttering pieces of paper were a horrible reminder of just how much we were all risking. Perhaps Francesca would change her mind now and decide the dangers Harry faced in trying to escape were offset by the mortal danger his presence on the estate put us all in.

At the villa's gates, I jumped down and pushed back the bolts, standing aside to let Francesca drive the horse through before carefully closing them again. But I couldn't summon up my usual feeling of reassurance at being safely back in our own private sanctuary. Francesca always used to say we worked hard to keep the wolf from the door. But now the wolves were on the prowl all around us and even those high iron gates seemed to offer very little protection any more.

As if to drive home how horribly vulnerable and exposed we now all felt, the following morning Umberto paid one of his calls. Our little lookouts came running to warn us that he was coming up the drive, once again giving Harry time to take off into the woods until the coast was clear.

The children were playing around the pool, some jumping a skipping rope and others engrossed in an intense game of marbles taking place in the *limonaia*, whose tiled floor made it the perfect surface on which to play.

'Come and join us, Beatrice,' said Francesca. I had no desire to spend any time in Umberto's company but I could tell she wanted my support, perhaps thinking my presence as a chaperone might deter him from trying to kiss her hand again. So I went to fetch the tray of tea things and took my place at the table on the terrace, from where I could still keep an eye on my small charges.

There was something different about Umberto that day. His usual air of bonhomie had slipped a bit and I thought there was an obviously aggressive edge to the peremptory nod he gave me by way of acknowledgement. I wondered whether the dropping of those leaflets the previous day had anything to do with it.

As Francesca poured the tea, he leaned back in his chair and watched her closely, his scrutiny making her hand shake so that she spilled a few drops. He took the cup and saucer she passed him without a word of thanks.

'Tell me,' he said. 'All those young men you used to have working here on the estate . . . how many of them joined up when they were called upon?'

Francesca carefully set down her own cup and lifted her gaze to meet his. 'Every single one of them, Umberto. Why do you ask such a question?'

'And none of them has returned? Perhaps having thought twice about serving their country?'

She gestured with a sweep of her hand. 'As you can see from the state of our grounds, the only ones left on the estate are the older farmers, who can scarcely manage to work the vineyards and harvest the olives now their sons have gone. Their younger children – who've so far been spared – help out where they can. The eighteen-year-olds have gone already, and we dread the day when the seventeen-year-olds are conscripted too. Who knows how we'll be able to keep the farms running then. We're hardly managing as it is, with all these extra mouths to feed. Miss Crane and I do what we can to maintain the gardens and we have to rely on the children's help too. Last week, as you probably know, our new German neighbours came and took most of our supplies. So we are barely scraping by.' I could tell she was trying to keep her voice level but a mixture of hatred, anger and fear still made it shake. 'But why do you ask?' she said again.

He sipped his tea, his eyes never leaving her face. 'I ask, Francesca, because the other day I happened to take my boots to the cobbler in San Quirico. They needed mending urgently, but he told me I would have to wait until he'd finished working on a heap of shoes that Signora Robbia from the Villa delle Colombe had brought in. He showed me the pile sitting on his bench and I couldn't help noticing a rather fine pair of men's boots among the children's shoes. They were made of strong leather. I thought how fortunate Carlo is to own such a fine pair of boots and then, of course, I realised they couldn't possibly belong to him – not with his bad leg. The soles of these boots were quite normal, you see. So that got me thinking . . . who might they belong to, these stout boots of such quality? They were the sort perhaps a soldier might wear.'

Without missing a beat, Francesca replied, 'Those were Edoardo's. An old pair that I was having mended so that one of the older children can have the use of them if I pad the toes with sacking. Their own shoes are worn through. We have to make the most of everything we have.'

Umberto's eyes widened. 'Forgive me, dear Francesca. How lucky the children are to have such a considerate patron. I apologise for seeming suspicious. But, naturally, I have to report anything out of the ordinary to my superiors. We've been asked by our German neighbours' – he deliberately stressed the phrase she'd just used – 'to be on the lookout for any suspicious behaviour and report back to them. You'll have seen the leaflets they dropped on the valley yesterday, I'm sure? So, you see, it's my duty to check on anyone who might be thinking of sheltering rebels.' He attempted to make light of it, but there was a sinister edge to his words.

Then he continued, with scarcely a pause, 'And tell me, how is that sweet little boy doing? The one who doesn't eat pork?' He put a hand up to shield his eyes from the sun's glare as he scanned the groups playing around the pool. Alfredo wasn't among them. I knew he'd be in the thick of the marble competition with Gio, crouching on the tiles inside the *limonaia*, whose windows reflected back the sunlight.

The back of my neck prickled with fear and hatred then and I wished I could pick up the teapot and throw it and its scalding contents in Umberto's smug face. Francesca didn't reply. I think she was struck dumb suddenly by the depth of his malice.

'You know,' he said, 'I should really report him to the authorities. But of course, since we are such close friends, I suppose I could be persuaded to keep it between us.' He slid a sly glance in my direction, then reached for Francesca's hand. 'What do you think, Francesca? We are very close friends indeed, are we not?'

She snatched her hand away as if she'd been burned. 'Please, Signor Ciccone, I beg you to leave us alone. Haven't you done enough already?' It was the closest she'd ever come to accusing him of playing a part in Edoardo's death. I could see he knew exactly what she was referring to because his fat face flushed puce with fury.

'I see. That's how it is to be, is it, Signora Robbia?' His voice cut the air like a steel blade. 'Very well. You have made your position very clear. I had hoped by now you'd have come to see sense, but it appears you persist in clinging to your old beliefs, despite where that got your own husband. There is no place in the new order for children like that one. Nor for liberals like you and your foreign friend here. Perhaps she, too, should be reported to the authorities.' He reached for his cap and got to his feet, giving the table a shove that sent the cups rolling, slopping tea in all directions.

Francesca stood too and took a deep breath to steady herself. Then, to my horror and disbelief, she put a hand on his arm in a conciliatory gesture. 'Umberto, wait. I'm sorry. We have all been under a great deal of strain recently. Sometimes I scarcely know what I am saying. Of course we are friends. Very close friends, as you say. Please,' she begged him. 'Let us talk again. Why don't you come back this evening, when we are less distracted and the children are in their beds? Come and have a nightcap with me. I still have a little grappa in my wine cupboard. We should discuss this like the civilised citizens we are. I certainly don't want to break any regulations. I don't want to cause any problems for you or for anyone else.'

Mollified, he took her hand in his. He scanned her face with another searching look, but she'd lowered her eyes and all he read there was an expression of capitulation. 'OK,' he said. '*A dopo*. I'll see you later. *Arrivederci*, Francesca.' He gave one last triumphant look in my direction as I stood there, my mouth open in shock at what had just taken place. And then he swaggered off towards his car, settling his cap on his head at a jaunty angle.

We watched in silence as he drove away and then I turned to Francesca.

'What on earth are you thinking?' I couldn't keep the fury out of my voice. I was terrified, of course, for myself as well as for Alfredo, but I couldn't bear to think of my friend sacrificing herself to that monster in order to save us.

'Don't worry,' she said. 'I'll do anything to protect you and Alfredo. Harry too. All of you.'

'No,' I retorted, my voice quaking with anger. 'Not this. You can't. Being with him will destroy you just as surely as any bullet would. We should go. Harry, Alfredo and I. We can make a run for it.'

She shook her head. 'It's too dangerous. If you're not here this evening, he'll suspect something's up and send them after you. The Fascists, the Germans, either way they'll kill all three of you. And it'll put the rest of us at risk too. This is the only way.'

I reached for her and held her tight. She was trembling uncontrollably as I sobbed against her shoulder. But then an idea occurred to me. I lifted my head and wiped my eyes defiantly with the back of my hand. 'No, Francesca. There is another way.'

I looked across at the children playing, oblivious to what had just unfolded, their laughter as innocent as birdsong in the sunlit air. And in that moment, I knew just how far she and I would be prepared to go to save them.

Chapter 30

Tess – 2015

I take a break from writing up the latest part of Beatrice's story, stretching my arms above my head to ease the ache in my back from hunching over the keyboard. It's been a long day. The sun has set beyond Monte Amiata but the air is still as hot and heavy as it was this afternoon. I expect it'll be another night of tossing and turning, trying to lie still on top of my crumpled sheets until I can fall asleep at last.

To cool down, I decide to go for a late swim in the pool, so I grab my towel and walk up the lane. Gio is just finishing up in the vegetable garden behind his house, tying unruly tomato vines in place and plucking the flower heads off the onion plants, which have bolted in the heat. I wave and he raises his hoe in a salute.

He's always a bit unsure of me, I sense, and all the more so since I was the one to deliver Marco's message about their eviction. This is Gio's childhood home, after all, the place he grew up under the watchful eye of his mother, Silvana, and where he learned his gardening skills from Carlo, his father. And it's also the place where Alfredo spent so much time, sleeping over at his friend's house. But when I look at Gio as he works in the gardens, I can't see any trace of the boy he once was. Beatrice has described him as a lively, enthusiastic and carefree child, but the Gio of nowadays seems to carry the weight of the world on his shoulders. His expression is habitually wary and a little closed when I'm around and I'm not sure he thinks it's a good idea for Beatrice to spend so much time talking to me about her memories of the war years. The threat of eviction is a heavy one too, of course, and I can see how it must break his heart to have to leave the estate, the only home he's ever known.

I slip off my sandals outside the *limonaia* and lower myself into the pool, sighing with relief as the coolness of the water envelops me, feeling it draw a little of the heat from my body. I swim a few languid lengths, then climb out and sit on the side with my feet still dangling in the water. A bat swoops low over the surface of the water, hunting for insects on the evening air, and I duck my head reflexively at the whirr of its leather wings just a few feet above me.

You sit beside me and I hear you laugh. *I know*, I say, *you're going to tell me they use some clever sort of radar to navigate, so there was no way it was going to collide with me.*

So, you say after a few moments' silence, *just what lengths do you think Beatrice and Francesca went to in order to protect the children?*

I shrug. *How far would any of us go for love?*

We know quite a bit about that, you and I, don't we? you reply. *We know how, as my body shut down bit by bit, you cared for me and tended to me. I could see how much you hated having to do those things, knowing how shameful and humiliating it was for me, but you didn't flinch once.*

A single tear runs down my cheek as I remember. And then you had to decide when it was time. It was such a fragile equation: you'd need to judge it so that you could still administer the final medications yourself. The advice we'd received was very clear on that. Just by accompanying you on that final journey to Switzerland, I was risking being prosecuted for the crime of assisting a suicide. We'd looked up the guidelines, and although in England the Crown Prosecution Service differentiates between compassionate and malicious acts, assisted dying hasn't been decriminalised. We waited as long as possible. The specialist MND nurses, who came in each day and were sympathetic to your decision, were clear about what to expect. Although each patient's MND experience is different and each case can deteriorate at very different speeds, they could at least give us an idea of when they felt the time had come, so you'd still be able to make the journey.

At the beginning, when your MND was first diagnosed, you could manage most of the tasks of everyday living, even if you needed to ask me for help occasionally. But when you couldn't lift your arm high enough to get a spoon to your mouth, and the nurses inserted the gastrostomy tube because you could no longer swallow, we knew it was time.

You'd already put the wheels in motion, wanting to take control of the end for yourself, contacting the organisation in Switzerland that could help you do that and beginning your application. That was a part of the finely judged timing too – you had to send them three medical reports and an official record of your latest medical assessment, as well as a signed letter asking them to assist you in bringing an end to your own life.

Holding the pen to sign your name was the biggest challenge, but you managed to do it with grim determination, pushing my hand away when I reached out to help you. Afterwards, you looked up at me from your chair and saw the tears in my eyes. *I'll be setting us both free, Tess. But you know I have to do this the right way, to protect you after I've gone.* Your words were slurred but I could hear the strength in them. You were plotting out the final months of your life and, to you, they were as clear as any map you'd ever made.

You'd received back the 'provisional green light', which meant you could travel to Zurich where they would see you for further assessments. At every step, they gave you the opportunity to change your mind. But you were following the path you'd mapped out for yourself, and you weren't going to turn back.

The bat swoops past again and the light is fading fast now. I draw my legs out of the water and slip my sandals back on. I look around and all I can make out is the ghostly glow of the white plumbago in the centre of the parterre. Night is softening the geometric lines of the box hedges, casting its pall over the branches of the oaks, and blanketing the dovecot above the *limonaia*. You've gone again and I'm alone in the darkness.

A cloud crosses the moon and I shiver slightly, despite the heat of the night.

How far would any of us go for someone we love? The answer is, we'll go as far as is needed.

Chapter 31

BEATRICE'S STORY – 1944

The children were safely in their beds when we heard the sound of Umberto's car coming up the drive again that evening. They were worn out after helping carry our remaining supplies from the secret chamber in the maze back to the kitchen and barn that afternoon. Everything was ready.

Even in May, the nights could be a little chilly sometimes, so Francesca had lit a fire in the drawing room and set out a tray upon which sat the remains of a bottle of grappa and two glasses. I greeted Umberto at the door and ushered him through, evidence that I was still there and nothing was out of the ordinary. Then I excused myself, pleading tiredness and saying I wanted to retire to my room with my book, leaving the two of them alone.

As I pulled the door shut behind me, I heard the sound of the cork being pulled from the bottle and the faint clink of glasses. Umberto's voice said, '*Salute!* To us, Francesca.' And then there were a few moments of silence before there came a gasp and a heavy thud.

I pushed the door open again immediately and ran to Francesca's side, gripping her arm and pulling her away from where

Umberto's body convulsed on the hearthrug, his face a livid scarlet, his mouth frothing. It happened so quickly. His eyes rolled back in his head as his heart stopped beating and death swiftly claimed him. She gave one solitary sob, more of relief than anything else I think, and then, pulling herself together, said, 'Go and get Harry.'

I picked up the tray and Umberto's glass, which lay on the floor beside him, the last of its contents oozing into the rug. It still contained a few drops of the grappa that had obscured the taste of cyanide. I'd taken the capsule from the inner pocket of Harry's greatcoat in the cottage earlier. We'd agreed not to tell him of our plan, knowing full well that he'd take it upon himself to confront Umberto if we did, trying to protect us. It was best this way. I dumped the glasses into the kitchen sink, rinsing them quickly, and then ran down the lane to the cottage.

I explained to Harry what we'd done as we hurried back to the villa. He remained remarkably calm and seemed to take it in his stride that we'd stolen the poison capsule from him and used it to dispense with Umberto. I suppose his SOE training must have prepared him for all sorts of eventualities, murder included.

Nothing had changed when we reached the drawing room. Francesca had sunk on to one of the sofas and was watching the fire as the logs slowly collapsed in on themselves, consumed by the flames. Harry quickly looked around, assessing the situation. He crouched on the rug and pressed his fingers into the folds of Umberto's neck, just above his shirt collar, making sure there was no trace of a pulse. Then he drew the edge of the rug over the body and straightened up.

Francesca seemed deathly calm, her face white with shock as she turned to look at Harry. 'We need to get him into his car and roll it into a ditch somewhere. That way it'll look like he had a heart attack on the way home after dropping in for a nightcap with me.'

He didn't reply immediately. He was staring at Umberto's boots where they protruded from the end of the rug, deep in thought. I tugged at his sleeve. 'Help us,' I said.

He looked at me and slowly nodded his head. 'Of course I will. But I think there's a better way.' He drew me down on to the sofa across from where Francesca sat. And then he explained his plan.

◆　◆　◆

The day before the funeral, Umberto's body lay in his open coffin on a pair of trestles in the drawing room, just as Edoardo's had done – only with the lid closed – some three years before. I think that reminder of what Umberto had been capable of helped both Francesca and me feel our crime was even more justified. We were protecting Alfredo and we were avenging Edoardo's death too.

The doctor had examined the body and listened to Francesca's account of how shocked and upset she'd been when Signor Ciccone had suddenly fallen to the floor and stopped breathing during an evening visit to the villa. Once he'd officially declared the death to be the result of a heart attack, the undertakers accepted Francesca's gracious offer to allow the body to remain at the villa with some relief. It saved them having to move the heavy coffin back to Umberto's cramped bachelor apartment in San Quirico and up the narrow stairs there, before its final journey to the graveyard outside Bagni San Filippo.

He'd never been a man who made close friends, and none of his Fascist colleagues came forward to claim either his body or his car. Silvana told us Umberto had been an only child, and she couldn't help adding it probably accounted for him being such a selfish bully – although she quickly made the sign of the cross and offered up a plea that the Good Lord might forgive her for speaking ill of the dead. Ever practical, Carlo suggested we hide the vehicle in the stables. If anyone asked about it, we could always say we'd

217

been keeping it safe until an heir could be found. Not that there were any, as far as anyone knew.

One by one, those who'd come up to the villa to pay their respects filed past, each glancing at Umberto's face, which was peaceful in repose now. Most of the mourners were members of the local Fascist party, along with one or two German officers, including the one we recognised from the raid on the estate. Umberto's connections had certainly been dark ones. A few other locals came too, friends of Francesca's who were there to offer her their support and to check that Umberto Ciccone – the bully who'd made so many of our lives a misery – was well and truly gone.

At last, the final mourners left and peace fell. I'd been keeping out of the way in the schoolroom with the children. They'd behaved themselves impeccably, understanding the gravity of the situation. We filed out of the library just as Francesca was closing the door of the drawing room behind her, pulling off the black veil she'd been wearing as she did so.

'Right, everyone,' she said briskly. 'Let's have supper outside tonight.' It was just about warm enough that evening and Silvana had spread cloths over the two long tables on the terrace where we dined al fresco in the summer. We were all a little subdued, I think, conscious of the coffin behind the closed shutters of the drawing-room windows.

Francesca had played her role perfectly that afternoon – Edoardo Robbia's widow, grieving a friend of the family who often dropped in to make sure she was all right but who had so tragically collapsed and died of a heart attack while they were having a quiet drink together at the end of the day. Through the open window of the library, I'd even overheard one of the *Fascisti* saying, 'Still, it was a pretty good way to go, eh? Drinking one last grappa in the company of a beautiful woman. Typical Umberto! Would that we all could be so lucky.' She looked pale with exhaustion that evening, although she smiled as she urged Alfredo to eat a few more of his vegetables, ruffling his curls as she did so. We knew how important it was to make everything appear normal.

After we'd eaten, the older children helped Silvana clear the tables, shaking crumbs from the tablecloths on to the gravel for the birds. Carlo did his rounds of the terrace as usual, watering the pots of geraniums and snapping off dead flower heads, while Francesca and I herded the little ones into the villa to get ready for bed. Harry was nowhere to be seen. We'd agreed it was for the best, and the children didn't question his absence, not when the house had been so full of people all afternoon. We said our quiet goodnights as Silvana took Gio and Alfredo back to the farmhouse. Francesca and I sat on the terrace, watching Carlo finish up in the garden, waiting until the last of the children were safely asleep. Then Harry appeared from the direction of the lane. He nodded to Carlo. And finally Francesca and I got to our feet, and all four of us went back inside the villa.

The day of Umberto's funeral began with one of those soft, late spring mornings when tattered strands of cloud clung to the flanks of Monte Amiata. The once abundant fields of her lower slopes were barely tended these days and the fragile soil was already beginning to erode without the careful nurturing of the farmers. She bore the scars of bombs and fire, too, but the mountain still held her head high, as if in defiance of her suffering.

The pallbearers arrived – six of Umberto's sturdiest colleagues – and reverentially lifted the coffin from the trestles, hoisted it on to their shoulders and carried it out to the waiting cart, which Carlo had readied. They set it down gently, puffing a little at the weight of it, and then gave the Fascist salute before marching smartly off to their cars. It had been agreed that they would go on ahead to the graveyard just outside Bagni San Filippo, where Umberto's parents were buried near his childhood home. That way, they could notify the German sentries at the roadblocks along the route that the funeral cortege was on its way.

We draped the coffin with the Italian flag, weighting its edges with large stones to hold it in place. Then the rest of the children and I watched as Francesca, Silvana and three of the older children, who'd been chosen to represent the estate, climbed into Umberto's black Fiat. Carlo picked up the reins, Gio at his side, and the cart began to trundle down the drive, followed slowly by the car.

I felt a tug at my sleeve. 'Why are you crying, Beatrice?' Alfredo asked. 'We never liked that man much, did we?'

I pulled a handkerchief from my pocket and blew my nose. 'I suppose I was just thinking about other goodbyes,' I replied, trying to summon up a watery smile.

He nodded, understanding that sort of heartache far too well for one so young. 'But you have us. And Harry. We all love you.'

I drew him close and gave him a tight hug. 'We have said goodbye to Harry too, Alfredo. But just for a little while, I hope.'

His head went down and he looked crestfallen at the loss of his hero – the Scottish soldier who'd survived being shot and become a friend, lighting up any room he walked into with his smile. Then he looked up at me again, a grin of realisation spreading from ear to ear. 'He's gone to help us win the war, hasn't he?'

I put a finger on my lips but couldn't help returning his grin with a smile of my own as I did so.

He nodded, satisfied, then pulled at my sleeve to make me stoop down to his level so that he could whisper in my ear. 'Well then, he will come back to us soon.' He gave me one last hug and ran off to join the others.

I stood and watched as the cart carrying the coffin turned out of the gates on to the road below and disappeared from view.

'Please God, let it be so,' I whispered in my turn.

Chapter 32

Tess – 2015

'Harry's escape plan was a brilliant one.' In response to my questions, Beatrice fills in missing details.

'Before the pallbearers arrived, we removed Umberto's body from the coffin. Harry got into it, carrying his pack and wearing his greatcoat with his revolver in the pocket. Then it was sealed shut. Once Carlo had driven the cart through all the roadblocks between here and Bagni San Filippo – waved through each one by the German sentries – just before the cortege reached the churchyard, he pulled on the reins and drove the cart a short way down a forest track. There, he unscrewed the coffin lid and Harry got out. He hugged them all goodbye and said to Francesca, 'Look after Bea for me. I'll be back as soon as I can.' Then, without a backward glance, he headed south, shouldering his pack – which we'd filled with as many rations as we could spare – and keeping to the tree line along the edge of the fields.

'Remember I told you we'd put some heavy stones into the cart to weigh down the flag we'd draped over the casket? Well, Francesca, Carlo and Gio put them into the coffin, wrapping them in blankets that they'd been sitting on so they wouldn't rattle and give the game away, and replaced the lid and the flag. Then they drove on the rest of the way to the graveyard, where the priest and the pallbearers were waiting.

'No one suspected a thing as the coffin was lowered into the grave alongside the one where Umberto's parents lay. Francesca did a good job of appearing to grieve from behind the black veil she wore draped over her hat. And on the journey back to the villa, as she drove Umberto's car behind the horse and cart once more, the sentries at every roadblock stood to attention and saluted her.'

I must admit, I'm pretty impressed at how Francesca and Beatrice – two such genteel ladies – managed to carry it off. I look at her, with her white hair pinned back into its usual neat bun and the clear blue of her eyes clouded only very slightly with age. Who would ever have known she was an accomplice to murder, committed right here in the villa's elegant drawing room? But what choice did they have? They'd known Umberto's threats weren't empty ones: he was perfectly capable of turning in both Beatrice and Alfredo. The Germans might well have sent Francesca to the concentration camps as well. And what would have become of the other children then?

As if reading my thoughts, Beatrice puts a hand on my arm. 'I know it's shocking. We killed Umberto. But you have to remember, Tess, it was war.'

'And Harry got away safely?' I ask.

'He did.' She doesn't elaborate though, and her hand goes to the buttercup brooch pinned above her heart. I can see how tired she is. Talking about these difficult memories has been hard for her. I'm beginning to realise the truth about some of the shadows that loom in her background, constantly threatening to overwhelm her. All these years, she's lived with the guilt of Umberto's murder.

One last thing occurs to me as I set down my pen and notepad. 'But Beatrice, if the coffin they buried that day contained nothing but rocks, what did you do with Umberto's body?'

She shoots me a shrewd look. 'Why Tess, haven't you guessed? We buried him at the centre of the cypress maze.'

She laughs, watching my expression change from bewilderment to comprehension as the penny drops. But then her eyes cloud over again with the memory of that night.

'It took the four of us – Harry, Carlo, Francesca and me – to carry Umberto's body up the hill. He weighed a ton and was still wrapped in the hearthrug, which added to the bulk. I don't think any of us could stomach looking at his corpse and Francesca certainly didn't want the rug back. Every time she saw it, she'd have seen his final convulsions too. We carried him into the maze, to the very heart, where the darkness engulfed us all. That journey is seared into my memory. I remember every step, every twist and turn as we navigated our way to the centre, struggling with the burden we carried. And I recall looking up at one point, desperate for a glimpse of the moon or a few stars, but all I could see was the profound blackness above us.

'We laid Umberto to rest in the secret chamber and closed the trapdoor once and for all. I've never gone back there again – it holds too much horror for me. The memories of what we had to do that night still haunt me.' Her hand trembles as she pushes back a wisp of hair that's come loose from the clasp holding it in place. She stares at the path leading to the English garden, her gaze unfocused. I sense it's not the box-lined gravel she's seeing, but the shadowy alleyways of the maze on a starless night all those years ago.

'As you know, Carlo made sure the entrance to the heart of the maze was obscured. But before he sealed it off, Francesca asked him to make a wooden cross to mark the grave. We did at least attempt to pay him that respect, you see, out of human decency.'

Despite the summer heat, I give an involuntary shiver. Beatrice's fear is catching. Those dark cypress walls seem more forbidding than ever now I understand what they conceal. Nothing would entice me to walk there again.

◆ ◆ ◆

The text from Marco arrives out of the blue. 'Are you free tomorrow? Would you like to accompany me to Siena for the day to watch the Palio?'

I show it to Beatrice. 'Of course I'm not going to go,' I tell her.

'But Tess, why ever not? Don't you see, he appears to like you. And this is a man who doesn't seem to like the rest of us one bit. Spending the day with him will be an opportunity for you to try to get him to see reason about his plans for the estate. Not that I'm asking you to plead my case, of course . . . oh, well, actually I am,' she says with a rueful smile. 'But now you know what we did with Umberto's body, you understand my desperation, don't you?'

I nod miserably. I haven't been able to get the thought of what now lies at the centre of the maze out of my head since she told me. I couldn't stop thinking about it last night, about what it could mean for Beatrice. I wondered whether the authorities would be lenient about the concealment of a long-cold corpse? She was the willing accomplice to a murder and then covered it up for several decades. And now she's confessed her crime to me, does that make me an accomplice as well? Will I now have to try to keep the secret too? That's if we can persuade Marco not to destroy the maze but to leave it undisturbed?

In the sleepless hours, as I ruminated over the implications, I also realised that Gio must have been aware that the coffin they were transporting contained a very-much-alive Harry, rather than a very-much-deceased Umberto. So might he, too, be culpable in some way as an accomplice? I now understand that Beatrice has been protecting many people down the years, not just herself and Francesca.

'In any case,' she continues, not allowing me to dwell on these tormenting thoughts, 'you can't pass up an invitation to see the Palio. It's the most extraordinary spectacle – a madcap horse race around the city's main piazza. The race itself lasts only about a minute – thankfully, as it's so dangerous – but it's all the pomp and ceremony leading up to it that's worth seeing.'

I'm really in no mood for a day out, but she does have a point about it being an opportunity to speak to him again, and it seems he's extended the invitation in the spirit of friendship. So, only slightly reluctantly, I reply to Marco and am ready and waiting when he turns up at the villa the next day.

It's less than an hour to Siena and we bowl along the country roads where the wheatfields are being harvested, combines and tractors plying up and down, leaving neat cylinders of baled hay in their wake. Marco drives at a steady pace, despite the obvious power of his black Ferrari, and he looks happier and more relaxed than I've seen him before. I hope his good mood means I'll be able to find the right moment to ask him again to reconsider his plans for the estate. Even if he would just postpone them for a few years, that would allow Beatrice to see out her days in peace in the little apartment that's been the only home she's ever had in her adult life. After that, he can do what he likes with the place. But we talk about safe topics like the weather and he asks me about my camera equipment, which I've brought with me, hoping to capture some good images of the Palio.

Siena is abuzz, already thronging with excited crowds. Coloured banners hang overhead, each bearing the emblem of the local neighbourhood or *contrada*. Marco explains there are seventeen of these *contrade* and twice a year they select ten of them to compete in the Palio. He navigates the narrow streets with ease, clearly familiar with the city, and parks in a reserved spot behind an office building near the town centre. The banners adorning the streets here are orange and green with a white border, bedecked with a design of oak leaves, and Marco tells me this is the Selva – or Forest – *contrada*.

As we get out of the car, a shout attracts our attention. Marco is immediately engulfed by a group of people, and I stand back as they hug him, exclaiming excitedly.

'*Salve, Selvaioli!*' Marco responds. 'Tess,' he says, ushering me forward, 'permit me to introduce the Voltolini family. They have trained one of the horses running in the Palio today, so it's a big day for them.'

Vincenzo Voltolini is about Marco's age or a little younger, I estimate, and appears to be a particular friend of his. I just about manage to follow his conversation with Marco, which seems to be about the condition of the horse, Allegro.

Just then, a church bell begins to toll a couple of streets away. '*Andiamo!* We must hurry,' says Vincenzo. 'The blessing is about to begin.'

We file into a small chapel, already crowded with people, and manage to find a couple of seats towards the back. Marco waves to an older couple who sit a few rows in front of us. The woman has white hair, pinned up in a bun, and the man sits in a wheelchair in the aisle beside her. 'Vincenzo's parents,' Marco murmurs to me.

Silence falls as the church bell stops ringing and we wait. Then the priest, wearing richly embroidered robes, steps on to a small podium and the congregation begins to sing. As they do so, the door behind us opens and, to my amazement, a man enters leading a bay horse. As its hooves strike the tiled floor, the sound echoes around the walls of the chapel. Allegro is a beautiful creature, draped with an embroidered banner bearing the same orange and green motif as the flags in the street outside, his flanks gleaming as the muscles beneath his shining coat ripple with each step.

The service is to bless the horse and its jockey, and it ends with the priest declaring, 'Allegro, *vai, e torna vincitore!* – go, and return a winner!

Outside, the August heat is stifling as the congregation spills into the piazza in front of the church. Marco introduces me to Vincenzo's parents and Signora Voltolini gives me an appraising look. 'Any friend of Marco's is a friend of ours,' says her husband, reaching up from his wheelchair to shake my hand. 'You'll come to the farm for dinner, won't you? Whether Allegro wins or loses, we'll be needing a few glasses of wine later.'

The horse is led away and we take our leave of the family as the sound of another, deeper bell begins to toll in the distance. 'We'd better go if I'm to show Tess the *Corteo Storico*,' says Marco. 'We'll catch up with you later.'

He leads me through the streets, taking my hand so we won't be separated as he threads his way through the gathering crowds, and we climb the steps in front of the cathedral. 'This is the best place to watch the procession,' he explains. 'You'll be able to get some good photos from here.'

To the insistent beat of a drummer, a cohort of men march into the square, dressed in red and blue medieval costumes and carrying flags. '*Contrada della Pantera* – the panther,' Marco says. As the beat of the drum grows to a frenzied crescendo, the two main flag bearers perform a series of sweeping movements and then throw their banners high into the air, where they cross, expertly catching them one-handed before they can clatter on to the cobbles. Then, following the drummer, they march onwards and the next band of men enters. The process is repeated seventeen times until every *contrada* has performed. We cheer especially loudly for the Selva cohort and

227

I recognise a couple of the standard bearers, carrying their orange, green and white colours, from the service in the chapel.

I snap away with my camera, trying to capture the movement and the colours and the evident sense of passionate pride the Sienese have for their city. 'Each *contrada* is way more than just a neighbourhood,' Marco explains. 'It's a family.'

'So have the *Selvaioli* adopted you?' I ask, after another friend wearing an orange, green and white scarf tied around his neck comes up to greet him like a long-lost brother.

He laughs and shrugs. 'I suppose you could say that.'

Once the procession is over, we follow the thronging crowd, which surges like a wave towards the Piazza del Campo. Marco grabs my hand again and leads me down a narrow alleyway that slopes steeply towards the city's heart. The sight that awaits us there is simply breath-taking.

The cambered square is packed with people. Some have crowded into the central area, while others stand around the sides, leaving free the track on which the horses will race. We take our seats in one of the grandstands by the city hall and I gaze around, taking it all in. There are more flags everywhere, as the Sienese proudly display their loyalty to the different *contrade*. Above us, bright red geraniums spill from balconies around the piazza where still more people crowd to watch the spectacle unfolding below them. Marco explains the significance of the pageantry preceding the race – the religious significance (the August Palio is run on Assumption Day), the competitive flag-throwing, the laurel garland carried by four young page boys, the cart drawn by four white oxen carrying the dignitaries of the Palio, and the fierce competition between the *contrade*. 'Each one had its allies and its enemies,' he says. 'Often the origins of those alliances and divisions are lost in the mists of time. Everyone wants to beat the *Nobile Contrada dell'Oca*, though – the noble goose *contrada* – because they've won the most times.'

Trumpeters blow a fanfare and the horses are led into the piazza one at a time for the crowd to admire, tossing their heads, their muscles taut with anticipation. The jockeys will ride bareback, with only a bridle to hang on to, and I'm relieved to see there are police and paramedics standing by. 'What about the horses?' I ask Marco. 'Isn't it dangerous for them as well?'

'*Si, certo*,' he replies. 'There is veterinary help here too. And in recent years a few more safety measures have been put in place, particularly on the most dangerous turns in the course. Like any horse race, though, there are still risks.'

Allegro looks calm as Vincenzo leads him into the arena. 'He's one of the more experienced horses,' Marco tells me. 'He's seen all this before. He hasn't ever won, though, and this is probably his last chance.'

The horses are led away again and then, after a good deal more flag-waving and throwing, the riders enter on horseback. An expectant hush falls over the piazza as the drums and trumpets fall silent and the crowd holds its breath. The riders canter around the circuit at first, taking their time, familiarising the horses with the course. Then there's a loud bang, signalling the race is about to begin. Nine of the horses gather at the starting area, between two ropes, and as the tenth horse enters, the *mossiere* – or starter – drops the rope. In an explosion of sound and fury, the horses thunder around the three laps of the track and my heart is in my mouth as they stream past us, only just missing the barriers at the tight corners of the piazza. By the second pass, several of the horses have lost their riders, but they race on, swept up in the frenzy. It's over in less than a minute and then chaos ensues as the crowd erupts in cheers and people run on to the track to catch the riderless horses and congratulate the winner. It's all happened so fast, I couldn't quite make out who won, but then I realise it's the *Selvaioli* who are jubilant, the square filling with a sea of orange and green flags.

'He did it!' Marco cries and he clasps me in a tight hug, carried away by his excitement. To my surprise, I find I'm hugging him back and then, suddenly self-conscious, I let go abruptly and draw away from him. 'Come on, Tess,' he says, appearing not to notice my awkwardness. 'Let's go and find Vincenzo. The family will be thrilled!'

It takes a while to make our way out through the milling crowds, but then we're swept into a jubilant riptide of *Selvaioli*, each wearing an orange, green and white scarf tied over their shoulders, making their way in triumph to the cathedral following the winner's banner. In front of the *Duomo*, Vincenzo proudly leads Allegro into the piazza and the horse is cheered all over again.

It's late in the evening by the time we extricate ourselves from the celebrations and drive a short way out of the city to the Voltolini family's farm. It's little more than a smallholding – a simple house and a few sheds, including a stable for Allegro, with a vegetable garden, some olive trees and a few vines. Vincenzo takes us to pay our respects to the victor. Safely home, Allegro is pulling wisps of sweet hay from a string bag hanging on the wall, completely oblivious to his new stardom. I snap a few more photos of him in the simple comfort of his home.

'Is he OK?' Marco asks. 'The front of that hock looks a little swollen.'

'I know,' says Vincenzo. 'I've put some liniment on it. He's a little lame, but he should recover with some rest. He's had his moment of glory and we'll retire him now, Pappa has decided.'

We leave Allegro in the peace and quiet of his stall and go to take our places at the long table that has been laid beneath a vine-covered pergola. Signora Voltolini brings out platter after platter of food and her husband fills our glasses with dark red wine as we tuck into delicate fried *zucchini* flowers, cannellini beans cooked with garlic and sage, sauteed wild greens, and chicken roasted in a delicious *Vin Santo* sauce. We raise our glasses time after time to Allegro, and to the jockey who rode him to victory, drinking their health. Surreptitiously, I take a few more pictures of the party, thinking I'll send them to the family later as a way to say thank you.

I'm sitting next to Vincenzo and he asks me if I've enjoyed the day. 'Very much,' I reply. 'I loved the processions and the feeling of being a part of the city's history. Although to be honest, I'm not quite sure why I'm here at such a special celebration now. I've hardly earned it!'

'But you are a friend of Marco's, Tess. And he is part of our family – like a brother to me and a son to my parents.'

'I can see that,' I say, watching Marco across the table where he's deep in conversation with Signor Voltolini, quietly helping him to more food when he can't reach it from his wheelchair. 'But I didn't know there was such a close bond between you.'

Vincenzo tops up my glass. 'Ah, *si*, that's our Marco. He's not exactly one of the great communicators of this world, is he? Well, I can tell you. I used to work for him in Rome. I trained as an architect and met him when I was brought in to work on a development project he was involved in.'

I recall Marco saying something about a meeting with an architect on the day he rescued me from the maze, and realise Vincenzo must be working on this latest project too.

'My father trained horses for the Palio here on our farm, once he and my mother moved out of the Selva district of the city, and one day he was thrown while on a gallop. He lost the use of his legs and has been in that wheelchair ever since. Of course, his accident meant he could no longer train horses, nor could he manage to do everything here on our small farm, and so I had to leave my job in Rome and return to live with my parents to help them. Marco heard what had happened and he helped us in all sorts of ways. He made sure my father got the best medical treatment and the best equipment – that chair of his is state-of-the-art. And he helped us financially too. It's his generosity and kindness that's allowed us to keep Allegro on. So winning the race today is far more than just a victory for us. It's a way of paying Marco back, of thanking him for all he's done for us as a family. He still gives me work, too, and that's allowed me to support my family as well. We really owe him.'

I'm quiet as I digest this. The Marco who Vincenzo is describing seems most unlike the Marco we first met at the Villa delle Colombe, the man who's going to turn Beatrice, Gio and Vittoria out of their homes and destroy all that they've spent so many decades nurturing. Perhaps he does have a heart after all.

'He's a complicated man, Tess,' Vincenzo continues. 'He lost his mother when he was young and he didn't have an easy relationship with his father.'

'Did you ever meet Alfredo?' I ask.

'Yes, only once. He was quite reclusive and didn't mix easily in company. I got the sense he was very shut off from everything and everyone. I suppose that's why Marco finds it hard to be in close relationships as well. He doesn't find it easy talking to people and it takes him a while to be able to trust. He uses silence as a wall to protect himself, just as his father did before him. Marco told me he never talked to him about his past.'

I nod, carefully placing my knife and fork on my plate.

'Here,' he says, 'have some more chicken?'

'I couldn't eat another thing,' I laugh. 'But thank you. Marco seems to find it easy with you and your family though,' I continue.

'I suppose that's in part due to the Palio. It's helped give him a sense of belonging, a sense of identity that I don't think he ever had before. We have adopted him, you see. Being part of the *contrada* has helped him feel part of something, a sort of family, I suppose.

And he needed it. He is like a lost boy sometimes, with no real sense of direction in life other than doing another deal and making some more money. I guess being so isolated with his father for much of his young life made him feel that was a way to protect himself. It's taken a few years, but he's more relaxed with us now. His helping us shows his true colours. He has a heart of gold, really, beneath that smart exterior with the haircut and the fancy car!'

Marco senses we're talking about him and calls across to Vincenzo, 'Hey! What are you telling her?'

'Nothing good about you, you can be sure of that, my brother,' Vincenzo teases him.

Signora Voltolini ruffles Marco's hair as she passes behind him, clearing plates. *'Lascialo, Vincenzo! È un bravo ragazzo, il nostro Marco.'* Leave him, Vincenzo! He's a good boy, our Marco.

After dinner, we take our leave of the family and go with Vincenzo to bid a final goodnight to Allegro in his stable. Moonlight fills the stall, where the horse seems to be asleep on his feet.

'I still don't like the look of that hock,' says Marco. 'The swelling seems to be getting worse.'

'I know,' Vincenzo nods. 'I just hope it's not the bone. It's a little hot.'

'You'll call the vet in the morning then?' Marco says.

'Sì, naturalmente. I'll keep you posted.'

◆ ◆ ◆

We drive back to the villa in silence for much of the way. It's well past midnight and I'm full of so much good food and wine I can hardly keep my eyes open. But I haven't had a chance to talk to Marco about his plans for the villa yet, so I know this is an opportunity to try to broach the subject.

I swallow, my mouth drying with nerves, knowing how much is riding on it. Then I say, a little tentatively, 'Thank you for such a great day, Marco. I enjoyed meeting Vincenzo and his family.'

'They are good people,' he says. 'I'm glad you liked them.'

'Vincenzo told me how much you've done for them, how kind you've been. It made me wonder whether you might consider a small kindness towards Miss Crane as well. If you could just allow her to see out her days at the villa, it would mean such a lot to her. She's not in good health and I'm worried that the stress of this move is going to be too much for her.'

He drives on in silence, focusing on the sweep of the headlights illuminating the road ahead. My words hang in the air between us, but he still doesn't answer them. Frustration rises in me at his lack of response. Perhaps he enjoys the power he wields over us, I think. I can't resist goading him a little.

'You know,' I say, deliberately keeping my tone light, 'Vincenzo also told me you were a bad communicator. He says you use silence as a wall to protect yourself.'

Marco frowns and I instantly regret overstepping the mark. 'Did he now?' he snaps. 'Well, that might be true, but at least I don't use a camera to filter out the real world, the way you do. You spent the whole day hiding behind it instead of putting it away and actually living. We all have our defences, Tess, don't we?'

The warmth that had grown between us over the course of the day seems to fade abruptly. I've blown it, I realise. Marco is as skittish and nervy as a Palio horse and one false move scares him back behind his cold wall of silence. I don't dare try to break it again as he drives the rest of the way, his foot heavier on the accelerator now, making my stomach lurch at every twist in the road.

I ask him to drop me at the gates to the villa. 'I don't want to wake Beatrice if she's sleeping,' I say.

He shrugs. 'As you wish.'

'Goodnight, Marco. And thank you, I really did enjoy the day.'

He doesn't reply. I shut the car door and he drives off, heading for his hotel room in Pienza once more.

Quietly, feeling utterly drained, I sling the heavy camera bag over my shoulder and walk back to the cottage on my own.

◆　◆　◆

The next morning, I'm still a little bleary-eyed as I walk up to the villa. Beatrice is sitting at the table on the terrace when I arrive.

I tell her about my day. But I also have to admit to her that I've made no progress with Marco.

She slumps a little in her chair, then draws herself up straight. 'All right,' she says with a little of her habitual briskness. 'Let's get the rest of my story down then. We're running out of time.'

I pour myself a cup of coffee, take out my notepad, and she continues . . .

Chapter 33

BEATRICE'S STORY – 1944

I felt I was holding my breath in the days following Harry's escape. At the time, we had no way of knowing whether or not he'd made it out safely, but I hoped and prayed he'd managed to evade the Germans and rendezvoused with the Allied forces who were making what felt like torturously slow progress northwards. The BBC radio reports spoke of a mile or two's advance at a time, with the fighting raging back and forth as the two sides struggled for control. We heard, too, of increased efforts by the partisans to rise up against the resurgence of the Fascist Republic, but what little news we received from our local sources was garbled and chaotic.

Francesca and I tried hard not to let our fear show, keeping ourselves busy with the demands of the children's day-to-day care. We told them that the maze was out of bounds because the central part of it had fallen in and become unsafe. It was true, in a way, I suppose. It was now a grave. Carlo dug up one of the cypresses from the outer section and replanted it to fill the way into the centre, leaving the once neatly trimmed hedges at the maze's heart to grow and spread, until they'd knit together to form an impenetrable barrier. If anyone did enter the maze, they wouldn't be able to find a way through. We'd made sure the riddle, wrapped in a mystery, inside an enigma had become even harder to solve.

◆ ◆ ◆

For two weeks I watched and waited for news from Harry. On the wireless, General Alexander issued a broadcast to Italian patriots saying the hour of their rising had come at last and urging them to destroy roads, bridges, railways and telegraph lines. Italy was a battlefield, with the front line in the tug-of-war between the Allies and the Germans shifting back and forth, and our quiet isolation at the villa became a thing of the past. Every day, we would find people at the door, all of them asking for help that we were ill equipped to give. We shared our food with partisans and refugees, stretching our supplies even further to make them go round. Our meals now consisted mainly of watery soups, scant helpings of risotto flavoured with a little garlic and a handful of wild mushrooms from the woods, or slivers of chestnut polenta. The early summer brought its bounty of fresh produce, but there were more visits from the German soldiers occupying the valley and we had to hide what we could, stashing supplies away in the cellar, the stables and the barn. Carlo showed Gio and Alfredo where to unearth the white summer truffles that could add a deceptively hunger-quelling depth of flavour to any dish with just a few wafer-thin shavings. Milk and eggs were our most precious commodities and we saved them for the children where we could, although it was hard to deny some of the starving and desperate people who trudged up the drive or appeared like ghosts out of the woods, begging for our help.

The fact that there were many more partisans in the valley gave us hope. They appeared silently, materialising out of nowhere, asking for food or medicine. Francesca recognised one or two of them as the sons of local families and those meetings were joyful ones, if necessarily muted. Some of the boys who'd left the valley four years earlier had returned at last, toughened and scarred by the hardships they'd endured living rough in the hills, and by the things they'd seen and done. Many more would never return.

Even though the German presence was stronger than ever, we felt the tides of war shifting and surging around us and that, at least, was progress. We heard reports from our neighbours of regular raids by the Germans on their food supplies, too, and several of the larger houses in the area had been commandeered as billets for German soldiers. But thankfully they continued to leave the villa alone, perhaps because Francesca had painted a large sign to hang on the gates saying that it was a children's home.

I scanned every face that passed through our gates, hoping each one might have news of Harry – a note, a message, some sign that he was alive and hadn't forgotten us. As midsummer approached, the long days seemed to stretch into endless, empty hours without Harry there beside me. The ache of hunger in my belly was eclipsed by the craving in my heart.

One morning, Silvana had been grumbling that she had nothing but a few handfuls of beans for supper, so I'd taken a basket to pick the very last of the wild garlic in the woods. The leaves tasted bitter by that point in the summer, but at least their pungent flavour would give us the illusion of a hearty meal and, to be honest, I craved a few moments of solitude, away from the constant niggling of the children and nagging of Silvana. All our nerves had grown frayed over the course of those weeks. I walked beneath trees whose thick mantle of green leaves shaded me from the sun, stooping here and there to pick whatever I could glean. The snap of a twig made me freeze, before straightening up quickly to glance back the way I'd come. And there he was, standing in a little patch of sunlight and smiling that smile that made my heart lurch. With a sob, I dropped the basket and ran to him, hugging him, laughing and crying all at the same time.

'I knew I'd find you here,' Harry said, wiping the tears from my cheeks with his thumb once we'd stopped kissing each other for a moment.

There was so much to say, so many questions to ask, so many stories to hear. But for those first few minutes it was enough just to be together again, there in the quiet of the forest, with only the sound of birdsong above our heads.

At last, he picked up my basket and, with his arm around my waist, we walked back to the villa together, while he told me how he'd made it to Rome. The city had fallen to the Allies at the beginning of June, so he was there for the final push. He'd rendezvoused with a band of partisans in the hills above Rome and they'd told him a battalion of Scotsmen who spoke just like him were camped out in a valley to the south. And so it was that he'd found his comrades in the Sixth Battalion of the Black Watch again – those who'd survived the months of bitter fighting at Monte Cassino, at least. He'd been able to give the Allied command useful information about the positions of the German defences in our region. The Royal Highlanders were moving north. And now they'd sent him back here to prepare the way for them, establishing communications with more groups of partisans, who would help liberate the valley.

'They're coming,' he told me, his hand caressing the lines of my face as if trying to smooth the sharp angles of the bones, chiselled by hunger and anxiety. His expression was tender with love. 'Don't worry, we will drive out the enemy and one day soon Italy will be free again.'

He explained he'd been sent on ahead of his battalion to prepare the partisans for the push that was to come. He'd found a band of them hiding in caves on the other side of the valley and had been with them for a few days. He'd stolen a few hours to come and find me before he had to return. Although I knew the fighting was far from over, knowing he and his brothers-in-arms were nearby rekindled the belief in all of us that we could win.

Harry also told us there had been drops of ammunition in the valley for the partisans. 'There is hope all around,' he said, as he kissed me goodbye. 'Everyone believes victory is possible at last. We just have to keep going.'

◆ ◆ ◆

I hadn't thought I'd see him again so soon, but a couple of evenings later he appeared at the villa. The fact he would take such a risk, and the grim expression on his face, immediately told us something was wrong. He didn't waste time on any pleasantries.

'The Fascists have given a list of names to the Germans. They're doing a sweep of the valley, rounding up anyone they suspect of harbouring Jews or foreigners. They're shooting people who don't give them the information they're looking for. My informant has seen the list. Beatrice, your name is on it. And I'm sorry, but Alfredo's is too.'

The blood drained from Francesca's face in the sickly glow of the paraffin lantern, which we used whenever the electricity was cut – a frequent occurrence by then. He went on, 'Umberto might be dead and gone, but I'm afraid he left behind a notebook, which has recently fallen into the hands of the local Fascist leader. We have to get you and Alfredo out of here.'

I was too stunned to speak.

'But where can they go?' Francesca asked.

'We need to try to get them south of Rome,' answered Harry. 'It's the only place they'll be safe, in Allied-occupied territory. And they have to leave tonight. The Germans could already be on their

240

way. Carlo will need to take them in Umberto's car – that way, if they're stopped it will look as if they're a refugee family like all the others fleeing south. I've drawn a map showing the safest roads to stick to. Bea, put a few things in a bag as quickly as you can. Francesca, you'll come with me to tell Carlo and Silvana?'

It happened so fast we scarcely had time to think, let alone to raise any objections or try to think of an alternative plan. If Alfredo and I were found, we'd be deported to the work camps in Germany. That's if we weren't shot on the spot – and Francesca too.

By the time I hurried to the stables, where we kept Umberto's car hidden behind the wooden cart and camouflaged with some planks of wood, the others had gathered there. In the flickering light of an oil lamp, their faces were pale and drawn. Carlo was readying the vehicle, pouring a precious jerrycan of fuel into the tank, while Silvana and Gio stood off to one side, coats thrown on hastily over their nightwear. Alfredo shivered, despite the warmth of the summer night, dressed in his clothes for travelling. His face was white, expressionless with shock.

Gio stepped forward to stand next to his friend. 'Pappa,' he said. 'Can I come with you?'

Silvana reached out and grabbed his arm, jerking him back to her side. 'Certainly not!' she hissed. 'Don't you understand how dangerous it's going to be?' Her face was white with ill-disguised fury in the lamplight.

I threw my bag into the boot of the car and turned to Francesca. 'Don't worry,' I whispered. 'I'll take good care of him.' I knew how agonising it was for her to let Alfredo go. 'And we'll be back, just as soon as it's safe again.'

Francesca nodded and tried to summon a smile, then hugged me tightly before standing back to let me go. She turned to Alfredo. 'Now, you must be a brave boy for Beatrice.' She did up the buttons on his coat. 'Keep warm. I've put your medicines in the bag

241

for you.' She held him for a long moment, burying her face in his mop of dark curls.

When she let him go, he turned to Gio and Silvana to say his goodbyes. 'Here,' said Gio, reaching into the pocket of his coat and holding something out to him. In the beam of the lamp, I saw the glint of a sliver of glass. It was the Roman dove that he'd unearthed all those years ago when we were digging the maze.

'I can't take this,' said Alfredo, holding it carefully in the palm of his hand. 'It's your best treasure.'

Gio shook his head. 'It will keep you safe. And remind you where your home is, here with us at the Villa delle Colombe.'

Shyly, Alfredo put it in his pocket. Then he turned to Silvana, a little uncertainly, and reached up to hug her goodbye. But, to everyone's horror, she recoiled in anger. Her face contorted with rage, her bitterness overwhelming her.

'Just go!' she said, spitting the words into the night air. 'You've put us through enough already, making this place so dangerous for us all. This is all your fault! And now my Carlo has to risk his life, taking the pair of you God knows where. When will it ever end?'

Carlo stepped towards her and gathered her into his arms to try to calm her. 'Hush, Silvana,' he said. 'It's not the child's fault.'

But she pushed him away and collapsed to the floor, sobbing hysterically, her words becoming incoherent in the torrent of anguish that had been unleashed, at last, after so many years of war. I drew Alfredo to me and hugged him tight, whispering to him not to cry, that she didn't mean those cruel words, she was just frightened and upset.

Francesca moved towards Silvana and gathered her into her arms. She looked up at the rest of us. 'Go now,' she said softly. 'Ignore her – she doesn't know what she's saying. And she certainly doesn't mean it. It's just the strain of everything.' She reached out a hand to Gio, who stood wretchedly looking on. 'Come, Gio, let's get your mamma back home.'

Harry held me one last time. I was shaking – with anger at Silvana's outburst, with the fear of the journey that faced us, with hunger and exhaustion, and with terror at the possibility of losing those I loved the most in this world. All of a sudden, it seemed too much to bear. But I had no choice.

'You'll be all right, my love?' Harry asked me, and the sound of his voice made me pull myself together.

I nodded, still unable to speak.

'See you on the other side of all this,' he said.

And with that, I helped Alfredo into the back seat of the car, giving him a reassuring kiss on the cheek, then climbed into the passenger seat beside Carlo. We had to make it look as if we were a family, in case we were stopped, although I wished I could sit in the back and tell Alfredo over and over again, until he believed me, that Silvana's toxic words meant nothing.

As we drove through the gates, I turned to look back at the villa. Alfredo, though, sat frozen in his seat, his face pale and expressionless, staring straight ahead.

◆ ◆ ◆

Dawn was just beginning to creep over the tops of the hills to the east of Rome. 'Nearly there now,' I said, turning my head to look at Alfredo in the back.

He'd sat white-faced, frozen with a mixture of misery and fear, for the entire journey, never once closing his eyes to sleep. I reached out to try to take his hand, but he snatched it away.

'Are you all right?' I asked.

He shook his head vehemently, tears spilling from his eyes. Then he said, 'Why are you sending me away? Do you all hate me as much as Silvana does? You do, don't you, because I'm Jewish?'

Shocked that he'd been thinking such a terrible thing, I twisted myself round further and opened my mouth to tell him he was wrong, that of course we loved him, that Silvana was scared, that was all, she hadn't meant those horrible words. But before I could get the words out, I caught sight of the German plane in the sky behind us, swooping lower, then lower still, like a bird of prey intent on its kill. I saw the guns spit flames as they opened fire, spraying our car with bullets, shattering the glass, making Carlo's head jerk forwards as if he'd been punched. We spun out of control, the car leaving the road as it somersaulted towards the ditch, end over end, and everything went black.

◆　◆　◆

I swam upwards through the dark waters of unconsciousness, sinuous snakelike shapes just visible out of the corner of my eye, struggling for breath, struggling to kick towards the light. I couldn't see it, but I had to believe it was there, up ahead, if I refused to give in. I summoned up every last shred of my strength and kept going upwards, resisting the pull of despair, turning away from the siren song of a deep black sleep from which I'd never return. There was something important I had to tell Alfredo, although I couldn't remember exactly what it was. All I knew was I had to keep trying.

At last, one morning, I opened my eyes and found myself propped on white pillows in a hospital bed. A nurse in a crisp white apron hurried to my side and picked up my hand, although it hardly seemed to belong to me as it lay on the rough blanket covering the bed.

'You're awake at last,' she said in a perfect English Home Counties accent, checking my pulse and making a note on the clipboard that hung at the foot of the bed. 'We didn't think you'd make it.'

'Wh . . . ?' I tried to form the question, but my lips were cracked and sore. I ran my tongue over them and tried again. 'Where . . . ?'

'You're in a hospital in Rome,' she said, although that wasn't the question I was trying to ask. 'Hush now, take it slowly, you've been completely out of it for three days. A British Army unit found you in a shot-up car on a road to the north of here. The city's under Allied control now.' She held a cup of water to my mouth and I sipped a little, swallowing with difficulty.

'The others . . . with me?'

She shook her head. 'I'm so sorry. The man in the car with you was dead. Was he your husband?'

'Carlo. No!' Hot tears sprang into my eyes. 'Alfredo?' I struggled to sit up, trying to gather splintered fragments of memory together, but discovered I was bound to the bed by a series of straps to prevent movement and my neck was encased in a stiff collar. I later found out I'd fractured bones in my pelvis. The pain was excruciating.

'Was that his name? Carlo Alfredo? It was a terrible crash, and the car was riddled with bullet holes. He didn't stand a chance. You were very lucky to survive. And heaven only knows, those injuries could have been far worse. Your guardian angel must have been watching over you.'

Her smile was kind, but I pushed her hand away as she tried to get me to drink some more water. 'No. There were three of us,' I said. 'Where is Alfredo?'

She shook her head again. 'It was just the two of you they found. Are you sure there was someone else in the car? You've had a

245

terrible crack on the head so maybe you're just a bit muddled.' She picked up a syringe and patted my hand. 'Sleep is the best medicine for you now to help mend those broken bones. This will help.'

I struggled against the injection, desperate to tell her to go and find Alfredo. But as I tried to form the words, the sedative washed through my bloodstream and drew me back down into the darkness.

◆ ◆ ◆

The next time I woke, my hand was lying on the blanket again and I looked at it as if from a great way off. It appeared strange. I frowned, trying to puzzle it out. Then I realised that there was another set of fingers curled around mine, brown against the white of my skin. I must have moved a little, because suddenly the other hand squeezed mine. And then I heard Harry's voice saying, 'Bea, my love.' And he was there beside me and my heart gave another of those great lurches as I began to sob.

He'd come as soon as news of the crash reached the valley. He told me Carlo had been killed outright, hit by one of the bullets from the plane's machine guns as it dived at us, on a mission to kill anyone attempting to flee to the south. Alfredo was missing. Presumed dead.

'I saw the car, Bea. I don't know how you survived. The roof was smashed in, the back seat completely crushed. They found your bags in the boot, but no sign of him. If he was thrown clear as the car spun, he was probably hit by a bullet. His body must have ended up in the ditch. If he'd been alive, he'd surely have stayed with you.'

I frowned, struggling to think clearly. 'Surely they'd have found him if he'd been killed? Did they search?'

'Thoroughly. And I went back to look too. Not a sign of him.'

'How long . . . ?'

'It's been five days, Bea. I'm sorry.'

He sat with me day and night, so he'd be there whenever I woke up from another deep, sedative-induced sleep, haunted by dreams of Alfredo's white face and dark eyes and the frozen look on his face as we'd driven away from the villa.

Harry told me the Germans had arrived the morning after our departure, demanding to know the whereabouts of Beatrice Crane, an enemy alien, and Alfredo Verlucci, a Jewish child. Francesca had faced them down and told them, in all honesty, that the people they were seeking had once been at the villa but had left some time ago. Which I suppose was literally true, a few hours being 'some time'. After a cursory questioning of the children, who corroborated what Francesca had said, the Germans hadn't returned since and were now far too preoccupied with fighting off the incursion of Allied forces from the south to have time for more searches.

I'd been dozing one afternoon and awoke to find Harry gone.

'He said to tell you he's just popped out for a while – he'll be back soon,' the nurse told me.

When he reappeared, he presented me with a little red leather box. I opened it to find a golden brooch in the form of a buttercup. 'It's not exactly the ring I want to give you, but it's a step up from your last engagement gift. It was the most fitting thing they had left in the jeweller's shop. Their stock is a little depleted just at present,' he said with typical understatement. I could only imagine the lengths he'd gone to, to find anything like that in Rome in the aftermath of the city's liberation.

'It's perfect, Harry. Better than any ring.' I pinned it to my hospital gown straight away.

I didn't want to waste time lying in a hospital bed. The next day, with a bit of grim determination, trying not to let the nurses see how painful it was, I hauled myself up and showed them I was able to hobble around on a pair of crutches. I knew full well how lucky I was not to have been left with any permanent paralysis.

'I've found a place in town to move you to,' Harry said. 'The fighting's well north of here now, so you'll be safe.'

I wove my fingers between his. 'No,' I said. 'I'm going back.'

'But Bea . . .'

'Please, Harry. I have to go back. Francesca and the children need me. Without Carlo, how will they manage in the garden? How can they feed everyone? How is Silvana coping?'

'Not well,' he admitted. 'She's taken the news of Carlo very hard, as you can imagine. But Bea, it's still too dangerous. There are Germans occupying pockets of the valley, even though most have retreated further north now. The fighting isn't over yet.'

'Then that's all the more reason for me to be at the villa. Francesca needs my help with the children. I can't sit here, knowing they're still in danger. You, of all people, have to understand that, Harry Priestley.'

He nodded slowly, the lines of his face relaxing into a smile of surrender. 'Very well. I do understand, Bea,' he conceded. 'I'm heading north in a few days' time to rejoin the Black Watch boys. They've advanced as far as Perugia, along with battalions of other Commonwealth troops. You should see it, we're fighting alongside boys from South Africa, Canada, India . . . We're all in this together, and we won't abandon Italy. There's a big push planned, to break through the German line near Arezzo. Don't worry, my love, I'll get you home.'

I was glad I could go with him and that he'd be close by the estate. After all those months apart, I wished there would never be any distance between us again.

◆ ◆ ◆

The villa seemed shrouded in shock and grief. Even in the radiance of the late June sunshine, an intangible pall covered the estate and its inhabitants. I'd only been away a couple of weeks, but it felt like a lifetime.

I moved slowly, gingerly, hampered by my crutches. It wasn't only because my own broken body was still mending, though, but because there was a fragility in all of us. The years of war had stretched us all to our limits. I discovered then that physical pain is easier to cope with than mental anguish – easier to heal from as well. The children's games beside the pool were subdued affairs, their laughter and shouts replaced these days by a quiet murmuring, which seemed to echo the sorrowful cooing of the doves from the roof of the *limonaia*.

The loss of Carlo was a devastating one. We all missed his calm good humour and kindness. His body was returned to us, finally, and we buried him in the local churchyard within sight of Edoardo's headstone.

Gio seemed to me to have taken on his father's responsibilities for supporting us all, and it was heartbreaking to see. His young shoulders were far too slight to carry such a heavy burden. He'd taken over the care of the vegetable garden and, with the help of some of the other children, was making a manful effort to ensure the produce on which we so depended continued to thrive. His mother seemed unable to support him. Silvana's grief had enveloped her in a tight chrysalis from which it seemed she might never re-emerge. She went through the motions in the kitchen, but Francesca and Elisabetta often had to take over her duties or the meals would never have reached the table. She couldn't look me in the eye. I suppose I was too painful a reminder of the accident. After all, her bitter words the night we left had turned out to be prophetic. There was a stony resentment in her expression that spoke volumes – why hadn't I been the one to die, instead of her husband? I could understand it. It was a question I pondered too. I wanted to tell her that I wished it had been that way round as well. I felt so guilty for having survived when the other two were lost.

Francesca's grief was heartbreaking too, in its own way. There was a dull resignation in her eyes. I suppose losing her own son and husband had primed her for the loss of Alfredo, although it made it no easier to bear. The only time I saw her eyes light up with a flicker of genuine gladness was when I climbed out of the Red Cross ambulance that had brought me home to the Villa delle Colombe and she ran to me, enfolding me in her arms. 'Thank God you survived,' she whispered. 'Losing you too, Beatrice, would have been too much.'

She spent every spare moment she could muster – in between looking after the children, dealing with the daily stream of refugees and partisans who continued to knock on our door asking for help, and making sure we were all fed three times a day – writing letters to anyone she could think of who might be able to find out news of Alfredo. We knew the most likely reality was that he had been killed in the accident. Perhaps his body had lain in the ditch and been removed by a passer-by following that same escape route, to be buried in a little grave somewhere. Or perhaps it had been dragged into the woods by some wild animal. I couldn't bear to think of such scenarios. Like Francesca, I preferred to live in hope. I told myself perhaps he'd somehow survived the accident, been thrown clear and knocked his head so he couldn't remember who he was and where he'd been going. Perhaps someone kind had found him wandering in the woods and taken him in. We had to keep the hope alive, no matter how improbable it might be: it was all we had left.

And so Francesca wrote letter after letter, imploring the Red Cross, the British Army, the Italian administration, the hospitals and orphanages around Rome, to check their records and see whether an Alfredo Verlucci had recently been taken into care.

On the days when the telephone worked – which were few and far between as the lines were continually being cut by one side or the other – she'd make call after call, following up possible leads or trying to find new lines of enquiry. She was driven, possessed by the belief that he was still out there somewhere. She once told me it would have meant the world to her and Edoardo to have passed the estate on to their own son – knowing the next generation would build on the family tradition. But losing little Edo, and then having both Edoardo and the horses taken from her by the cruel tides of the war, had destroyed every shred of that hope. So she'd decided the estate was to be left to Alfredo as proof of her love for him, a gesture of recompense for what he and his own family had suffered. I suppose it was an attempt to turn the nightmare back into the dream she'd once had. But all her efforts to find him came to nothing. She drew a complete blank.

Chapter 34

Tess – 2015

It seems pretty futile sending Marco the manuscript of Beatrice's story, but there are only ten more days to go before we have to vacate the villa and it's all I can do. There's been no word from him since that day we spent in Siena, just more of that stony silence. So I compose an email to him, attach the document and press send. The email says how important it is that he reads the account of Alfredo's life with Francesca and Beatrice. Whatever he decides to do with the estate, he needs to understand how much his father was loved and the lengths those two women went to in trying to protect him.

I've sensed a change in Beatrice over the past few days. There's a sense of relief overlying her resignation and fear for her fate. But there's also a new fragility about her. It's as if now she's told me her secrets and they've been set down on paper, she's lost something that had been keeping her going all these years. When I told her I'd sent the email to Marco, she just nodded and then went into the garden and carried on deadheading the roses as if it were just another normal day. I suppose she wants to tend the garden until her very last day at the Villa delle Colombe, keeping her promises to Francesca until the end.

The full ramifications of Marco's plans are dawning on me. When the maze is destroyed, Umberto's grave will be discovered, and Beatrice will have to explain herself to the police. She's staked her freedom on telling the truth. She kept the secret all those years in the hope that Alfredo would return. And she had to continue to keep the garden alive because it meant she was keeping alive her faith that he was still out there, somehow, somewhere. But now he's gone, I suppose telling the truth is the final thing she's been able to do for Alfredo.

I check my emails several times a day, impatient for a response from Marco, conscious of time slipping away minute by minute, hour by hour . . . but there is only silence.

Beatrice said that after the car crash, she discovered physical pain is easier to bear than mental anguish. That's something we never articulated, did we, all through your illness, but I realise how right she is. You faced the physical challenges with such courage and determination, religiously doing the exercises the physiotherapist gave you, forcing down those liquid meals – pre-prepared and nutritionally complete and completely disgusting – to try to keep the weight on and hold back the wasting of your body. You tolerated the discomfort and the pain and the exhaustion, and the indignity of it all, calmly accepting the loss of each function, the insertion of every new tube and the cruel, inexorable creep of the disease. But I heard you crying in the bathroom when you thought I was out one day, and I saw how the fear and the emotional distress ate away at you too. You wanted to protect me – and everyone else you loved – from that anguish. The decision to end the suffering was taken bravely. You took that decision for us all.

It's not only Beatrice who has changed. Something has shifted in me too. Marco's cold retort in the car that night really stung me.

Do you think I take refuge behind my camera? I ask you. *Am I using it as a barrier between me and the real world? But then again, if it means it keeps me in the limbo where you still exist then maybe I want it to.*

You don't answer me, though, and I realise it's been a while since I felt your presence. Something else has changed too. The anger I used to feel has gone now, replaced by something calmer, something with more clarity: acceptance. I no longer feel I'm running, scared and lost, through the maze of my grief. I'm still walking through it, but now I feel I have a map to show me where I've been. I understand that I will be able to get out when the time is right. When I'm ready. But I know, too, I have to go through it. There's no way round or over, no way to take shortcuts or avoid the path I have to walk. Like a butterfly in a chrysalis, the struggle through my grief is a necessary part of being able to escape and leave it behind, helping me grow strong enough to spread my wings and fly again.

I wonder about Alfredo's silence for all those years, his misplaced bitterness, and about Marco, who inherited his father's grief and turned it into another sort of carapace, surrounding and imprisoning himself in it.

Will the truth set him free, even as it takes away Beatrice's liberty? That's the price she's willing to pay.

I refresh my emails, checking again to see whether there's a reply yet from Marco, but there's nothing. I need to start doing my own packing and clean up the cottage ready for my departure. But where will I go? I'm not ready to head home yet, and Beatrice may need my help if she is arrested and sent to jail for murder.

Suddenly, out of the blue I hear your voice. *Come to the garden,* you say.

But I have things to do here, I protest.

Tess, come to the garden now. There's an urgent insistence in your tone that I've not heard before and it startles me.

I close my laptop and walk up the track, slipping through the gate into the English garden. The last flowers have fallen from the wisteria now and the pergola is covered with a thick thatch of leaves. Soon, they too will drop, leaving only a bare skeleton of twisted stems. And then they'll be ripped out by Marco's team of developers. There won't be another cascade of blossoms next spring.

I look for you, wondering why you've summoned me here. And then I see the slumped form on the bench at the viewpoint and I run, shouting, calling Beatrice's name, but there's no response.

◆ ◆ ◆

Beatrice insists it was just a 'funny turn'. The doctor says she suspects it was a minor stroke and that I should keep an eye on things and let her know if there's any deterioration in Beatrice's condition in the next few days. Above all, she should avoid stressful situations. I wonder how we're going to manage that, given what waits just round the next corner for us all.

The next morning, I perch on the end of her bed, making sure she stays put. She's already attempted to get up once. When she's finished picking at her breakfast, by way of a distraction I gently ask her if she'd like to tell me the rest of the story of those war years. I want to know what happened to Harry, but I know I mustn't pressure her into talking about things if she doesn't want to. Her face still lights up when she thinks of him, though, and she wears the little gold buttercup pinned to the lapel of her dressing gown.

Her eyes grow misty with memories as she begins to talk . . .

Chapter 35

BEATRICE'S STORY – 1944

The sound of the bombardment ebbed and flowed, sometimes drawing closer and at other times receding into dull thuds in the far distance that we scarcely registered as we went about our daily tasks. Even so, the villa still felt like a safe refuge, but we soon realised it was a false sense of security.

One morning, at the beginning of July, a young partisan appeared at our door with a message from Harry. 'You need to leave,' he told us. 'Take everyone and go to Montepulciano, where you can take shelter underground. There's no time to spare. Take water, and whatever else you can easily carry, but go quickly. And make sure you keep off the roads – they've been mined by the Germans. Stick to the edges and cut through the fields where you can. Captain Priestley said to tell you he'll come and find you in Montepulciano when the battle is over and it's safe to return.'

We received the news in silence. Our only option was to walk. We'd be heading deeper into German-occupied territory, through a war zone, exposed to attack.

'Can't we just go down into the cellar here?' I asked him. 'We can squeeze in and sit it out.' My broken bones had mended by then, but my legs and back still ached terribly if I walked too much. I worried that I might hold the others back, that I might not be able to make it all the way to Montepulciano.

He looked at me, pityingly, shouldering his rifle as he prepared to leave. 'No, *signorina*, you don't understand. This whole valley is about to become the front line in the war. We know the Germans are trying to make a stand here, setting up artillery posts on every piece of high ground. They'll be here before long, and we think they've earmarked the villa for one of their gun emplacements. The safest place for you all will be the Montepulciano tunnels. Good luck, and may God protect you.'

'You too,' whispered Francesca as he slipped away into the woods from which he'd materialised.

We didn't hesitate. The young man's message carried such urgency, and we knew Harry would never tell us to take such a risk unless there really was no other option. We rounded up the children and Silvana, filled every bottle and jar we could find with water, bundled up what food we had to hand, and quickly helped the little ones tie their bootlaces. Then we set off, walking down the drive through the striped shadows of the cypress trees and unlocking the gates. 'Don't bother to shut them again,' Francesca said. 'There's no point.' She glanced back just once towards the villa on the hill above us, then squared her shoulders and led us across the road to begin our journey. 'Spread out a bit,' she told me and Silvana. 'That way we won't make such a concentrated target.' We each took charge of a group of children and urged them to follow us in single file as we picked our way along the grass verge. It was mid-morning and the sun pounced on us immediately, scorching our shoulders through our clothes. The children carried their tattered coats and jackets, which we knew we'd probably need later when the heat went out of the day – we had no idea where we might be sleeping that night. Francesca held the hands of the littlest, and

Silvana and I lugged the sacks on our backs containing our supplies of food and water.

Our progress was slow. We had to walk at the pace of the slowest and we were all soon exhausted by the heat because we were so under-nourished after so many months of scant rations. The noise of the shelling followed us and it seemed to be approaching faster than we could flee, closing on us, growing louder and more intense with every mile we managed to cover. Round one bend in the road, we stopped in our tracks when we stumbled across a scene of devastation. A car – its inhabitants no doubt attempting to flee southwards – had hit a mine. What was left of the vehicle sat askew in the crater left by the explosion.

I approached Francesca. 'Do you think there's any chance they survived?' I murmured.

She shook her head. 'Let's take the children through the fields. Don't let them see.'

I followed her glance and saw the remains of a body, flung to the far side of the road. It was impossible to tell who it might have been. One of our neighbours, perhaps?

Francesca led the children away into the field of wheat and it was a small relief to feel the green stems brush our legs, safe in the knowledge that the crops had been undisturbed. But the ground beneath our feet was less even and the going was harder, slowing our progress even more. Biting insects swarmed around us, feasting on any bits of bare skin they could find as we trudged and stumbled on over the clods of sun-baked clay.

We heard the sound of the plane approaching long before we saw it. It materialised out of the dazzle of the sunlight and then changed course, making straight for us.

'Lie down!' Francesca shouted.

We dropped on to our bellies, the wheat engulfing us as the plane swooped low overhead. Every muscle in my body tensed in anticipation of a shower of bullets from the machine guns mounted on its fuselage, and the pounding of my heart in my ears was so loud it seemed to drown out the roar of the engines. But the plane soared off, climbing back into the white-hot sky, the pilot searching for other more profitable targets.

We stayed where we were, lying in the dirt, until silence fell once again and then the crickets resumed their endless screeching song. At last we got to our feet, brushing dust and crawling insects from our clothes with trembling hands, and carried on our way.

After about three hours, several of the children began to whimper with tiredness. Their feet were sore, and we were all covered in furiously itchy red lumps from being bitten by the numerous mosquitoes that constantly swarmed around us.

I estimated we were probably only about halfway to our destination, having recently passed Pienza on its hilltop as we pressed on through the fields. My back hurt so much it made my breath catch, but I tried not to let on to the others how much I was struggling. We found a place for lunch in the shade of a cluster of pines and handed round thin slices of bread and salami, washing it down with some of the water. 'Don't let them drink too much,' Francesca murmured. 'We need to keep some for the rest of the journey.'

We stayed where we were for a couple of hours, giving the children time to rest during the hottest part of the day. The sound of shelling continued to fill the air from the direction we'd come and we realised that Harry had been right – the fighting must have engulfed the villa by now. I couldn't bear to think of what might be happening there. The hilltop refuge that had kept us safe for so long might be no more: the house bombed to oblivion, perhaps, or its walls riddled with machine-gun fire, the *limonaia* destroyed and the gardens we'd so carefully planted and tended laid to waste.

Eventually, we got back to our weary feet and gathered up our belongings. I thought back to the day I'd left the prison at Santa

Verdiana and trudged through the hot streets of Florence dragging my suitcase. I'd struggled to believe, then, that my life had been so reduced. But now the thought of a suitcase full of belongings seemed an unimaginable luxury. All that remained were the clothes we wore and the half-empty bottles of water we carried with us. I walked on doggedly, biting my lip to stop myself from crying out at the pain in my back and legs.

We tried to keep to the verges in the afternoon, where the going underfoot was a little easier. But the heat reflected off the white dust of the road and our pace grew even slower as the children became ever more tired and dehydrated. We eked out the water, saving it for the little ones, and by the time we reached the approach to Montepulciano, my head pounded with a vicious ache that made my vision blur.

The town sat high above us on its hilltop perch, close by now. But we were so exhausted that the climb seemed as impossible as ascending Mount Everest. Silvana sank to her knees at the foot of the hill, unable to go on despite the encouragement of Gio, who tried to get her to stand. 'Look, Mamma, we're nearly there.'

'I can't.' Her lips were parched and she struggled to form the words. She turned to look up at Francesca. 'You go on, take them to safety.' One or two of the children started to whimper, but most of them were too drained to summon up any more tears. And then, one at a time, they sank to the ground too. Thankfully, I joined them.

'We'll rest here,' Francesca said. 'Let's get our breath back and wait for evening to fall, when it will be a little cooler. Then we'll be able to climb the hill.'

The thud of falling bombs was louder now, but even that couldn't scare up enough adrenalin to start the climb that would take us to safety. Francesca and I exchanged a worried glance. We'd made it so far. But was our journey going to end here, within plain sight of our destination? I felt so helpless in that moment, and I believe we'd all given up hope, drained by the struggles of the past months and years that seemed to have led us here, to this moment of despair and surrender.

My head still ached as I looked up at the walls of the medieval town, high on the hill above us. And then I blinked, trying to clear away the fog of pain that blurred my vision as I saw something move. Had I imagined it? But no, I blinked again and saw another movement.

I put out my hand and touched Francesca's arm. 'Look.' My voice was barely a whisper, but the emotion in it made her turn her head and follow my gaze.

From the gateway above us, a swarm of people emerged. They began making their way down the steep hill towards us. They weren't soldiers but civilians, the local people of Montepulciano, who had seen our straggling progress from far off. They'd watched as we stumbled and fell at the final hurdle along the way. Now they were streaming out of their walled town, despite the danger that threatened on all sides, and coming to help us.

They brought water and helped the children drink thirstily. A stout man – who we later learned was the mayor – scooped up two of the little ones, one in each arm, and led the way back up the hill. Others carried the children who were too tired to take another step, or offered a helping hand and words of encouragement. '*Andiamo.* You are safe now, don't worry. We'll take care of you.' Most of the townsfolk were strangers to me, but I recognised the wine merchant, at whose shop we'd dropped off a barrel of wine, and the local priest. The pair of them helped Silvana stand and supported her, one on each side, as she began the climb. An elderly man, seeing I was limping, handed me his walking stick without a word and took my arm in his to help me up the path. And my chest swelled as it filled with hope once again at the sight of so much kindness and compassion from these strangers, who took us into their hearts and welcomed us into their town.

◆ ◆ ◆

I'd never seen the cellars beneath Montepulciano's streets, although Francesca had told me of their existence on one of our trips to the town. I don't know what I'd imagined, but it certainly wasn't the awe-inspiring series of caverns and tunnels into which the mayor led us. At first, it was such a blessed relief just to be out of the heat of the day and to know we'd made it to safety that I didn't really take in my surroundings. But gradually, as my headache subsided and the ache seeped out of my tired limbs, I looked around and could hardly believe my eyes. Vast columns rose from the cellar floor to the ceiling far above us, making the underground hall look more like a cathedral than a simple cavern. Massive wooden barrels were stacked around the walls, breathing the soft perfume of Montepulciano's famous *Vino Nobile* into the air around us. It was quiet and cool, and a hush fell over the children. I think they were as awed as I was to find themselves in those majestic surroundings. The constant sound of shelling that had accompanied us on our long march couldn't penetrate the thick stone. It might not have been the paradise we'd known at the Villa delle Colombe, but this underworld was no hell. It was another sanctuary, and one where we were supported by the town's inhabitants. They brought us milk for the children, and meals of rice and vegetables, sharing their own precious supplies with us. At first, we were on our own, but over the next few days, more and more of the townspeople came to join us, leaving their homes and seeking refuge underground as the wave of war broke over Montepulciano too.

They were frightened and spoke in hushed tones as they told us what was happening in the streets outside. The town had been taken over by the Germans; fierce fighting continued on the plain as the Allies punched through the German line of defences and the air was filled with the smell of smoke and the sounds of the battle.

One woman whispered to us, so that the children wouldn't overhear, that the German soldiers had hanged a young partisan from a lamppost in the main street. They'd given orders that the body should be left there for twenty-four hours as a warning to others. The priest, who had helped us climb the hill just a couple of days earlier, had defied the soldiers and gone to deliver the last rites to the boy as he died. 'We all closed our shutters, so we wouldn't have to see him hanging there,' she said, with tears running down her cheeks. 'But the sight of what we witnessed still haunts us all.'

She'd left her home when they started blowing up some of the houses in her neighbourhood to block the streets into the town. 'I saw the Medici arch fall,' she said. 'But the statue of the Madonna that adorned it landed on top of the rubble, unbroken. Surely that's a sign?' She crossed herself as she spoke, and I think we all sent up a silent prayer that it was indeed the sign of a miracle that would save us. She'd brought with her a case containing her best table linen and a framed photograph of her husband, dragging it down the narrow stairs into the cellar. 'He's fighting with the partisans,' she told us when she showed us the picture, with pride in her voice mixed in with the fear.

We lost all sense of time, cocooned underground, but knew several days must have passed. The children's fear subsided enough for them to become bored and so we kept them busy with songs and games. Then, at last, the mayor appeared to tell us the Germans had left, shelling the Palazzo Ricci and blowing up the bridge behind them. 'Allied soldiers are coming up the hill,' he announced, and his voice trembled with triumph and exhaustion in equal measure.

We filed out into the piazza, blinking in the glare of the day-light, and stood, stunned, trying to take in the scene that awaited us. In just those few days, while we'd been cocooned underground, the town had been battered by the fighting. Some buildings had

although we'd never met before. 'Are you, by any chance, Miss Beatrice Crane?'

'I am! You know him!'

He hesitated a moment, then took my hand in his. 'Miss Crane . . . Beatrice . . . I'm sorry. Harry didn't make it. I'm here in his place. He told me if anything happened to him, I should come and find you in Montepulciano. He asked me to look for you and the children in your care. To find you and take you safely home.'

◆ ◆ ◆

We jolted back to the villa over the battle-scarred roads, which had been cleared of mines now. The army truck lurched over potholes and swerved around craters left by the shelling as we skirted Pienza and San Quirico, re-entering the valley. We may only have been away for a couple of weeks, but it felt like a lifetime since we'd made that endlessly long trek to Montepulciano. So much had changed.

We discovered that the villa had indeed been used by the Germans as a gun emplacement. They'd driven their trucks over our carefully planted flowerbeds and set up their heavy artillery at the end of the English garden, where the hillside falls away, commanding the view across the valley. The villa itself was still standing, but there were shell holes in the roof. The library had been ransacked, the globe crushed, Edoardo's books scattered across the floor and some pages torn out to be used as lavatory paper, as evidenced by the stinking mess in one corner of the room. The last pieces of Francesca's good furniture were smashed to bits. But in the middle of all that devastation, the only time I saw her cry was when we found the remains of her letters from Edoardo. Their charred remnants lay in the fireplace. Why anyone had wanted to attempt to light a fire in the middle of the summer was not clear. Perhaps it was just a part of the mindless destruction of war.

There were bullet holes in some of the walls, and the occupiers had evidently departed in a hurry, leaving bedding and other detritus scattered through the rooms.

I left the house, where Silvana, Francesca and the children were setting things to rights as best they could, and walked out into the garden. I followed the path through the gap in the hedge, past the cypress maze to the English garden, where the flowerbeds had been mangled and crushed by the fury of war. I stood for a while at the end of the arbour, looking out across the valley, remembering Harry's smile and his kindness and his love for me, and I felt utterly empty. As I raised a hand to brush the tears from my cheeks, my fingertips came to rest on the buttercup brooch pinned to my blouse. I closed my fist around it and suddenly felt his presence. I shut my eyes and saw his smile, heard his laugh, remembered the look in his eyes when he bound a living buttercup around my finger that day in the orchard and pledged to love me forever. The surge of emotion I felt was stronger than the destruction all around me. It was so powerful I knew it could never die.

I glanced down at the flowerbed beside me, where some lavender that had been uprooted was still flowering. I knelt down and scooped a hole for it, settling its roots into the soil, gently pressing it back into place with my fingers. Then I reached for another plant, and another, the tears still running down my face as I worked.

After a while, I realised I wasn't alone any more. Francesca had come to find me. She watched for a moment, then came to kneel beside me, digging with her hands as well, helping me settle the roots of a broken rose bush back into the ground.

Then, one by one, the children appeared through the gap in the hedge and they, too, fell to their knees and joined us in our work. And together we began replanting the garden, with hope for a better tomorrow.

Chapter 36

Tess – 2015

Beatrice insists on getting up the next day. By the time I knock on her bedroom door, she's managed to get herself dressed, pre-empting any attempts to make her stay in bed. 'Don't fuss, dear, I'm absolutely fine,' she says. But she does take the arm I offer her, and obediently sits down at the table under the oaks while I bring her breakfast out to her. She lifts her face to the sunlight, closing her eyes, drinking in the day along with her morning cup of tea.

'Can we have an outing today, Tess?' she asks. 'There's some-where I'd like to go. But first, we need to go to the orchard.'

I agree a little reluctantly, worried that she's overdoing it. But then, I think, what is there to lose? I don't blame her for wanting to make the most of her last days of freedom.

I hold her arm and walk her to the orchard where, with my help, she gathers a posy of wildflowers. Afterwards, I suggest we rest for a while and drink a glass of water. But she insists we set off in the car straight away, and directs me to the little town of Foiano della Chiana, halfway between Montepulciano and Arezzo. I pull up outside the gates of the war cemetery there. It sits on the edge of the little Tuscan town, with houses and the church tower overlooking it on one side and a field full of sunflowers on the other. Beatrice pushes open the black metal gate and we step into the neatly kept grounds. The grass is mown to perfection and beyond the tall stone cross stand row upon row of white headstones, set in precise lines. At the end of each row there's a neatly trimmed topiary ball, reminiscent of the box hedging on the *terrazza* back at the villa. We walk towards the markers and I read the names that are carved there. There must be a couple of hundred of them at least, the young men who fell on the battlefield here in July 1944.

Beatrice makes her way towards the far corner, carrying her posy of cornflowers and buttercups. In the shade of one of the tall trees that stands like a sentry along the boundary, she shows me Harry's stone. It's just like all the others in the cemetery, a simple white marker. His is carved with the emblem of the Royal Highland regiment – St Andrew bearing his cross – and his name: Captain H. E. Priestley. Beneath it are his service number and the words

The Black Watch

6th July 1944. Age 29.

Beatrice bends down and places the bunch of wildflowers at the foot of the headstone. In the neat, narrow flowerbeds that flank it are planted a white rose – the one called 'Peace', just like the ones in the English garden at the villa – and a rosemary bush. I run my fingers over the rosemary's spiky leaves, releasing its aromatic scent into the air.

'Rosemary for remembrance?' I ask, and Beatrice nods.

'You see, Tess,' she says, 'he promised me that the Allies would never abandon Italy. All these young men, not just from Britain but from Canada and South Africa and India too, remain here, where they fell. They gave their lives to help save Italy. To help save people like Alfredo and Francesca, the children we sheltered and their families. To help save me.'

I see, now, that this is another reason why Beatrice never wanted to leave Italy. Harry never abandoned her. And she would never abandon him.

I leave her standing by his marker, giving her some time alone with her memories of the man she loved, and wander among the serried ranks of white headstones. I think of you – the same age as many of the men who fell here – and the personal battles you fought. I think about sacrifice, about courage, about wanting to protect those we love.

And in that beautiful, dignified, unutterably sad place, I find a sense of peace in the knowledge that those battles are over now.

Chapter 37

Tess – 2015

As the final week of August approaches, the heat makes it impossible to spend much time outdoors. It seems to have sapped all the energy out of Beatrice, who spends her days in the relative cool of the library. She surrounds herself with Francesca's sketchbooks. They seem to bring her solace, to calm and settle her as she waits for what comes next.

'Come back to Britain with me,' I urge her. 'You can stay in my flat until you find your feet. Or I know Granny would love to have you. You need somewhere to go though. Surely you're not going to stay here until Marco comes and turns you out?'

She shakes her head. 'That's very kind of you, dear. And oh, how I'd love to see Philly again after all these years. We're the two remaining Triplets from our schooldays, after all. But it's too late for me to leave Italy. I've lived here most of my life and the ghosts of the people I've loved the most are here. How can I leave them? There's nothing for me in Scotland now. My parents were killed before the war ended by a stray bomb that destroyed our house. I only learned of it – far too late – when I tried to get in touch in 1945 to let them know I'd survived the war in Italy and was still alive and well. I'm sorry they never knew. I have no other living relatives there and no friends now either, since Ella died earlier this year. No Tess, if I'm going to be arrested for murder, I might as well make it easier for everyone by staying put.'

'No one is going to arrest you,' I say. 'Anyway, perhaps Marco will change his mind about his plans and leave the maze in place.' I've tried calling him a few times, but there's been no reply and I haven't left a voice message as I know he'll see my number and realise what I'm ringing about.

She smiles faintly, showing a glimmer of her old spirit, but it fades away again quickly. 'I very much doubt his idea of a swanky hotel includes having a body buried in the garden. And anyway, he'll need all the land for his blessed golf course. Not to mention the fact that both you and he are now duty-bound to go to the police with my confession.'

Part of me thinks she's wildly exaggerating the danger she's in, but the thought of turning her over to the Italian police makes me shudder, as I remember the morning the British police turned up at my door about a fortnight after I got back from Switzerland. They questioned me for over an hour, asking for details of the trip and my involvement in your death. We'd known it would happen, of course, and I'd been prepared for it. I showed them the letter you'd written, absolving me of any coercion and stating that I'd repeatedly tried to talk you out of contacting the clinic. The policewoman called me a few weeks later to let me know the Director of Public Prosecutions had decided not to press charges of culpable homicide against me. By then, though, the trauma of everything we'd been through together made the risk of prosecution seem almost irrelevant. I no longer cared what happened to me.

I'd always considered myself to be strong and independent, but without you I felt exposed and vulnerable, as if my strength had been stripped away as I'd watched yours diminish, my resilience eroded. Alone in the flat, I felt hopelessly weak. Every minor set-back – the light bulb in the bedroom blowing, the car's oil light coming on, the kitchen sink becoming blocked – felt like another major blow that knocked me sideways. I had to force myself to go through the motions of life.

'Can I bring you anything?' I ask her. 'A cup of tea? Or a glass of water? You need to drink lots in this heat.'

'Thank you, Tess, it's kind of you to take such good care of me, but I'm fine, really. I think I'll have a nap now. Why don't you take the afternoon off? And feel free to take the car if you want to go out anywhere.'

She clearly wants some time on her own, so I go back to the cottage and reluctantly begin tidying a few things away.

◆ ◆ ◆

It's Gio who finds Beatrice this time. He'd gone to do his evening rounds, tidying away cushions and watering pots. Perhaps it was the heat, or the stress of awaiting her fate, but she'd wandered into the garden late in the afternoon, her secateurs in her hand as usual, and collapsed. Vittoria comes to fetch me, telling me Gio has carried Signorina Crane to her bed and called the doctor.

It's a more severe stroke this time, dragging down one side of her face, making her speech almost indistinguishable. The doctor wants to call an ambulance so we can get her to the hospital in Florence as quickly as possible, but Beatrice shakes her head vehemently. She clutches at my hand with surprising strength and pulls me close to make sure I can hear her. 'No,' she slurs. 'I . . . stay here.'

As I show the doctor out, she tells me it's just a question of time now. It's very likely Beatrice will suffer another major stroke, she says, especially since she refuses to go to hospital where they might be able to stabilise her a little. 'You should be prepared,' she warns me. 'Call me any time you need to.'

Back in the bedroom, Beatrice lies in her bed, her white hair fanning out across the pillows. She seems so small and fragile, her arthritic fingers brown against the sheets. She beckons me to come closer. 'My brooch,' she mumbles. Her hand lifts towards the gardening smock I've folded over the back of a chair. I pin the little gold buttercup carefully to the collar of her nightgown and one side of her mouth lifts in a lopsided smile. All at once, she looks more relaxed than she has done for weeks. She mutters something else and I bend close to make out what she's saying. 'Better like this. Sets me free. You too.'

I know what she's trying to tell me, and I don't know how to reply. So I just sit with her as night falls, holding her hand, watching over her as she slips away a little further, step by step, along the path she must walk alone.

◆ ◆ ◆

There's not much change in Beatrice's condition the next morning. She flits in and out of consciousness and refuses to eat any of the breakfast we bring her.

Gio and Vittoria hover outside the room, wanting to help if there's anything she needs. I only vaguely register the sound of a car pulling up outside, and when I hear the knock on the door I expect it to be the doctor coming to check on Beatrice again. But, having gone to answer it, Vittoria summons me downstairs and there in the hallway stands Marco.

'Tess, I'm sorry to hear Signorina Crane is so unwell. I've just finished reading her account of my father's time here in the war and I came as quickly as I could.' He takes my hands in his and I see Vittoria's eyebrows shoot up in surprise. 'Please,' he says, 'may I be permitted to see her?'

Gio, who is sitting on a chair in the corridor outside Beatrice's bedroom, gets to his feet as Marco approaches. His face grows dark with anger and for a moment I fear he's going to lash out.

'It's OK, Gio,' I say, putting out a hand to calm him. Still scowling, he gives a curt nod by way of greeting but remains on his feet, wary and protective. I turn to Marco. 'Please wait here a moment. I'll just check whether Beatrice can see you.'

She is lying against her pillows with her eyes closed, but they open as I approach the bed and she smiles her lopsided smile again.

'Marco's here,' I tell her. 'He's read it. He wants to speak to you. Is that all right?'

Her smile fades, but she manages to slur a 'Yes.'

I usher Marco into the room, but he turns to Gio first. '*Prego*,' he says. 'Please. Would you come in as well?'

Gio, Vittoria and I hover in the background as Marco pulls up a chair at the bedside and reaches for Beatrice's hand. He clears his throat and swallows. I can see what an effort it is for him to allow the words to come. But then he begins to speak.

'Signorina Crane, thank you for telling me what happened to my father here in the war years. He never spoke about it, you see, and his silence gave me the impression that something terrible must have been done to him. I suppose in a way it was – Silvana's anguish wounded him to the core and must have made him feel even more responsible for the death of Carlo.' He turns to Gio. 'I am so sorry you lost him in that way, when he was trying to save my father. And I understand, now, that you lost your best friend as well as your own father that day.'

Gio quickly drops his eyes but not before I catch a glimpse of the sudden tears that spring into them.

Marco turns back towards Beatrice. 'But here's what I know about the accident. He never spoke to me of it, but these are the threads of my father's life that I managed to glean from my mother before she died. It ties in very much with the story you have told Tess.

'After the car was hit, Alfredo clambered out, thinking you and Carlo were both dead. And he thought it was all his fault because Silvana's words must still have been ringing in his ears. He was just a child and he didn't understand why he'd been sent away when the other children hadn't. He only knew he wasn't wanted at the Villa delle Colombe. He didn't know where his own parents were either, just that they were in the north and he had to go south.

'He ran away from the car when he heard traffic approaching on the road, and he spent several days hiding in the woods, terrified and alone. He foraged for food – thankfully you had taught him how to do that, Signorina Crane, and it helped him survive – and he drank water from a stream . . . But soon he became ill. He was found in the woods, dehydrated and starving, by a local farmer out hunting rabbits. The farmer took him home, but my father was unable or unwilling to speak. He told no one his name, nor where he was from. The farmer and his wife were elderly and they couldn't help the young child, so eventually they took him to an orphanage in Rome. There, he still refused to tell the staff his name, so they gave him a new one.

'Many children in the city had been orphaned by the war and the orphanages there were full to capacity. My father was sent south, where a place had been found for him in Sorrento. The staff there were kind and gentle and finally managed to coax him to tell them his parents' names. But once the Red Cross traced them, Alfredo was told they'd been dead for years. I guess that may have made him feel even more betrayed by Francesca, and he still believed he'd brought nothing but shame and danger to everyone at the villa. So he refused to say where he'd been since his parents died. He grew up in that orphanage and did well in school.' He smiles and gently squeezes Beatrice's hand. 'You gave him a good grounding, Signorina Crane. He became a lawyer in Rome. And I know, now, that he received a letter from Francesca, who never gave up trying to find him, but he didn't reply. He ripped it up without reading it. He'd lost trust in humankind, you see. Although you and Francesca kept him safe, you couldn't protect him entirely from the corrosive anti-Semitism that the war stirred up. His shame and guilt must have been overwhelming. Alfredo spent his life living in their shadow.'

He pauses, swallowing again, then goes on. 'This summer, I've come to understand the power of silence. It was the mechanism my father used to be able to keep going, but it also created a vacuum into which fear, distrust and misunderstanding seeped. I know now that silence allows doubt and fear to grow – and it needs to be broken. Unfortunately, my pride and stubbornness – which I think I probably inherited from my father – got in the way of me doing that. When I first heard I'd inherited the villa, I wanted nothing more than to obliterate the place I thought had caused my father so much anguish and made him the uncommunicative, unhappy man he was for so much of his life. The wall of silence he built to protect himself turned out to be a tragic impediment that ruined many lives. It kept in the fear and distrust, and it kept out so much joy and love. If only he'd reached out earlier. If only he'd replied to Francesca's letter. If only he'd understood a little better . . .'

He stops again and the expression on his face is one I haven't seen before. I think he's asking for forgiveness but can't quite form the words.

Beatrice's eyes close for a moment and a single tear runs down her lined cheek. Then she opens them again and squeezes Marco's hand.

'There's something else,' Marco says, reaching into his jacket pocket. 'It turns out my father never did forget you all and the kindness you'd shown him. I found this among his things after he died. I didn't know what it was. But now I do.'

He opens his hand. In the palm sits a sliver of worn glass, misted with time.

Gio leans forward to look and then a sob rises in his throat. '*È la colomba di vetro,*' he exclaims. The glass dove.

Marco turns towards him. 'When I read that you gave this to Alfredo, Gio, and that he'd kept it all these years, I realised how much you all meant to him. You told him it would keep him safe, and it did. And you said it was to remind him where his home was, here at the Villa delle Colombe. So, while he felt he'd been exiled twice over – firstly from his home and his parents in Turin and then from this place too – he never forgot. And I don't think he ever stopped wishing he could come home again and be among the people who had saved him.'

He puts the glass dove into Beatrice's hand and her fingers curl around it.

'I know now how much you and Francesca loved Alfredo, how much you did for him,' Marco tells her. 'And by keeping him safe here at the villa, you sacrificed your own safety too.

'You have also carried the burden of a terrible secret all these years,' he goes on.

Beatrice closes her eyes as if exhausted by that burden, which she's now ready to give up.

He folds his hand over hers again, so the glass dove is held in the cocoon of them both. 'Don't worry,' he says. 'We will sort this out. It's time for the cypress maze to give up the darkness at its heart and to let the light of a new day flood in again. For all of us. There's already been enough grief in our lives. I promise you, I'll take care of the estate. I'll take care of everything. I'm putting the plans on hold for now. I think we need a bit of time to get to know each other better.' He turns to Gio and Vittoria. 'Please would you consider staying on? You know the villa and its gardens so well. The farmhouse is yours for as long as you want.'

Gio puts an arm around his wife, and she rests her head on his shoulder and closes her eyes in a gesture of infinite relief. 'Thank you,' he says. 'We would like nothing better.'

Beatrice mumbles something and I bend closer to make out what she's trying to say. It sounds like 'home'. She presses the little glass dove into Marco's hand and I understand.

'She's telling you this is your home,' I say.

He smiles at her. 'You are a very wise woman, Signorina Crane. I should never have underestimated you.'

One corner of Beatrice's mouth lifts again and she closes her eyes.

'I think we'd better let her sleep now,' I say, and I shoo the others out of the room. I make sure she's comfortable and turn to go, leaving her in peace. But as I do, she says three words with absolute clarity.

'Thank you, Tess.'

Chapter 38

Tess – 2015

As autumn comes to the valley – the season of letting go – there are two funerals to organise.

The first is Beatrice's. She left us peacefully one evening, as the last light of the day bathed the garden in its mellow light. She'd slipped into unconsciousness the day before and I hadn't left her side, knowing the end of her life's journey was approaching.

It's believed that the last sense to fade is hearing. That's why I held your hand and told you I loved you, that day in Zurich, once you'd depressed the plunger of the second syringe and your eyes closed. It's why I kept saying it, over and over again, as your breathing slowed and then stopped. I hope you heard me.

Knowing that, I'd been reading aloud to Beatrice from the leather-bound copy of Dante's *Divine Comedy*, which held the buttercup Harry had given her pressed between its pages. She still wore the little gold brooch pinned to her nightgown.

> The nature of the universe, which is still
> At the centre while all the rest moves round it,
> Begins here from its starting point.

And this heaven has no other location
Than the divine mind, in which is lit up
The love which turns it and the power which
        rains down from it.

As I read that last line, she gave a deep sigh. And when I glanced up, I realised it had been her final breath.

For her funeral, we bury her ashes in the churchyard next to Francesca's grave and I place a bouquet of late summer roses over them on the freshly turned earth. But I keep back one small handful of her earthly remains. I dig it into the ground beneath the rose called 'Peace' that she'd planted alongside Harry's marker in the war cemetery at Foiano della Chiana.

The night after Beatrice Crane finally leaves the villa she'd called her home for most of her life, I have a troubled dream, in which she and I are walking in the maze together. 'It's time now,' she tells me. 'Time to open up the heart of it again.'

Her voice sounds so real that I awake with a gasp. I try to call out to her, but it's your name that I say. It hangs on the hot air in the darkness of my bedroom, just beyond my reach. I shove my feet into my sandals and grab a torch, running up the track to the villa. As I turn the corner on to the parterre, I nearly jump out of my skin at the sight of a figure sitting beneath the oak trees, illuminated by a vast, copper-coloured harvest moon that seems to hang in their upper branches. He shouts, '*Chi è là?*' – who's there? – sounding as alarmed as I am. My heart calms a little as I realise it's Marco.

'It's OK, it's me – Tess,' I reply. 'Can't you sleep either?'

He stands, coming towards me. 'What are you doing, running around like a crazy woman at this time of the night?'

'We have to open up the maze,' I say, knowing that my explanation must only serve to confirm his opinion of me as I wave my torch towards the path leading through the gap in the hedge.

To my surprise, though, he doesn't argue. He doesn't even ask any more questions. He just gives me a long, searching look and then says, 'OK. In that case, we'll need some tools.'

He disappears for a few minutes and then comes back and leads the way, carrying a torch of his own as well as a pair of loppers and a handsaw. We pause at the entrance to the maze, just for a moment. He turns to look at me and I nod, determined to see through what we've begun. Then we plunge into the darkness, the high walls shutting out the moonlight, our torches casting long shadows on the path ahead that quickly close in behind us again as we pass. At last, we come to a solid barrier of dark, interlaced branches and know we've reached the chamber. Without a word, Marco hands me the pair of loppers and sets to with the saw, hacking out a section of the cypress wall. It's hard work – the trees have grown strongly, and their trunks have thickened over the years – but at last we cut through and fling aside the final boughs, then step through the gap we've created. We stand in silence, taking in the simple wooden cross. By the light of Marco's torch, I can make out the name carved into it. *Umberto Ciccone*. And the date, *6 maggio, 1944*.

I don't know what I'd expected to feel on finally penetrating the heart of the cypress maze. But as we stand there, side by side, all the fear, all the anxiety and panic – the dread of what it might contain – evaporate.

The beam of my torch flickers, then dies. I shake it, trying to get the batteries to work, but they've run out. Next to me, Marco switches off his own light too and the darkness envelops us. Then I look up and see a million stars, tiny, bright pinpricks scattered across the vast eternity of the universe.

I reach for Marco's hand, and we stay there, side by side, watching in silence. Understanding at last that what lies in the heart of the maze of grief is, very simply, acceptance. And once we unlock that hidden chamber, there is nothing left but peace.

◆ ◆ ◆

The second funeral that autumn is Umberto's. Marco reports to the authorities the discovery of a body buried in the middle of the maze, apparently dating back to the war years. No further questions are asked, once the authorities learn that the elderly *signora scozzese*, who might have known how it came to be there, has died. The wooden cross gives them the information they need: an investigation of the coffin buried beneath the headstone of Umberto Ciccone in the churchyard at Bagni San Filippo proves it to contain nothing but a number of heavy stones wrapped in an old blanket. And so, with due respect, his body can finally be moved to its rightful resting place. The heart of the maze has relinquished its secret at last.

◆ ◆ ◆

Marco has moved into the villa now. And I've moved into Beatrice's old apartment while we work together on a new project.

We've started small, renovating the old stable block and putting down a thick layer of sand in the yard there. The Villa delle Colombe has opened its doors to those in need of a sanctuary again: it's become a refuge for retired or injured Palio horses. Allegro is the first to arrive, from the farm outside Siena. The vet has diagnosed arthritis in his hocks. He's soon joined by three more horses, and we have plans to build more stabling to accommodate others, as well as a water therapy pool, using the underground spring as its source. Vincenzo is helping draw up the plans, staying in the cottage a couple of days a week so he can be with Allegro and still help his parents run their smallholding.

On fine days, the horses are turned out into the orchard, where they can graze among the buttercups, nosing out the last windfalls from beneath the apple trees. Sometimes we saddle up two of the horses that are sound enough to be ridden and go for hacks through the beechwoods as the leaves begin to fall, forming a deep carpet on the forest floor. As we ride, we talk. Because we've both learned that silence can be the worst thing of all. Talking can be painful too, sometimes, but it stops grief from sinking its roots down into the dark loneliness of silence and wrapping its tendrils around your heart. The horses seem instinctively to know the way, their hooves kicking up clouds of sunlit dust as we climb a farm track to the top of the valley and dismount there, letting them crop the last of the autumn wildflowers. Marco takes me in his arms and we kiss. Then we stand together, looking back the way we've come, over life's maze of winding paths.

On the ride home, we meet Gio coming back with a basket of *porcini.* He shows us a single black truffle wrapped carefully in his handkerchief. He's been continuing my education in horticulture and says I'm getting pretty good at it these days.

More and more often, I set aside my camera so I can sink my hands into the rich earth, preparing the garden for winter and the spring to come next year. As I do so, the last butterflies flutter among the drifts of pale cosmos, sipping nectar from the black-eyed Susans that flower in the garden's final autumnal sunburst. They're a good reminder to me that sometimes it's important to go through your own struggles, shut in the chrysalis of your grief, but that there are others alongside you – there to support and encourage you – the ones who have learned how to become stronger through struggles of their own and now fly free.

A wise woman once said that grief is love that has nowhere to go. At last, I'm exploring new directions, finding the way, navigating the paths that will transform my grief into new love. Creating a map of my own making. The garden and the villa both feature on it. Marco does too. He and I have become inseparable. Our grief is individual, deeply personal, but we know that together we can help each other to heal. Sometimes we walk in the maze. It's lost its darkness now that we've managed to find our own ways through and we know we can return at will to the garden in all its beauty. We've both come to realise that what was left, once we managed to find the way to acceptance and peace at the heart of the maze of grief, was simply an empty space. And emptiness can be filled with other things. Like joy. And love.

Sometimes, in the liminal moments at dawn and dusk when I walk in the garden, I still catch a fleeting glimpse of you and hear your voice. I'm taking my own time to say goodbye.

You're nearly there, Tess, you tell me. You're going to be all right.

And I know I am.

AUTHOR'S NOTE ON SOURCES AND RESOURCES

ITALY:

On a trip to Tuscany, I visited the beautiful gardens at La Foce, the estate that belonged to Iris Origo (which members of her family have since inherited). It was there that I discovered the story of the children she sheltered during the war. Her diaries of those years – *A Chill in the Air* and *War in Val d'Orcia* – make fascinating reading and I drew much inspiration from her eyewitness accounts of what daily life was like as the winds of war raged back and forth across Italy.

The complexity of Italy's Second World War history is covered extensively in online sources and in many excellent reference books. I found two books particularly relevant to my research for *The Cypress Maze*: Caroline Moorehead's *A House in the Mountains: The Women Who Liberated Italy from Fascism* and Roderick Bailey's *Target: Italy: The Secret War Against Mussolini, 1940–43*, which details SOE operations in the country. Eric Newby's *Love and War in the Apennines* is also a wonderful account of his experiences in wartime Italy, where he was captured while on a covert mission and subsequently met the woman who was to become his wife.

Joan Marble's book *Notes from an Italian Garden* describes the trials and tribulations of carving out a garden from scratch. And Pamela Sheldon Johns' recipe book *Cucina Povera: Tuscan Peasant Cooking* provided some of the culinary details.

THE PALIO:

The name of the winning horse in the August 2015 Palio (Polonski, ridden by the jockey Giovanni Atzeni for the Selva *contrada*) has been changed for the sake of my story. *Il Palio* is considered controversial and animal rights protestors continually demand that it be stopped. In recent years, new safety measures have been put in place for the race, such as limiting the number of horses taking part and installing protective barriers on the most dangerous turns in the Piazza del Campo. It inspires very mixed feelings but is certainly a seminal event for the city of Siena, and the history and passion involved in the pageantry of the day's events are enthralling.

The idea of making the Villa delle Colombe into a sanctuary for retired horses was inspired by the State Forestry equestrian centre near Radicondoli. Now managed by the Carabinieri Biodiversity Group (*Raggruppamento Carabinieri Biodiversità*), the centre was established specifically to house old and injured Palio horses, on a farm called Il Caggio, about fifteen minutes' drive south-west of Siena. Here, Palio horses are cared for in their retirement in a safe and peaceful environment on a nature reserve.

A Note on Dante's *Divine Comedy*:

In the smallest of nutshells . . . having been guided by the Roman poet Virgil through Hell (*Inferno*) and Purgatory (*Purgatorio*), Dante arrives at the threshold of Paradise (*Paradiso*). There he is met by Beatrice, who leads him through the successive ascending levels of heaven. Written in the fourteenth century, it remains a powerful allegory for today, not least in helping us navigate the paths of life and death, of grief and hope. There have been many different translations down the years. I drew on a combination of these and adapted them slightly for the quotes used in this book.

The quote at the very beginning of this novel is from the opening of *Inferno* I, 1–3:

> In the middle of life's journey
> I found myself in a dark forest
> Where the straight path was lost.

The quote in chapter 26 is from *Paradiso* XXXIII, 7–12:

> That love was lit again within your womb;
> By whose warmth, in the everlasting peace,
> Was this flower allowed to bloom.
> For us above, you are a noonday blaze of love,
> And there below, on earth, among the
>   mortals,
> You are a living spring of hope.

And the quote in chapter 38 is from *Paradiso* XXVII, 106–111:

The nature of the universe, which is still
At the centre while all the rest moves round it,
Begins here from its starting point.
And this heaven has no other location
Than the divine mind, in which is lit up
The love which turns it and the power which
rains down from it.

MOTOR NEURONE DISEASE AND ASSISTED DYING:

I knew these would be emotionally difficult and painful subjects to research, but I was moved to explore this strand by the personal stories of two very brave people in particular. One was Richard Selley, a former colleague and a friend, who was diagnosed with MND in 2014 and took the decision to end his life at a Dignitas facility in 2019. His book *Death Sits on My Shoulder* is an account of his experience of MND, and the blog he wrote – *Moments with MND* – explores the reasons why he chose the route he did. The other is Elsie Carnegie, who helped and supported her husband, Dave, all through his illness and was at his side when he died at home in 2019.

The courage, grace and dignity of those two men and their wives through those devastating times is both heart-rending and awe-inspiring.

Information and a support helpline for families where there is a diagnosis of MND are available via the Motor Neurone Disease Association's website: www.mndassociation.org. There is also a facility there to support research into MND by making a donation.

ACKNOWLEDGEMENTS

Thanks to my friend Wendy Carter, who first told me about Iris Origo and the gardens at La Foce, and to the wonderful Suzanne Branciforte of Grapevine Experience (https://grapevineexperience.com) for taking me there.

Thank you, too, to two inspirational women, Elsie Carnegie and Elaine Selley, for allowing me to refer to their husbands' stories of living and dying with Motor Neurone Disease.

Grazie mille to the helpful and friendly staff at Castello Banfi – Il Borgo, which must surely be one of the most beautiful hotels in the world. I found much inspiration for the Villa delle Colombe in the Tuscan landscape surrounding Montalcino, Montepulciano and Pienza, as well as in the Val d'Orcia itself.

Huge thanks, as ever, to the Lake Union team at Amazon Publishing: Sammia Hamer, Victoria Oundjian, Victoria Pepe, Eoin Purcell, Nicole Wagner and Bekah Graham. And to my patient and meticulous editors, Mike Jones, Jenni Davis, Swati Gamble and Silvia Crompton. Thank you, too, to Emma Rodgers for all her fabulous cover designs.

Undying gratitude to the team of superstars who support me and cheer me on at the Madeleine Milburn Agency – especially Maddy, Liv and Rachel, and Liane and the International Rights team.

Love and thanks to the friends and family who've supported me through the ups and downs of writing this book and particularly to all those who helped me in my hour of need, most of all my friend Lesley Singers. I promise not to climb any more very high ladders!

Special mentions to Sarah Wimberley and Rachel Jaggard for their assistance, and to Lesley, Eva and Livvy for their contributions to my storytelling, including our conversations about horse-riding and true love.

And last, but never least, love and thanks always to my sons, James and Alastair.

ABOUT THE AUTHOR

Photo credit: Willow Findlay

Fiona is an acclaimed number one bestselling author whose books have sold over a million copies and been translated into more than twenty languages worldwide. She draws inspiration from the stories of strong women, especially during the years of the Second World War, and her meticulous historical research enriches her writing with an evocative sense of time and place.

For more information, to sign up for updates or to get in touch, please visit www.fionavalpy.com.

Follow the Author on Amazon

If you enjoyed this book, follow Fiona Valpy on Amazon to be notified when the author releases a new book!

To do this, please follow these instructions:

Desktop:

1) Search for the author's namse on Amazon or in the Amazon App.
2) Click on the author's name to arrive on their Amazon page.
3) Click the 'Follow' button.

Mobile and Tablet:

1) Search for the author's name on Amazon or in the Amazon App.
2) Click on one of the author's books.
3) Click on the author's name to arrive on their Amazon page.
4) Click the 'Follow' button.

Kindle eReader and Kindle App:

If you enjoyed this book on a Kindle eReader or in the Kindle App, you will find the author 'Follow' button after the last page.